"She's lying," Iuna blurted. "My father bought her as a slave from Thay. Everybody knows that Thay is full of wizards."

"Halt!" At the command, Ythnel stopped, watching the nobleman from the corner of her eye. He circled her slowly, examining her from head to foot. "Your height, skin tone, and shaved head all mark you as Thayan. And the tattoo, is it not also a custom for wizards of that land to wear such decorations?"

"Many who are not wizards also bear such decorations, milord, so as not to stand out." Ythnel noted that the nobleman's hand was now firmly wrapped around his sword hilt.

"Regardless, I think it prudent that you be questioned further. In the name of House Karanok, I order you arrested. Guards, take her."

Chosen from five hundred submissions in an international open call, Kameron M. Franklin brings to life a realm of evil that can only be saved by

THE PRIESTS

THE PRIESTS

THE
PRIESTS

MAIDEN OF PAIN

KAMERON M. FRANKLIN

MAIDEN OF PAIN

©2005 Wizards of the Coast, Inc.

Distributed in the United States by Holtzbrinck Publishing. Distributed in Canada by Fenn Ltd.

Distributed to the hobby, toy, and comic trade in the United States and Canada by regional distributors.

Distributed worldwide by Wizards of the Coast, Inc. and regional distributors.

Printed in the U.S.A.

Cover art by Marc Fishman
Map by Rob Lazzaretti
First Printing: June 2005
Library of Congress Catalog Card Number: 2004116899

9 8 7 6 5 4 3 2 1

ISBN-10: 0-7869-3764-5
ISBN-13:978-0-7869-3764-6
620-96709000-001-EN

U.S., CANADA,
ASIA, PACIFIC, & LATIN AMERICA
Wizards of the Coast, Inc.
P.O. Box 707
Renton, WA 98057-0707
+1-800-324-6496

EUROPEAN HEADQUARTERS
Hasbro UK Ltd
Caswell Way
Newport, Gwent NP9 0YH
GREAT BRITAIN
Please keep this address for your records

Visit our web site at **www.wizards.com**

To Bacon,
because I promised Grimbones.

Acknowledgements

·

The author would like to thank the following, without whom this book would not have been possible: Karen Kirtley's PSU Spring 2003 Book Editing class, Peter Archer, Ed Greenwood, Scott Bennie, Eric L. Boyd, Phil Athans, and my wife Joanne.

THE PRIESTS

PROLOGUE

The Year of the Bow

(1354 DR)

The two handmaidens carried Yenael between them. The pain was overwhelming, and the strength had left her legs. They had made her walk until she could not do so on her own and was forced to lean heavily on the two women supporting her.

Yenael was humiliated. It didn't matter what she was going through, what had been done to her. Pain was a Loviatan's tool, her constant companion. To have her sisters see her succumb to it like this shamed Yenael.

They brought her into the round, stone chamber beneath the manor, maneuvering her onto the slab of dark metal resting in the middle of the room. Its cool touch was a minor balm to her burning flesh. While one of the handmaidens lit each of the lanterns that hung on the walls, the other secured the clamps around Yenael's ankles. It was an extra measure to make sure she did not endanger herself or anyone else should the last of her self-control fail.

No sooner had they finished than it started once more.

Yenael gritted her teeth against the pain, refusing to release it in the primal scream she could feel building in the back of her throat. She brought this on herself. She would endure the pain. No, she would conquer it. That was what was expected of her by her goddess.

Headmistress Mylra swept into the chamber as the wave of pain passed. She was dressed in the robes of her office, a red so deep it was almost black, highlighted by crimson and gold thread along the cuffs and hem. Her head was covered in a ceremonial hat of similar material that was shaped to resemble two horns protruding from the sides of her head, with a thin, gold charm hanging from each tip.

"How are things progressing?" the headmistress inquired.

"Swiftly, Headmistress," one of the handmaidens replied. "We should be finished here in a few minutes."

"Excellent. You are doing so well, Daughter," Headmistress Mylra said from her place behind one of the handmaidens at the foot of the table.

Pain gripped Yenael again, and she stiffened. She found no comfort in the headmistress's words. They weren't meant to comfort, though. The headmistress's tone conveyed that much. Giving comfort would have defeated the purpose and gone against all that Loviatar taught. Everything had been arranged to eliminate any possibility of relief from the pain. Even the comfort that came from her initial contact with the table was gone. The metal had quickly absorbed Yenael's own body heat, causing her skin to stick to the smooth surface. Sweat flowed from every pore, pooling wherever her body touched the table top. The clamps bit into the flesh around her ankles like little insects.

No, Headmistress Mylra was not trying to comfort her. She was merely expressing her pride in Yenael, and her pleasure at seeing Yenael suffer.

"You realize, of course, that the ritual serves a dual purpose in your case," the headmistress continued as the level of pain subsided from a relentless wave crashing against the breakers to something more like the tide sliding across the sand. "Not only does it exemplify the pain that is inevitably inflicted upon us from the moment we enter this life, but it is also a fitting punishment for the lack of discipline you displayed, wouldn't you say, Sister Duumin?"

"Yes ... uhn ... Headmistress." Yenael grunted through another wave of pain. Strands of matted hair stung her eyes, but she paid them no mind. The contractions of her uterus, like a giant's hand crushing her lower abdomen, relegated everything else to the status of mere annoyance.

"I'm glad you agree. Your indiscretion has jeopardized our influence with the powers of this city."

Headmistress Mylra circled the crude table, the hem of her voluminous robes sweeping the dark stone floor of the candlelit chamber. Her right arm was folded across her torso, supporting her left elbow, while she idly tapped her lips with the index finger of her left hand. Her eyes held no mercy.

The headmistress was right. Yenael deserved this suffering, but it was all she could do not to cry out in agony. It was humbling to realize she was so weak. She prayed Loviatar would forgive her then laughed at her own inanity. Loviatar did not forgive.

Yenael's laugh was cut off by a moan as another contraction hit her.

"The head is crowning," an attending handmaiden said. "Keep pushing, Sister."

Yenael took three short breaths and pushed. Her fists clenched into balls, nails biting into white flesh and drawing blood. Tears streamed from eyes squeezed tightly shut. Yenael felt something rip and nearly lost consciousness. From somewhere distant, she thought she could hear the screaming of tiny lungs.

"It's a girl."

"Congratulations, Sister Yenael." Headmistress Mylra took the newborn in her hands. A hint of pleasure flashed in Mylra's eyes, but her smile was ice cold. "It appears that Loviatar still favors you. Have you chosen a name?"

Yenael tried to lift her head to see the infant, but the movement only filled her sight with swirls of blackness. "Ythnel." She sighed.

"Welcome, Ythnel. May you suffer and deal suffering in kind." The benediction given, Headmistress Mylra passed the baby back to a handmaiden then nodded toward Yenael. "Clean her up, and see that she gets some rest. She has served well today."

The Year of the Tankard (1370 DR)

Saestra Karanok loved parties. She adored being the center of attention, receiving compliments on how beautiful her thick, dark tresses were; how the sparkle of her jeweled earrings set off the twinkle in her deep, brown eyes; or how the sleeveless, full-length gown of light purple silk she wore made her look so much like her mother. Some said she was too vain; Saestra preferred to think it was her way of honoring a mother who died giving birth to her.

It was no different with this party. In fact, because it was her eighteenth birthday, Saestra seemed to have an unending line of well-wishers. She stood in the midst of a continuous swirl of friends and relatives, minor nobles and rich merchants, all trying their best to come up with dazzling and original remarks about her beauty and their desires for her continued health and happiness.

She paid them only nominal heed tonight, smiling and nodding absently at them as they passed. Her attention was elsewhere, on a small group of young men huddled a few feet to the right of where she stood in the great audience hall of the Karanok family palace. Her older brother, Naeros, was among the men, but it was not him she watched with interest. No, it was the young man next to him, Augustus Martiro, who kept drawing her eyes. He had a round, soft face, framed by thick waves of brown hair. A thin band of gold held his mane away from warm, brown eyes that reflected the broad smile he wore. She glanced away whenever their gazes crossed, only to return after she was sure he wasn't looking.

A chime sounded once, twice, and the audience hall quieted. Saestra recognized the signal and watched the single door at the far side of the hall. Moments after the second chime faded away, the door opened, and two regal figures strolled in. The first was Saestra's father, Jaerios. The firm set of his jawline and the dark curls slightly touched with gray at the temples gave him an air of confidence and wisdom. If his nose were not so dominant, he would have been considered quite handsome. Saestra was glad she really did take after her mother.

The figure on Jaerios's arm made Saestra's normally dainty features twist involuntarily into a snarling pout of annoyance. Her twin sister, Kaestra, usually did not attend the parties the family threw in the palace. Unlike Saestra, Kaestra cared little for her looks and the attention garnered by them. She never made an effort to do anything with the long, thin strands of her mousy brown hair, simply letting them fall straight to the middle of her back. Her face was plain and hard, her complexion pale from hours spent buried in books. It didn't matter what others thought about Kaestra; they were sycophants to her.

Tonight, however, Kaestra's hair was pinned up, her cheeks had a healthy glow like sunlight through rose petals, and she wore a white silk gown with a flowing train that practically floated behind her. The pair climbed the dais at the back of the hall where the family sat whenever they presided over official occasions. Earlier that day, two new chairs had been added to the three that were there before. Jaerios stopped in the center of the dais and turned to face the gathered attendants.

"Welcome, everyone. I am so glad you could join our family in this celebration," Jaerios began. Saestra made her way forward in anticipation of her father's introduction, but halted, confused, as he continued without even glancing in her direction.

"There is always some sadness when a father's little girls grow up. But there is pride, too. And nothing makes me prouder than to announce my dear Kaestra's decision to join the church of Entropy."

Applause and murmurs of approval rose to meet

Jaerios's broad smile. Saestra could barely keep her jaw from dropping. What was going on? This was supposed to be her party, her night, but everyone was flocking to Kaestra now. Shock quickly turned to anger, yet Saestra could see no way of rescuing the evening. Frustrated, she stormed from the hall, stomped up the stairs, and slammed the door to her room.

She did this on purpose, Saestra fumed as she paced angrily. I knew she was always jealous. And this proves it. I can't believe she ruined my evening like this. I'll find some way to get her back.

A knock at the door interrupted Saestra's train of thought.

"Go away," Saestra growled.

"I'm sorry about the party, Saestra." It was Naeros, her brother.

"Why would you be sorry? This is the kind of thing you usually find funny."

"True. However, I'm not here to gloat."

"Oh? Don't tell me you stopped by to make me feel better."

"Actually, I'm just delivering a message, though it will probably have that effect."

"I doubt there is anything you could say that would change how I feel," Saestra sighed.

"Oh, I don't know about that. You remember Augustus, right? The man you were staring at all night." Saestra could practically hear Naeros leering on the other side of the door. She blushed. If Naeros had noticed, how many others had seen?

"Anyway, a bunch of us were going to head over to my tower. The party here is getting a bit too stuffy. Augustus begged off but wanted to know if you'd like to meet him over by the Crypts."

"Why would he want to do that?" Saestra was suddenly suspicious of Naeros. This wouldn't be the first time her brother had tried to pull a prank on her. She wasn't in the mood for any of his tricks tonight.

"How would I know? What do young couples normally do in cemeteries? I can't believe I'm even discussing this with my sister. It's bad enough I had to ask you for him."

Saestra's heart skipped a beat. It was true that lovers were known to stroll through the Crypts at night, sometimes stopping for other activities. Some of her friends had shared their firsthand experiences. If there was even a chance that Augustus wanted to meet her there....

"So, what should I tell him?" Naeros was getting impatient. He probably was in a hurry to return to the new place Father had just built for him and get drunk with his friends.

"Tell him ... tell him I'll meet him there in one hour."

"Will do. Have a good night."

Saestra let go of her breath as she heard Naeros's footsteps fade away. It was all she could do not to race out of her bedroom and make for the Crypts straight away. A lady did not rush off to a clandestine rendezvous with her lover, however. Saestra got up from where she sat at the edge of her bed and strode over to her vanity. Her hair was still immaculate, but she primped anyway. It would be cool outside in the early morning hours, so she needed something to cover her arms and shoulders. Saestra sorted through her wardrobe until she picked out the perfect wrap, its fur lining sure to keep her warm.

When she decided she had waited long enough to arrive fashionably late, Saestra slipped out of her room and made her way back downstairs. Not wanting to be seen by anybody at the party, she used the servants' hall and let herself out one of the palace's side entrances. It was a balmy summer night, but Saestra tingled with enough excitement that gooseflesh rose on her arms. The moon was full in the cloudless sky, outshining the closest stars. Saestra could not ask for a more perfect setting. The evening had truly taken a turn for the better.

The Crypts was a large graveyard situated near the center of Luthcheq. It covered a block of land nearly three-quarters of a mile long and a quarter of a mile wide. Used almost exclusively by the nobility of the city, the grounds were dominated by sculpted mausoleums belonging to each house. Lesser nobles and some of the richest merchants rested in plots marked by ornate headstones near the front of the cemetery.

A fence of black iron bars, meant to keep the public out, wrapped around the exterior of the Crypts. Several of the bars had been bent in various places, however, granting entrance. Taxes funded the grounds keeping, and Saestra's father employed a large force of workers specifically to maintain the Crypts, but it seemed someone forced their way in as soon as old bars were replaced. Saestra figured that as long as no real damage was done to the property, it would probably go on that way.

Saestra slipped through the fence and glanced around for Augustus. The marble of the mausoleums glowed eerily in the pale moonlight, and she shivered involuntarily as her eyes moved across them. Saestra thought she saw someone peeking around the corner of one of the buildings, but when she looked back, there was no one there.

She was silently chiding herself for letting her

imagination play tricks on her when a cold hand grabbed her shoulder from behind. She started with a shriek, whirling about to see Augustus holding on to her as he came through the fence.

"Sorry." He grinned. "Hope I wasn't keeping you waiting too long."

"No." She quickly recovered. "Though don't think I would have waited here much longer."

"Of course not." He still wore that broad smile Saestra remembered from the party. "You ever been to the Crypts before?"

"No," Saestra answered, unable to think of anything but his beautiful, round face. She had been here before, when they laid her mother to rest. That was during the day, though. She'd never been here at night.

"I should show you our family's mausoleum, then." He clasped her hand in his and led her into the cemetery. They strolled past sepulchers of various shapes and sizes. Some were decorated with celestial figures escorting departed souls to their final resting places. Others were adorned with grotesque visages of stone meant to ward off evil spirits.

Saestra paid them little heed. Her mind was focused on the connection formed by Augustus's hand wrapped around hers. Were her palms too sweaty? Could he feel her rapid heartbeat through the tips of her fingers?

"Hey, is that door open?" Augustus had stopped at the edge of a gravel path that wound its way up to a slant-roofed mausoleum. Saestra could see that the door, framed by a pair of Ionic pillars, was slightly ajar.

"Is that your family's?" she asked.

"No, but let's go check it out. Maybe there's grave robbers inside." He started forward but turned back when Saestra didn't budge. "I was only kidding. Besides, I'd protect you. I'm sure there's nothing inside there bigger than a rat. Come on." He flashed that smile, and Saestra let herself be dragged along reluctantly.

When they reached the entrance of the mausoleum, Augustus motioned for Saestra to wait while he took a look inside. She hugged one of the columns as he disappeared into the darkness, putting the mass of marble between her and the open doorway. Time crawled while she chewed on her lower lip, waiting. It was eerily quiet. Then something moved inside the tomb, the faint sound of shuffling feet drifting out. Saestra tried to hide behind the column, but could not pull her eyes from the doorway. A shape appeared at the threshold, just beyond the edge of the moonlight.

Augustus stepped out, and Saestra let her breath go with an audible sigh.

"Don't do that," she scolded, moving out from behind the pillar to meet him.

"What?" The mischievous grin on his face belied the innocence in his voice. "It's empty inside, except for a couple of sarcophagi. Which are closed," he quickly added. "Come in with me."

Saestra bit her lip, hesitating for a moment before nodding her consent. Just inside the doorway was a small landing. They stood there for a few minutes, letting their eyes adjust, before descending a short flight of steps. By the faint traces of moonlight that barely pierced the darkness beyond the door, Saestra could make out two large, rectangular objects that occupied the center of the chamber. The thought of somebody's decaying remains still being inside the sarcophagi, just a few feet away, made her shiver.

"Are you cold?" asked Augustus.

He came up behind Saestra and held her to his chest. His arms were strong, and she felt secure with them wrapped around her. She turned in his embrace and looked up, meeting his gaze. Slowly, he leaned in. Saestra wet her lips with her tongue and closed her eyes.

A harsh, grinding noise immediately drew their attention to the thick stone door of the mausoleum. Someone was pulling it shut! Augustus bounded up the stairs but was too late. The last sliver of moonlight was cut off, and the pair was plunged into darkness as the door sealed with a solid thud.

"Hey! Open the door! Let us out!" Augustus shouted, vainly pounding the slab of marble.

"Are the young lovers scared?" a familiar voice taunted. "Enjoy your first night together. See you two in the morning."

"Naeros, I hate you!" Saestra's scream was met with muffled laughter.

"This isn't funny, Naeros. Let us out," Augustus demanded. There was only silence in reply. Saestra heard Augustus come back down the stairs, but she still jumped when he touched her.

"I'm going to look around," Augustus said, his voice just above a whisper. "My uncle always told me that a lot of these mausoleums had hidden rooms and were connected by catacombs that led to the city sewers. I bet we can find a way out."

Saestra nodded, even though they couldn't see each other in the dark. When he pulled away, however, she reached out and grabbed him, suddenly overcome with fear.

"It's all right, Saestra. Nothing's going to happen."

She let him go and huddled against one of the sarcophagi, hugging her fur-lined wrap to herself. It didn't keep her from shivering as a chill settled into her bones. Her ears picked up the sounds of Augustus moving along the walls of the chamber. Saestra imagined his hands moving over the surface, looking for some trigger or mechanism that would reveal a secret door. She'd heard the same stories he had, but even if they were true, the chances of finding something in total darkness was close to impossible. More than likely, they would end up spending the night inside this creepy room together.

They were all alone—by themselves. It wasn't such a bad thing, now that she thought about it. She was just about to suggest that Augustus give up his search when he cried out in discovery, accompanied by the grating of stone against stone. Saestra looked in the direction of the sound and could see an area of dark gray interrupting the blackness that surrounded them.

"There's some kind of light down there," Augustus said.

Saestra saw his silhouette separate from the darkness to stand in the center of the gray area. She moved toward him, her arms outstretched in front of her searching for anything that might be in her way.

"Where does it go?" she asked when she reached him.

"Looks like some stairs leading down to another room. Hold on to me," he said as he started forward.

"Be careful. Go slow."

She thought his silhouette nodded. They crept down the stairs, hugging the wall and each other. The gray began to lighten as they descended, and Saestra caught a hint of smoke in the air. When they came to the bottom of the steps, they found themselves at a dead end. There were no doors on the landing.

"There has to be a door here," Augustus said, his voice thick with frustration.

Saestra glanced around but noticed nothing that looked as if it would grant entrance. Then a faint yellow glow flickered out along the edge where the wall on her right met the floor. It disappeared so quickly she wasn't sure she actually saw it.

"Over here," she said. "I just saw some light through a crack."

Saestra began to push on the wall, looking for a knob or release that would give them access. She could hear Augustus doing the same beside her. This time, it was her turn to find the catch.

The wall slid open to reveal another chamber lit by a solitary torch set in a sconce a few feet away from the stairs on the left wall of the room. Shadows danced across demonic faces carved into the stone, their hungry leers eternally frozen. Saestra gasped.

"What is this place? Waukeen, protect us," Augustus hissed.

Saestra followed his stare to the middle of the room where another sarcophagus lay, its lid pushed open. Next to the stone box, a figure hunched over something, its back to the pair. A cold wave of fear washed over Saestra, and she trembled uncontrollably, rooted to the spot.

The figure turned, finally aware of the presence of intruders. Torchlight revealed taut skin, so white it was almost translucent, stretched across a ghastly face with red eyes that seemed to burn Saestra's soul as they fastened upon her. Wild, wiry strands of hair sprouted in random places from its scalp, and blood dripped from its fanged mouth. One clawed hand was wrapped in the hair of its victim, a woman who now hung like a rag doll from the monster's grip, her life flowing out of a wound on her neck.

"Saestra," Augustus shouted at her, trying to break her paralysis.

He took a step, perhaps to put himself between her and the creature, but the thing intercepted him, moving faster than Saestra could blink. One instant it was by the sarcophagus; the next it was at Augustus's side, the burial robe it wore eerily motionless. It took Augustus's head in both hands and twisted. Saestra shrieked when she heard bones snap.

"I'm sorry. Did I frighten you?" A raspy voice, like dry leaves rubbing together, issued from between the monster's bloodstained lips. It focused its beady red pupils on Saestra and smiled. "Where are my manners? I haven't had dinner guests in such a long time, I've forgotten to even introduce myself. My name is Posius."

Posius drifted over in front of Saestra and gently took her chin in his hand. She tried to recoil at his cold touch, but his grip was inescapable.

"My, my, aren't you a pretty one. I think I'll keep you."

His gaze captured Saestra, and she felt some inner part of her falling into his soulless eyes. She offered no resistance when he tilted her head to the side, and only a slight shudder as he embraced her.

THE PRIESTS

CHAPTER I

The Year of Rogue Dragons

(1373 DR)

Summer in Bezantur was known by the locals as the Reeking Heat. Piles of refuse scattered throughout the city had slowly grown through the year, and now baked in the sun, their ripe stench carried about the city by stiff winds that blew in off the Sea of Fallen Stars. The citizens of Bezantur dealt with the Reeking Heat in their own ways, most of them ineffectual in actually providing any sort of sustained relief. Even those who resided in the Central Citadel, the home of the city's ruler, resorted to an archaic method involving cauldrons of incense and fans.

Fortunately, the master of the Central Citadel had other means available to him. Aznar Thrul, tharchion of the Priador and zulkir of the school of Evocation, warded himself from the heat and the stench with his magic. Crisp air from some faraway mountaintop filled his nostrils and flowed over his skin, the result of a simple invocation he had learned when he was just an apprentice.

Regardless, it was not helping his mood, but that had more to do with who he was meeting, not the weather.

Aznar sat tapping his fingers on the ornately carved oak table that stretched out before him. While most audiences were held in the throne room, the conference chamber had been selected for this particular meeting. It was one of several concessions Aznar was forced to make in order to get Samas Kul, master of the Guild of Foreign Trade, to come to him. He had also forgone the normal rule that all visitors entered his presence naked. It was worth the risk to his person not to be subjected to the sight of Kul's fleshy rolls jiggling before his eyes.

The doors to the conference room swung open, and Aznar's chamberlain entered.

"O, Mighty Tharchion, Mightier Zulkir, I present Samas Kul, Master of the Guild of Foreign Trade." The sticklike servant bowed and stepped to the side to reveal a corpulent mass in red silk and leather. A red skullcap rested atop Kul's shaved head, which was so lumpy it appeared the man was having some sort of allergic reaction to multiple bee stings. The high, flaring collar of his tunic tried unsuccessfully to hide the layers of excess skin that flapped under his chin. Leather shoulder pads studded with gems struggled vainly to add any sort of form to Kul's upper body. The sleeves of his tunic ended in leather bracers that covered his forearms. His fat fingers swelled around the thick bands of gold that adorned each hand. Brown hosiery and knee-high leather boots completed the outfit.

Samas waddled in and dropped his bulk into the chair at the opposite end of the table from Aznar. At a nod from his liege, the chamberlain bowed once more and stepped out of the room, closing the doors behind himself.

"Thank you for coming, Guildmaster Kul."

"I must admit, I was rather surprised to hear from you." Kul's voice was a wet rattle in the back of his throat. "My past requests for your time always seemed to . . . conflict with other pressing matters of state."

It was obvious Kul knew Aznar was simply avoiding him.

"I would be remiss in my duties as tharchion if I did not keep abreast of all that happened within my city." The statement was meant more as a subtle reminder to Kul of Aznar's position above him. It was infuriating that he even had to provide such a reminder. The man was an accomplished transmuter, but nowhere near a match for the Zulkir of Evocation. It was Kul's political clout that kept Aznar from crushing him like a fly. Samas Kul controlled the Guild of Foreign Trade, the vast, bureaucratic body that oversaw the running of every Thayan enclave around Faerûn. Aznar had to be careful. If he wanted to keep control of this meeting, he could not tip his hand too soon. "So, tell me how things fare with the guild?"

"Exceedingly well, as I am sure you know." Kul's fleshy lips parted in a toothy smile. "The coffers overflow with coin from the enclaves. Their success is more than anyone imagined, I dare say."

Aznar clenched his jaw to keep from rising to the bait. Kul knew of his stance against the enclaves when the idea was first proposed. He knew what a thorn in

Aznar's side it was to have all that gold sitting in his city, yet be unable to touch but the barest portion of it through tariffs and municipal fees. That was going to change.

"That is good to hear," Aznar said, leaning forward, "because it is time I started seeing more coin from the guild."

"And how do you propose to make that happen?" Kul seemed unfazed.

"I was thinking the guild's increasing usage of the city's port facilities wasn't accurately reflected in the leasing fee it pays."

"I see. That would certainly net you a few more coins, once the fees cleared all those layers of bureaucracy."

Aznar's eyes widened, and his nostrils flared. Was that a threat? No, he reasoned, it was the simple truth. Aznar held no illusions about the corruption within his city's government. After all the bribes and skimming off the top, he really wouldn't see that much of an increase.

"If I may suggest an alternative that would be mutually beneficial?" Kul was watching him closely. Aznar nodded for him to continue.

"Were you to sponsor a few enclaves of your own, you would receive a direct cut of the profits. No intervening agencies to bother with, just straight to your own purse."

Aznar sat quietly, letting the silence draw out. So, it came back to this. It was not the first time Kul had approached him about sponsoring an enclave. The idea was a bitter pill to swallow, considering how vocal his criticism had been.

"I assume you've cut similar deals with the other zulkirs?" Aznar already knew the answer to that.

"It's just business, you understand."

"Of course. I will think more on your . . . suggestion. Thank you for coming, Master Kul." Aznar smiled politely while silently signaling for his chamberlain. Kul stood and followed the man out of the chamber.

As soon as the master of the Guild of Foreign Trade left, Aznar Thrul's smile twisted into a snarl. The obese mound of flesh tested his patience, speaking to Aznar as though he were an equal. Regardless of the wealth the guild generated, Aznar was a zulkir and tharchion, and Bezantur was his city. Perhaps it was time to show Samas Kul exactly where he stood.

Unfortunately, Aznar needed Kul and the guild. The admission made him grimace. He had opposed the enclaves at their inception, ridiculing the notion that Thay could gain power by selling magic rather than taking what it wanted by force. He had been proven wrong, and now had little share of the enormous profits that flowed through the guild's coffers. Not that Aznar lacked resources, but he would not stand idly by while the purses of the other zulkirs grew at an alarming rate.

However, his demands of a greater portion had been politely refused by Kul time and again. The guildmaster's audacity to repeatedly suggest that Aznar perhaps sponsor the opening of more enclaves, thereby increasing his cut, was maddening.

Aznar slammed his fist on the table and stood up from his chair. As angry as it made him, Kul was right. Aznar was not so inflexible as to ignore the recommendation. The question, then, was where. There were already enclaves in almost ninety percent of Faerûn's major cities, but sponsoring one in someplace smaller than Saerloon, Baldur's Gate, or even Hillsfar was hardly worth his time and effort.

That left cities in nations that opposed either the

Red Wizards or the arcane in general. Aznar quickly eliminated Aglarond, Rashemen and Mulhorand as possibilities. There was too much bloodshed by Thayan hands in those places, and there was no one of any significance Aznar had a hold over.

Then it came to him.

Aznar strode down the hall toward his study, a predatory grin on his face revealing the triumph he felt as the pieces of his plan began mentally falling into place. The last question to resolve was what catalyst would be used to set things in motion. It could not be himself, or any of his underlings. No, the agent had to have nothing to do with the Art at all if this were to succeed.

When he reached his study, Aznar grabbed several sheets of parchment and sat at his desk. There were many people who owed him favors but only one he could think of with the resources and competence to accomplish this task. They had met more than twenty years ago, before he became zulkir of Evocation. They had been introduced, really, at one of the many socialite parties thrown by some minor noble, where everyone scurried from circle to circle with hopes of elevating their own status. He still remembered it quite clearly.

Mylra, headmistress of Loviatar's Manor, sidled up to Aznar as he stood in a circle of fellow students from the school of Evocation. She wore a flowing gown with long sleeves and an empire waist. The green silk matched the tattoos that covered her shaved scalp. Thick lines of kohl circled her eyes, rouge powder coated her cheeks, and her lips had been painted a dark red, all in a vain attempt to hide her age. Aznar watched her approach from the corner of his eye. It had been like this all night, people coming to offer their congratulations or praise for his accomplishments in the Art.

This is the price of being a rising star, he sighed to himself. Aznar turned to greet Mylra, and saw she was with another woman, about twenty years old, standing quietly at her side.

"Master Thrul, don't you look...." The rest of what Mylra had to say was little more than buzzing in Aznar's ear. He smiled politely and nodded, but his gaze was fixed on the woman with Mylra. She was nearly as tall as Aznar, her head shaved except for a single stripe of long, braided hair that ran from her forehead back to her shoulders. She wore a simple dress of white, belted at the waist with a gold braid. What intrigued Aznar the most was her unwavering, dark eyes that seemed to drink in his soul.

"Well, if you'll excuse us, Aznar, there are some other people I wanted to speak with."

Aznar blinked, just now aware that the conversation had run its course and Mylra was turning to leave. What was the name of the woman with her? He realized he hadn't even asked. Mylra was already involved with another group across the room before he could open his mouth.

"Does anybody know who that woman with Mylra is?" he asked the others around him. Everyone shook their heads or said that they did not. Aznar excused himself and started toward Mylra and her companion, but he was intercepted by Lord Brusjen after only a couple of steps. The elderly patriarch of some minor noble house momentarily blocked Aznar's view of his objective, and the young Red Wizard craned his neck over and around the old man in an attempt to reacquire Mylra's position. She was nowhere to be seen.

Desperate, Aznar cut off Brusjen, physically moving him aside. He scanned the room and caught a flash of green silk exiting on the far side. The young woman trailed behind, but she stopped in the doorway and looked back, right at Aznar. Their eyes locked, and she smiled then followed her mistress out. Before he could chase after them, Milurkah Ilvable, a fellow student who had practically thrown herself at him this past tenday, snaked her arm around his and pulled him aside. Aznar frowned but resigned himself to the fact he would not learn the young woman's identity that evening. He allowed himself to be led away, and even worked up a smile at the thought that he would at least be able to take his frustrations out on Milurkah tonight.

He contacted the headmistress a few days later and was told the woman was a newly appointed Maiden of the Lash named Yenael Duumin. Mylra invited him to the manor to meet her. After participating in one of their pain rites, he and Yenael spent the night together. For the next year they shared a bed.

Then one day, without explanation, she disappeared.

Other things had kept him occupied: his rise to zulkir, the Salamander War, and becoming tharchion of Bezantur. He was never at a loss for companionship during those years and hardly thought of Yenael.

So it took him somewhat by surprise when she resurfaced just a few years ago, requesting his aid in a plot to replace Mylra as headmistress. He readily agreed, realizing the advantage of having a powerful temple in his debt.

While the ink dried on the parchment, Aznar mouthed a cantrip to summon his chamberlain. The man appeared in the doorway as Aznar pressed his seal into the hot wax on the back of the envelope. It was time to call in a debt.

"What is your bidding, O Mighty Tharchion, Mightier Zulkir?" the chamberlain asked with a bow as Aznar rose and walked over to him.

"Have this delivered immediately to Headmistress Yenael at Loviatar's Manor. I'll be in my bedchambers. Send her there when she arrives."

❧ ❧ ❧ ❧ ❧

The Year of Lightning Storms (1374 DR)

Prisus Saelis leaned against the port rail and watched the ship pull up to the pier, his breath visible before him as he exhaled into the chill air. A slight breeze ruffled his sandy hair; he shivered and pulled tight the collar of his wool overcoat. These trips were bittersweet. No city could compare to the clean, white stone buildings or the magnificent marble sculptures that lined the streets of home, certainly not Bezantur. From his vantage point, he could see the slave markets just beyond the wharf. Masses of filthy bodies milled about in pens while auctioneers yelled out bids. The markets rivaled the many temples as the dominant feature of Thay's largest city. He could see the spires of various religious structures rising above the tangled skyline. The whole city was a chaotic jigsaw whose pieces didn't quite fit. No, Bezantur was definitely not

Luthcheq. But much as he loved the sites of Luthcheq, they reminded Prisus of his wife, gone now these past five years.

With a sigh, Prisus warded off the homesickness and melancholy that typically followed these reveries. He was here on business; best to get it done quickly and be off. The ship had docked, and a gangplank was secured from the deck to the pier. He motioned his manservant, Leco, toward the bags and made his way down to the city. The pair waded through the bustling crowds toward Myulon's, the only inn where Prisus felt even a little safe. It was located near the North Gate, which meant passing by the Central Citadel, home of Aznar Thrul, a Red Wizard and ruler of the Priador. A mix of human, gnoll, and goblin guards lounged against the black stone of the massive building, harassing pedestrians who wandered too close. Prisus made sure to keep his distance.

When they arrived at Myulon's, a two-story building of gray stone with a tiled roof, Prisus went straight to the front desk and checked in.

"Master Saelis, welcome. I did not think we would see you again until the spring." Myulon was tall and lanky. His head was shaved, but the sallow skin of his scalp was bereft of tattoos. He wore the same smile Prisus remembered, broad and unsettling, as though the innkeeper knew something you did not. Myulon handed Prisus a note along with the room key.

"You be careful, Master Saelis," Myulon said. Prisus frowned, not sure what to make of the innkeeper's words.

"Oh, I did not read the note," Myulon quickly reassured, "but I saw who delivered it. Those types of maidens bring only pain. I could find you a nice girl, if you like."

"Thank you, Myulon. I'll remember that." Thoroughly confused, Prisus climbed the stairs to his room. He unlocked the door, entered, went immediately to the writing desk, and broke the wax seal on the letter.

Master Saelis,

If you wish to go through with our transaction, come to Loviatar's Manor at your earliest convenience after arriving in Bezantur. Ask for me.

Yenael

Prisus was slightly taken aback. He was aware almost every god in Faerûn had a temple or shrine of some sort in Bezantur, but what little he knew from his wife's involvement with the church of Loviatar still gave him pause. The goddess wasn't called the Maiden of Pain for nothing.

"I don't like this, Master Saelis." Leco had brought the luggage in and now stood over Prisus's shoulder, reading the note. "Do you really want to bring a Loviatan back into our household? Remember what it was like when Mistress Saelis—Waukeen bless her soul—was involved with that cult?"

Prisus sighed and nodded. Unfortunately, there weren't alternatives. Without his wife, their daughter, Iuna, needed a governess. The poor girl was not adjusting well to her mother's death. They had gone through four women in the past five years because of her mood swings. Finding new help locally was suddenly all but impossible. So Prisus started searching elsewhere, but a steady increase in taxes by the Karanoks made coin tight, and many of the candidates' fees were too expensive. He'd almost given up when he was contacted by a woman named Yenael.

Prisus left the inn right away. It was already late afternoon, and only a fool walked the streets of Bezantur after sundown without an armed escort.

The manor was just a couple of blocks east of the Central Citadel. It was built into a hillside, with extensive grounds consisting of graveled walkways that wound through well-manicured lawns. Prisus paused at the open front gate, unable to reconcile the church's reputation for painful torture with the peaceful landscape that stretched out before him. He approached the main building, a sprawling affair of stonework, unadorned except for the low relief of a barbed scourge carved above the lintel of the entrance, its nine tails spread out like a fan. Prisus banged the knocker on the iron-bound wooden door then stepped back to wait. Several minutes passed before it opened.

A robed figure surrounded by a soft nimbus of golden light stood in the doorway and said, "I'm sorry, but the manor is closed to the public while the rite is being performed."

Prisus could not see the face, as it was hidden under a hood, but he thought from the voice that it must be a woman.

"I am here to meet Yenael," said Prisus. "She's expecting me."

He showed her the note. He could feel the woman's eyes measuring him.

"You don't look like her typical subject. Loviatar calls all kinds, though." The woman moved back from the doorway, causing the nimbus to fade, and motioned for Prisus to enter. "Wait here while I find her."

Closing the door, the woman left Prisus standing in

the middle of a small entry hall. Her words had been unsettling, and he glanced about nervously. Candlelight glowed from small coves carved in the walls, creating more shadow than illumination. Opposite the front entrance was a great open archway that led into the main sanctum. Prisus gasped.

The room was lit with numerous candles. Little flames filled candelabras or flickered in groups on table tops. In the center of the floor sat a large circle of candles placed several feet apart from each other. For each candle on the floor, a man or woman danced naked around it. Each person was singing or chanting, though none of them seemed in unison. And each, at some time during their ritual, would pass a body part through the flame of their candle, often holding it there for several seconds.

Prisus's nose wrinkled at the strange odor wafting in from the sanctum. It took him a moment to realize it was not incense, but the acrid smell of burnt hair and singed flesh.

Prisus turned to the door, ready to leave, and came face-to-face with another woman. Instead of a robe, she wore a tight, sleeveless leather body suit buffed to a high shine. Her head was shaved, except for a thin braided tail that began at the base of her skull and ended between her shoulder blades. Blue tattoos of some unfamiliar design covered her scalp. Dark eyes reflected the wavering flames of the candles.

"Prisus Saelis? I am Sister Yenael." She smiled, a warm and friendly grin. "Let's go somewhere we can talk." She waited for a moment, sensing Prisus's shock. "Our Candle Rite happens every twelfth night," she explained, holding her hand out toward the sanctum. "Fire is one of the Three Pains. Loviatar teaches that pain brings strength of spirit."

Prisus shook his head then motioned her to lead on. They went up a flight of stairs and entered a small parlor. Red velvet drapes hid the hard stone walls, and plush sofas of crimson shared the floor with piles of dark red pillows embroidered in gold thread. Prisus had heard that the church of Loviatar often recruited from the ranks of the wealthy. It certainly explained the extravagance.

Yenael lounged across the pillows, leaving Prisus to his choice of sofas. A robed man entered shortly, carrying two goblets on a tray. He offered first to Prisus then to Yenael. She rose partway to take the cup and whispered something to the servant, who bowed and left. Prisus sniffed the drink, a honeyed mead, then took a sip.

"I hope your trip went well, Master Saelis. No sahuagin attacks?" Yenael took a deep draught as she waited for his answer, her eyes never leaving him.

"No, no attacks." He shifted on the sofa, uncomfortable under the stare. He desperately wanted to get past small talk to the business at hand and return to his room at the inn. "Um, I'm not sure . . . I don't think you're quite what I was looking for."

Yenael gave a small laugh. "All business, I see. I like that. Master Saelis, I apologize for the confusion. I am not the one you will be hiring." She set her goblet down then snapped her fingers. The servant returned, this time with another woman in tow. Nearly as tall as Prisus, she wore a simple linen dress that blended with her pale yellow skin. The left side of her head was shaved. A tattoo of a nine-tailed serpent ran the length of her exposed scalp, its open mouth framing her left eye. The dark hair that remained was pulled into a long, thick braid that hung to her waist.

With confident strides, she brushed past Prisus to

stand next to the reclining Yenael, who dismissed the servant with a curt, "Thank you. You may leave us." She turned to Prisus. "Master Saelis, may I introduce Ythnel."

Prisus stood as the servant departed. "I am pleased to meet you, Ythnel." The young woman gave a small curtsy in reply. "May I ask a few questions?" Prisus requested, looking at Yenael.

"You may speak directly to me, Master Saelis." There was no defiance in Ythnel's voice or eyes; it was just a statement of fact.

"Ah, yes. My apologies, then. Very well. If I may begin by asking how old you are?"

"Twenty-one summers, this Eleasias."

"Tell me a little about your education."

"I have studied the regional histories, lifestyles, and societies of Thay and its neighbors: Aglarond, Rashemen, Chessenta, and Mulhorand. I am also versed in the literary and performing arts."

"Remarkable."

"So, do you find her acceptable?" Yenael asked.

"If I might ask one more thing?" Prisus hesitated. His eyes bounced between the women, waiting for a signal. Both stared at him stone-faced. Clearing his throat, he turned back to Ythnel. "Why are you interested in becoming a governess?"

"I have lived my entire life within these walls," Ythnel said without pause. "I want to see with my own eyes what I have only read about in books. I wish to put to use what I have learned."

Prisus frowned. "I don't mean to offend, but I will not allow the dogma of Loviatar taught in my house."

"Do not fear, Master Saelis," Yenael said, finally standing. "Loviatans do not evangelize. Those who are interested seek us out." She smiled, but there was no warmth in it this time. "Is there anything else?"

"No, I think that is all. Here is the gold I promised as a commission." Prisus untied a swollen pouch from his belt and handed it to Yenael.

"The terms are agreed upon," Yenael announced. "You are free to go." She led them back to the entrance. "You may return in the morning for her things." Yenael opened the door. "Good night, Master Saelis."

"Good night, Sister Yenael." Prisus turned and led Ythnel away.

Yenael watched Prisus Saelis and Ythnel disappear from view then closed the door. "Good-bye, daughter," she whispered. It felt strange to think of the girl in that way. Yenael stood there for a moment, her hand still on the latch, wondering why the thought had even occurred to her.

There had never been a familial bond between them. Yenael had always treated Ythnel like another initiate. It was a purposeful decision on her part—a kindness, even, in Yenael's mind. There always came a point in a child's life when the parent was revealed to be only human, imperfect. That revelation was often a form of betrayal to the child. In an act of mercy even now Yenael could not explain, she chose to shield Ythnel from this pain. The girl had been raised as a ward of the manor, told she had been orphaned when she grew old enough to ask.

What's done is done, Yenael told herself, and she is better off for it. She does not need the distractions a family brings. They would only hinder her in the task she has ahead.

Shaking her head, Yenael turned down the hallway

into the manor. She needed to clear her own head, and performing her evening prayers would provide the focus she required. The only question was which whip she should use.

Ythnel rose from her bed and pulled back the curtains, letting the sun into the room Master Saelis had rented for her at the inn. She removed the shirt Master Saelis had provided as a nightgown, folded it, and placed it on the floor beside the bed. She then reached behind her neck to untie the thin leather strap from which hung a small, ceremonial whip with nine tails, the symbol of her faith. Ythnel knelt on the folded cloth and began a prayer chant. Every few seconds, as the chanting would reach a crescendo, Ythnel lashed herself with the whip, leaving pink welts on her smooth, sallow skin. With each lash, Ythnel felt a tingle of pleasure that transcended the pain.

A creak from the door brought the prayer to a halt. Ythnel quickly stood, just catching a glimpse of someone stepping back from the doorway. Remembering that she was still naked, Ythnel scooped up the nightgown, put it back on, and traded the whip for a towel and her clothes and walked out of the room. Prisus stood across the hall with his back to her. Ythnel tried to slip quietly past him, but he turned as she closed the door.

"I ... uh, I didn't mean to ... I mean, it wasn't my intention ...," Prisus stammered.

"Perhaps it would be best to knock first before entering in the future, Master Saelis," Ythnel said, unable to look directly at him.

"Of course." Prisus's cheeks were flushed. "I only

wanted to tell you that I've booked our passage. And
... and Leco has your things. I'll have him bring them
to your room. We can go as soon as you're ready."

"Thank you. I'm going to take a bath before I meet
you downstairs." She didn't wait for a response.

They made their way to the docks after morningfeast. The city was already buzzing with activity, but
Prisus seemed oblivious to it, lost in his own thoughts.
As they approached the pier, Prisus finally blurted
out, "Why do you beat yourself?" Several dockworkers
who were loading cargo looked askance at the pair.

The embarrassment from earlier in the morning
came rushing back. "I thought you were not interested
in my religion, Master Saelis?" Ythnel raised a questioning eyebrow. She did not want to talk about it, but
the deflection failed.

"I'm not," he replied a bit more discreetly. "To be
honest, my wife was part of a group that dallied a bit
in some of the less ... exotic rites of your faith. She quit
before we were married, thank Tymora. I just ... I don't
understand what could motivate someone to ... to—"

"To suffer?" Ythnel finished. Prisus nodded, but
Ythnel hesitated, unsure how to answer. She had been
told time and again by the clerics at the manor why
they served as they did, and had repeated the reasons
back just as often, but this was the first time she had
been asked to explain to someone unfamiliar, and
uncomfortable, with the Loviatan beliefs. "Why did
you come all the way to Bezantur to find a governess
for your daughter?"

"Because I love her, of course."

"And I love Loviatar. She is the only mother I have
known. I want to show her my devotion, just as you
wish to show your daughter how much you care for
her."

"I don't think the situations are necessarily equivalent, but I guess I can see your point." Prisus shrugged. The pair walked in silence to the waiting ship and boarded.

For the first two days of the voyage, Ythnel was violently ill. The roll of the ship on the waves of the sea wreaked havoc on her stomach, and she spent most of her time leaning over a rail on deck, or over a pail in her quarters. Master Saelis was finally able to procure some sort of root for her from another passenger onboard that, when chewed, prevented nausea.

By the fourth day, Ythnel was enjoying herself. Gulls soared back and forth with the ship, bolstered by the brisk wind that carried with it the briny smell of the sea. Sail-finned fish leaped from wave to wave before the bow, racing the ship. It was beautiful, this open world of air and water, and quite alien to Ythnel. She lingered at the starboard rail well after sunset, watching the stars twinkling in the night sky, her breath forming puffs of white before her.

She shivered, hugging herself and rubbing her arms to keep the blood circulating. The wind cut through even the thick coat and mittens she had borrowed from Master Saelis. It was probably best if she headed belowdecks for the night anyway, before he worried why she hadn't returned to the cabin she shared with Prisus and Leco.

Ythnel turned and noticed two sailors were watching her from their stations across the deck. Most of the crew was asleep; the current shift included a helmsman along with a single guard fore and aft. These two were supposed to be making repairs to the sails or mending lines or something. Their work lay at their feet.

The intent behind those stares was unmistakable. Ythnel had seen it many times before, though she usually hadn't been the target. If necessary, she was confident she could handle the two men but decided it was better to remove herself from the situation. She strode toward the hatch that would take her belowdecks, not even bothering to glance at the sailors.

The approaching sound of boots on wood planks told her they were not going to give up so easily. Ythnel stopped and pointed at one of them.

"Fall!" she ordered. Propelled by divine energy channeled from Loviatar, the force of the command struck one of the sailors and knocked him prone.

The sailor who kept his feet jumped slightly at the obvious use of magic. Then he visibly screwed up his courage. "You're gonna pay for that, witch." The man continued to advance, his face twisted into a lecherous leer.

"What's going on here?" Leco emerged from out of the hatch. Ythnel saw his eyes dart between her and the two sailors. "Master Saelis sent me to look for you." He pulled Ythnel past him and closed the hatch after they both had descended.

"Thank you for your help, Leco," Ythnel said as they started down the narrow corridor toward their cabin.

"Don't thank me. I'm just doing what Master Saelis asked of me. Those men could have had their way with you for all I care."

Ythnel pulled up short, shocked by Leco's harsh words. "Why? What have I done to you?"

"You are a Loviatan. I know what that means. Master Saelis's wife was a Loviatan before they were married. I told him it was a bad idea to hire you. Rest assured, I will be watching you. I won't let you hurt him or his daughter." He continued down the corridor without waiting for Ythnel to respond.

She stood there for a moment after he disappeared into the cabin, shocked. The man hated her simply because of her faith. She had heard stories about this kind of prejudice from sisters in the manor, but now that she had come face-to-face with such a situation, Ythnel realized she hadn't really understood what those sisters experienced. A deep sadness washed over her as she let herself into the cabin and quietly slipped into her bunk.

On the afternoon of the sixth day, they arrived in Luthcheq. The reflection of the sun off the white buildings created a dazzling brilliance that nearly blinded Ythnel, but she would not close her eyes. She had never been beyond the manor's grounds before; she had read of other cities besides Bezantur but had never seen them. All she had known were walls of dark stone. Here everything was so bright and clean. Even the movement of the crowds seemed orderly. Ythnel feared that if she blinked, if she looked away for just a second, it would all vanish like a dream.

Prisus had Leco run ahead to fetch a carriage while he and Ythnel waited with the luggage. As she watched people walk by, she noted how different they looked. There was a hint of olive to their skin tone, and their eyes did not have the same tilt as hers. Most of them were short, like Prisus. The men wore their hair cropped, with the bangs brushed down onto their foreheads. The women had their hair pinned up in back, with several loose strands of curls trailing down to their shoulders.

A carriage pulled up, and Leco jumped off the back and began loading their belongings. Prisus motioned for Ythnel to get in then followed, closing the door behind himself. Leco finished with the luggage and climbed up next to the driver. Ythnel's stomach began to flutter, and her palms sweated as the carriage started off. Prisus had gone over her new duties while they were aboard the ship, but now that she was moments away from meeting his daughter, she was nervous. The world outside the manor was so different. For the first time, she began to feel awkward about her beliefs. It seemed that they now served to alienate her rather than provide a common bond.

Ythnel wiped her palms on her dress and bit her lip. Prisus noticed the nervous gestures and smiled. "You'll do fine, Ythnel. I'm sure Iuna will like you. She's really a good girl. It's just that her mother's death hit her hard. It hit us all pretty hard."

Prisus sighed and looked out the window of the carriage. Ythnel gazed out as well, thinking the sights might help her to relax. They had left the docks behind and passed a solitary tower in the center of a well-tended garden. Four giant trees surrounded the tower, obscuring all but a single window at the top from view.

"The tower of Naeros Karanok," Ythnel breathed.

"So, you are versed in the politics of our city," Prisus chuckled. "Let's test that knowledge, shall we? Anything more you can tell me about the ruling family?"

"From what I understand, Naeros is also known as the Marker because he likes to disfigure prisoners. He's the grandson of Maelos Karanok, the family patriarch and ruler of the city, though that's mostly in name only. Jaerios, Maelos's son and Naeros's father, is the real source of power. I believe Jaerios also has a daughter, but I know nothing about her."

"Excellent." Prisus nodded. "What else do you know about Luthcheq politics?"

Ythnel thought for a moment as the tower faded from view. "The Karanoks have decreed that all arcane magic is outlawed. Wizards and sorcerers, and those who associate with them, are summarily executed—a policy that has caused tension with neighbors and hindered the economy of the city."

"An understandable point of view for one who comes from a nation ruled by wizards, and not without merit," Prisus conceded.

The carriage pulled into a private courtyard and stopped in front of a two-story building squeezed between its neighbors. It had a flat roof and an unremarkable exterior. A short flight of stairs led up to a plain but sturdy wooden door. Ythnel followed Prisus in.

"Iuna, precious, I'm back," Prisus called out when he entered. For a moment, they stood in silence in the middle of the living area. A beautiful woven rug covered most of the stone floor. Two sofas and a chaise lounge formed a semicircle before a marble fireplace where a small fire burned lazily. A doorway beyond the sofas led into a dining room.

"Papa!" A young girl of about eleven summers stood at the top of a staircase to the right. She wore a knee-length blue dress with lace ruffles at the shoulders rather than sleeves. Her dark hair was done up much like that of the women Ythnel had seen in the streets.

Prisus strode to the base of the stairs and opened his arms, catching Iuna as she leaped down the last two steps. He gave her a twirling hug then set her down. "I want you to meet someone," he said, turning her to face Ythnel. "This is Ythnel. She's going to help you with your studies."

Iuna's smile suddenly turned into a pout. "I thought we decided it was just going to be you and me, Papa."

"Now, Iuna, you know how much I want that. But I

can't always be here because of business, so you need someone to look after you when I'm gone."

Iuna crossed her arms over her chest, unconvinced. "I don't like her. Find a different one."

"There isn't anyone else," Prisus sighed. "Just give it some time, precious. Why don't you show her around the house? That will give you both a chance to get to know each other."

"All right, Papa. I'll do it for you." Iuna stood on her tiptoes and gave Prisus a kiss.

"Excellent." He smiled. "Now, I have to run to the Trade Center, but I'll be back by dinner. Have a good afternoon."

"Good-bye, Papa." Iuna waved as Prisus headed back outside. Then she turned to Ythnel. Her lips were pinched, and anger smoldered in her brown eyes. "Follow me."

Iuna led Ythnel up the stairs and down the hall to a small room with a single bed, a dresser, and a desk. Ythnel's belongings were sitting on the bed.

"This is your room. Not much"—Iuna sniffed—"but plenty for a slave." She looked pointedly at Ythnel then pushed past her. On the other side of the hall, they stopped before a closed door. Iuna opened it to reveal another bedroom. Dolls sat upon a chest at the foot of a four-poster bed. The floor was covered with several matching rugs. An elaborate vanity stood near a large window in one wall that looked out into the courtyard.

"This is my room. Slaves are not allowed in here without my permission." Iuna stepped into her room and turned back to Ythnel. "And that concludes the tour." She slammed the door shut.

It had been a long day, and Ythnel was glad to finally be in her room. She moved about in silence, unpacking her things. The emotional turmoil of the day manifested itself in a physical draining of energy, and sleep beckoned. Ythnel sat on the bed, fighting the temptation. It would be so easy just to lie back and close her eyes, to forgo the evening prayer for much needed rest. She wasn't at the manor anymore. No one would know.

I would know, her conscience scolded. And Loviatar would know.

Ythnel picked herself up and undressed. She took the whip from around her neck and knelt on the floor, her back to the door. The words of the evening prayer began to form in her mind, but she could not focus. Iuna's petulant face shattered Ythnel's concentration every time she closed her eyes. The spoiled brat infuriated her. Yet there was something about the girl that reminded Ythnel of herself. And there was the fact that her mother had been a Loviatan. Perhaps Ythnel's being here was a part of some greater purpose. Perhaps the Maiden of Pain had plans for the young girl.

First things first, she told herself. You've been hired to train this girl how to be a lady. Focus on and accomplish that before you start imagining you're here on some divinely ordained mission.

She sighed. It was an arduous task set before her, regardless. She would not be able to do it alone.

"Oh, Loviatar, the Willing Whip, I pray for the strength and wisdom to discipline this child. Let me help her, as I was helped."

Ythnel sat quietly for a moment, looking inward for that center of peace and order. A weight lifted from her heart, and she knew her supplication had been answered. With a calmed mind, she quietly began the chant of the evening prayer, letting the rhythm sooth and refresh her. She raised the whip.

A creak from the floorboards outside her door jerked Ythnel's attention away from the prayer.

"I thought we agreed to knock first, Master Saelis." She remained crouched, her head bowed while she waited for an answer. None came. "Master Saelis?" This time she rose. As she did, Ythnel heard the patter of little feet running away.

THE PRIESTS

When Ythnel made her way downstairs, she found Prisus and Iuna already seated at the table eating morningfeast. A place was set on Prisus's left, opposite Iuna. Assuming it was for her, Ythnel slid into the empty seat.

"Good morning, Ythnel," Prisus said, dabbing the corner of his mouth with a napkin. "We wondered if you were going to show." A middle-aged woman in an apron appeared with a plate of steaming sausage and two eggs, which she set before Ythnel. "I don't believe you've met Libia, our cook, yet." Libia gave a small curtsy before disappearing back into the kitchen.

"I apologize for my tardiness, Master Saelis. It seems I overslept. I will submit to whatever penance you see fit." There was no regret in

Ythnel's voice. It had been an honest mistake. She knew the importance of discipline, though, and did not fear punishment. Even a minor transgression like this received some sort of flogging back at the manor.

Prisus waved her off as he lifted a glass of water to his lips.

"Perhaps if you did not stay up all night casting spells, you would be able to get up with the rest of us," Iuna chided.

Water sprayed from Prisus's mouth.

"What?" Prisus yelled, all color draining from his face. He turned to Ythnel. "Is this true?" Without waiting for a response, he turned back to Iuna. "I don't care," he continued, "I do not want such things spoken in this house. Ever! Am I understood?" Iuna nodded sullenly.

"I was not casting spells, Master Saelis," Ythnel said evenly. She looked straight at Iuna, but the girl would not meet her gaze. "I pray every morning and evening as part of my daily devotion to Loviatar."

"Be that as it may—" Prisus paused, taking a deep, steadying breath. "—why don't we all just forget about the whole affair? I'm going to be in my study for most of the morning. I suggest you two finish morningfeast and begin Iuna's lesson." He excused himself and left.

Ythnel and Iuna continued their meal in silence. Ythnel efficiently cut up her sausage and ate each piece with a bite of egg. Iuna lethargically stirred her food with a fork for a few moments then sighed. Pushing her unfinished plate away, she got up from the table. Ythnel stabbed the last piece of sausage with her fork and shoved it in her mouth. She used the napkin to wipe off her face and followed Iuna. They climbed the stairs, Iuna seemingly unaware of Ythnel's presence behind her. At the top, Iuna surprised Ythnel and instead of continuing down the hall to the parlor next to Ythnel's quarters, turned to the right and walked straight to her bedroom, closing the door.

"Iuna?" Ythnel called through the door. "You heard your father. We should begin your studies." She waited, but there was no reply. "Iuna open this door."

Sudden anger at Iuna's disrespect welled up inside Ythnel. She wanted to fling the door open, charge in, and spank the girl. Undisciplined punishment teaches nothing, Ythnel told herself, pushing the emotion back. The vacuum was quickly filled with uncertainty. She felt as if she stood on the edge of a precipice as doubt fought with years of indoctrination. Her mind knew Iuna needed to be taught her place, but Ythnel's heart hesitated, questioning if it was her responsibility, if corporal punishment was the correct solution.

This is the reason I'm here, she mentally affirmed. Pain brings strength of spirit.

Ythnel opened the door and stepped inside. Iuna stood there, facing her with her arms crossed.

"I did not give you permission," she said defiantly.

"I don't need your permission. I am not a slave. Your father has employed my services to help raise you," Ythnel said sternly. "Now it is time to end this game."

Iuna's eyes blazed, and her arms went rigid at her sides, her hands balled into fists. "How dare you! You are not my mother, you pile of troll dung!"

Something stirred in the back of Ythnel's mind. A memory rushed back, sweeping her away.

Ythnel slumped at her desk, her head resting on her folded arms. Her stomach had been hurting since the morning, when she had discovered some blood in her undergarments. Sister Larulene, Mistress of Initiates, had told her it was a sign she was entering womanhood. It had done little to comfort her, and she was in a foul mood. All she wanted to do was go back to her room and curl up in bed. Instead, she sat in class, listening to Sister Yenael describing dwarf anatomy.

"Who can tell me the five most sensitive spots on a male dwarf?" the sister asked. The following silence was soon broken by the click of boot heels approaching on the hard stone floor. Ythnel slowly lifted her head to find Sister Yenael looming over her. "Answer the question, Initiate."

"I don't know," Ythnel sighed.

"Are we not feeling well?" Sister Yenael asked, her voice full of compassion. Ythnel nodded. "I don't care! Answer the question." The sister brought her fist down with a crash on the desk. Ythnel jerked upright in her seat.

"I said I don't know. Look, those two are raising their hands. Why don't you go ask them?" She glared are the sister.

Sister Yenael's eyes narrowed, and the two became locked in a battle of wills. From the corner of her vision, Ythnel saw something fly at her. She turned toward it instinctively but was not fast enough. She was struck across the cheek by the sister's hand. The blow knocked her out of her seat, bursts of light filling her vision. She started to cry as Sister Yenael walked back to the front of the class.

Iuna sat on the floor, rubbing her right cheek. Ythnel held her hand poised for a backswing.

"You ... you hit me," the girl sobbed in disbelief.

Then she started to scream. "Papa!" Ythnel heard footsteps pounding up the stairs and turned to see Prisus running down the hall toward them.

"What is going on in here?"

Iuna got up and ran past Ythnel into her father's embrace. "She hit me, Papa." Prisus bent down and cupped his daughter's chin gently in his hand, examining the red mark emblazoned on her cheek.

"I was disciplining your daughter, Master Saelis. She refused—"

"I thought I told you I didn't want Loviatar's teachings in my house."

"But Master Saelis, Iuna needs—"

"Enough! How dare you tell me what my daughter needs," Prisus roared. His face was flushed, and he was shaking. Iuna peeked out from behind her father, grinning maliciously. Prisus took a deep breath and exhaled slowly. "I apologize for losing my temper like that. Obviously, I didn't make my expectations clear from the start. I hope they are now." Ythnel nodded.

"Good. Now why don't you two head into the parlor and start your lessons. Go," he gently pushed Iuna, ignoring her frown. She took two steps then turned and tried again.

"But, Papa—"

Prisus shook his head and pointed to the parlor entrance. With a pout on her face, Iuna stomped into the room.

"See," Prisus said to Ythnel as she, herself, headed into the parlor. "You can get her to listen without beating her."

Ythnel looked at Prisus but gave no response. Apparently satisfied that she understood his point, he turned and went back downstairs.

The parlor was a well-appointed room obviously

used to entertain guests. A beautiful but modest crystal chandelier hung from the center of the ceiling. Colorful, oil-painted landscapes hung at intervals along the walls, their woodworked frames tactful enough not to draw attention from the brush-stroked canvas. Thick velvet drapes were pulled back to reveal a floor-to-ceiling window set in the far wall, supplying a view of the city. A single-keyboard harpsichord sat in front of the window, basking in the sunlight, its lid propped open to showcase the strings inside.

For now, the parlor was set up as a classroom. Iuna sat behind a small, portable writing desk, her hands neatly folded in her lap. Ythnel closed the door behind her and strode over to the lectern that stood a few feet away from the desk. She sorted through the lesson plan she had prepared last night before going to bed, reviewing the subjects she hoped to cover. Ythnel felt her stomach clench and realized she was just stalling. There really was nothing to do but get on with it.

"I thought we might start with something easy," Ythnel began, "something that will give me an idea of your level of knowledge and give you an idea of my teaching style."

Iuna raised her hand.

"Yes."

"Have you ever taught before?"

"I don't see how that is relevant—"

"I just want to be sure that *your* 'level of knowledge' is sufficient to—"

"Don't be rude," Ythnel snapped. With a deep breath, she regained her composure. "Your father has confidence in my skills. That should be enough for you. Now let's begin." Iuna gave her a mocking smile but remained silent.

"Why don't we go over some local history? In

what year did Chessenta break free from the Unther empire?"

Iuna sat silently, still smiling.

"All right, how about the name of the one and only king to ever unite all the city-states?"

Iuna continued to silently hide behind her smug smile.

"Fine, then can you recite which cities are currently aligned against Luthcheq, and which are her allies?"

There was nothing but the smile from the girl.

Ythnel trembled, barely able to keep her frustration in check. She wanted to storm over to Iuna, pick the girl up, put her across her knee, and paddle her. This would never be allowed to continue if she were back at the manor. But they were not at the manor. They were in Luthcheq, in the Saelis household, where Ythnel was only a hired governess and was required to follow the rules set down by her employer. Ythnel ground her teeth and resolved to plow ahead.

"I can see you're not interested in local history, so we'll come back to that later. Your father told me on the journey over here that you are quite good at geography. I'd love to hear you tell me all about the two major mountain ranges in Chessenta."

Iuna smiled sweetly.

So this is the way it's going to be, Ythnel thought. I can play this game, too. Without saying another word, she dragged a chair over from its place against the wall and sat facing Iuna.

They passed the morning staring at each other. Around highsun, there was a knock at the door. Ythnel stood and opened it. Libia stood there with a tray of sandwiches and drinks.

"I'm sorry, Libia, but we won't be having lunch today until Iuna finishes her lesson."

Libia nodded knowingly and turned to go. Ythnel thought she heard Iuna fidget and looked over her shoulder. The girl's brow was furrowed, and her mouth opened as though she were going to say something. But when she noticed Ythnel looking at her, she straightened up and was smiling once more. Ythnel closed the door and went back to her chair.

As the sun's reach into the parlor faded back through the window, the two were summoned to dinner. Iuna practically skipped from the room when Leco opened the parlor door. Ythnel rose to follow, but Leco stopped her at the door.

"I heard about your little starvation tactic this afternoon. I know the child is willful, but I will not allow that kind of stunt to continue. If I hear that you use it again, I will report you to Master Saelis."

"Then what do you suggest I do?" Ythnel asked. Her patience was about at an end. Did everyone in this house spoil the child?

"I'm not the governess. You figure it out." He ushered her past him and followed her down the stairs. Ythnel entered the dining room and took her seat.

"Ah, Ythnel, Iuna was just telling me what a wonderful day she had with you," Prisus said. "See, I knew you two would get along smashingly."

❧ ❧ ❧ ❧ ❧

Ythnel was not late to morningfeast on the second day. As she finished her meal and prepared for another day of sitting silently in the parlor, Prisus motioned for everyone to stay where they were.

"I thought that it might be nice to do something a little different today. How about we go on a trip to the Trade Center? This would be the perfect chance for

Ythnel to get out and see some of the sites, and we're going to need some supplies for the city's upcoming Midwinter celebration. What if we all go together and spend the day there?" Prisus smiled, looking around the table expectantly.

"Oh, yes, Papa, that would be so much fun," Iuna practically clapped her approval.

"If that is your wish, Master Saelis," Ythnel replied.

"It is. I'll have Leco ready the carriage." He excused himself from the table, leaving Iuna and Ythnel facing each other. Iuna stuck her tongue out at Ythnel then ran after her father.

Everyone rode in silence, shifting in their seats, not meeting the others' eyes. Tired of gazing at the gray winter sky, Iuna counted the streets as they neared the Trade Center. She tensed when they began to slow and leaped from the carriage before it had come to a full stop.

The Trade Center of Luthcheq was a unique marketplace. It was not unique in the sense that you could find something there you couldn't find elsewhere in Faerûn, but it was unique in its design. Rather than congregating in the middle of some square at the intersection of two large streets, the merchant guilds had purchased a large piece of property near the docks. The lot was shaped like a trapezoid, with a small leg jutting off the southeast corner, and took nearly the entire block. Erected over this area was a vaulted roof, supported every ten feet by fluted columns as tall and thick as an ogre, with ornate capitals decorated with spirals and leaves. On the underside of the roof were scenes depicting athletic competitions, painted on the plaster in the spaces between the vaults by local artisans.

The acoustics of the Trade Center added to the marketplace's atmosphere. The vaulted ceiling caught the myriad cries of merchants like a fisher's net. Yet each call reverberated clean and clear above the constant murmur of the crowd. Iuna could hear the bark of some jeweler from the other side of the center just as easily as she could the beckoning of the fruit peddler two feet away from where she now stood.

A hand on Iuna's shoulder made her jump.

"Now let's not go running off by ourselves," Prisus said, turning Iuna around to face him. Ythnel stood behind him. "Why don't you and Ythnel go find yourselves new dresses to wear for Midwinter? I'll meet you both back here in, say, a candle. Then we can grab some lunch." He smiled, patted Iuna on the head, and disappeared into the crowd.

Iuna started after him but was grabbed by her wrist. She turned around to glare at Ythnel.

"Don't touch me," she said, jerking free. She tried to sound angry, but a hint of fear crept in as she remembered what Ythnel did to her yesterday. Iuna hated being afraid of the woman, hated the control it gave Ythnel. She would find a way to get back at Ythnel, to get her fired. She would think of something her father couldn't ignore.

"Your father isn't here to protect you, Iuna. You will obey me." There was no malice in Ythnel's voice, just a sternness that spoke of consequences for failure. "Besides, he gave me the coin. If you want that dress, you'll have to stick with me." Ythnel smiled, her tone much more friendly.

Iuna's mouth twisted into a grimace, but Ythnel was right. It was no use forcing the issue without her father here to witness the result. She would just have to bide her time.

"All right." Iuna sighed. "But try to keep up." She marched into the marketplace without glancing back to see if Ythnel followed.

It was approaching highsun, and the center was at the peak of its activity. Iuna shouldered her way through the continuous flow of traffic, not even bothering to excuse herself as she careened into thighs and hips. The sweet fragrance of perfume filled Iuna's nostrils and mingled with the pungent aroma of some foreign spice carried through the center on a breeze off the Bay of Chessenta. She wrinkled her nose and pressed on.

At a convergence of lanes, Iuna veered right, diving into a new stream of shoppers. She could feel Ythnel's presence behind her and absently wondered what it would take to lose the woman. Suddenly, her father's words echoed in her head, not as a warning, but as the inspiration for a plan. She grinned wickedly and came to a halt.

"Is everything all right? Why did you stop?" Ythnel asked from behind her.

"Oh, everything is fine. We're here." Iuna pointed to a large, green-and-white striped canvas tent across the way.

The tent was easily twice the width of its neighbors and was so deep, it also occupied the row behind it. Iuna's father had told her it was run by a seamstress who owned a shop in town. Clothing was made and sold in the shop; the Trade Center tent served as an outlet for older pieces that needed to be moved to make room for the newer fashions. It was commonly patronized by well-to-do merchants who could not afford the latest styles worn by the nobility.

An armed guard stood by the open tent flap, but Iuna paid him no heed as she entered. Dresses, shirts, and pants hung from hooks on the walls. Stuffed mannequins stood at various spots on the floor, modeling outfits. Iuna drifted from item to item, lifting hems and sleeves with feigned disinterest as Ythnel trailed behind. It wasn't long before an attendant soon joined them.

"Do you see something you like?" the young woman asked. She was just a few summers older than Iuna, perhaps the seamstress's apprentice.

"No, not really," Iuna sighed. "What about you, Ythnel?"

"Oh, I don't know. I never really had a need for this sort of thing back at the manor." As if to emphasize her lack of fashion sense, Ythnel plucked at the skirt of the dark linen dress she wore.

It was like a shark sensing blood in the water. The attendant swept Ythnel up and rushed her over to several gowns hanging on a section of the wall on the other side of the tent.

"Oh, I know just the thing. You're going to love this. Now tell me, what's the occasion?" she chattered excitedly.

Iuna backed toward the entrance of the tent. She halted as she drew parallel to the guard and looked up, suddenly afraid he might notice her guilty face. He just glanced at her briefly and grunted. To her, it was like the blast of a horn that signaled the start of an arena race. She bolted into the crowd.

Iuna couldn't contain her laughter as she charged ahead. Her father would have to send Ythnel away now. How could he not, if the woman was so irresponsible as to lose track of his daughter because she was too busy trying on something frilly. Iuna couldn't wait to see their faces when she finally showed up at the carriage, crying because Ythnel had abandoned her.

As Iuna rounded a corner, she decided to take a quick look behind to make sure Ythnel had not caught up. She was nowhere to be seen. Iuna turned back, a triumphant smirk growing on her face, and slammed into something hard. The force of the collision knocked her backward, and she fell to the ground, stunned.

As her vision came into focus, Iuna noticed that a wide circle had been cleared around her in the marketplace traffic. She turned her head slowly back toward the direction she had been running and saw a man leaning over her. He wore a suit of hardened leather under a fur-trimmed cloak. A white letter K with a burning branch above it was painted on his breast. His dark hair hung in waves that reached to his neck. A golden circlet held it off his forehead. And though he smiled down at her, his brown eyes were full of cruelty.

"Do you know who I am?" he asked. Iuna nodded frantically. Anyone who hadn't actually met Naeros Karanok had heard enough stories that they would recognize him. "Then you have me at a disadvantage. I don't like being at a disadvantage, so why don't you tell me who you are? Or did your parents forget to name you as well as teach you manners?"

Iuna opened her mouth to speak but managed only a croak.

"I'm afraid the girl has been knocked senseless," Naeros joked with his men, who Iuna now noticed were responsible for clearing the space around her and their lord.

"N-n-no, I'm all right," Iuna stammered. "M-m-my n-name is Iuna."

"Well, Iuna, don't you know it's very rude to run into people? What do you think we should do to rude young girls?" Suddenly, Naeros's smile was as cruel as his eyes.

Ythnel's head was spinning. The attendant talked incessantly, throwing dress after dress at her without missing a beat.

"Enough!" Ythnel dropped the pile of garments that had accumulated on her outstretched arms to the ground. The attendant's face paled at the outburst. "I think you've spent enough time on me," Ythnel continued, taking a deep breath to calm herself. "Why don't you show some outfits to Iuna?" She turned, scanning the tent for Iuna. The girl was gone.

"She must have stepped outside," the attendant meekly offered.

"Painbringer's touch," Ythnel cursed. She stormed out of the tent, pausing in the street to search the crowd in both directions for Iuna. Remembering the guard, she spun around to confront him.

"The little girl I came in with, did you see which way she went?" He peered down his nose at her, his arms folded across his puffed-out chest, and grunted. Ythnel's face became a mask of fury. Quicker than thought, she jabbed him in the gut with her right hand, just below the rib cage. The guard's eyes popped in surprise, and he doubled over.

"Which way?" Ythnel asked again through gritted teeth. Gasping for breath, the guard pointed down the lane past her. Ythnel raced off without another word.

Even with her height, it was hard to see through the sea of bobbing heads and shoulders, and the morass of moving bodies prevented Ythnel from maintaining the speed with which she had left the seamstress. Finally, she reached an intersection. She stood at the corner for a moment, desperately searching for a glimpse of Iuna's small figure weaving in and out of the crowd. There was none. Ythnel silently cursed the child. Iuna could be anywhere by now. This was going to cost Ythnel her job. Why was the girl acting like this? Couldn't she see that Ythnel was just trying to help her?

A shift in the movement of the crowd to Ythnel's right caught her attention, and she swung her head to investigate. Something was parting the traffic a few yards down the lane, creating a bottleneck as the throng tried to continue on its way.

Ythnel was sure Iuna was somehow involved.

With a resigned sigh, Ythnel shouldered her way through the press. She emerged to find herself within a cleared space in the middle of the lane. In the center of the circle, a dark-haired man towered over a trembling Iuna. Ythnel could read the threat of harm in his body language. As she took a step forward, Iuna turned toward her and pointed.

"She made me do it," the little girl shrieked. "She's a witch. She cast a spell over me and my father. I saw her do it in the middle of the night."

At the mention of a witch, the crowd froze and a few cries arose from some faint-hearted citizens. The dark-haired man's head snapped up, his gaze following Iuna's outstretched arm and locking onto Ythnel. He straightened but made no move toward her.

"Is this true?" The man's hand dropped casually to the hilt of the short sword hanging in a leather scabbard at his side. "Are you a witch, as the girl claims?"

In a city were the arcane was forbidden, Iuna's charge had turned the situation from a childish prank into a potentially deadly encounter. From the man's arrogant bearing, he was obviously nobility, which meant he also probably thought he was invincible. Ythnel had learned how to interact with such people from her years at the manor.

"I apologize, milord," she began, bowing slightly at the waist. "The truth of the matter is that I am this girl's governess. I'm afraid she is not very happy with the arrangement and has been making every attempt to ruin me. I assure you I will see to it personally that she is severely punished for this display."

The nobleman nodded thoughtfully at this. Ythnel walked toward Iuna, hoping the matter finished and she could drag the girl off.

"She's lying," Iuna blurted. "My father bought her as a slave from Thay. Everybody knows that Thay is full of wizards."

"Halt!" At the command, Ythnel stopped, watching the nobleman from the corner of her eye. He circled her slowly, examining her from head to foot. "Your height, skin tone, and shaved head all mark you as Thayan. And the tattoo, is it not also a custom for wizards of that land to wear such decorations?"

"Many who are not wizards also bear such decorations, milord, so as not to stand out." Ythnel noted that the nobleman's hand was now firmly wrapped around his sword hilt.

"Regardless, I think it prudent that you be questioned further. In the name of House Karanok, I order you arrested. Guards, take her." The nobleman motioned, and Ythnel's attention was drawn to the several large, brutish men standing at the edge of the circle, acting as barriers between their lord and the

Trade Center crowd. She cursed herself for not noticing them sooner, assuming they were just gawking bystanders.

Ythnel felt a presence behind her and spun inward to her left. With her right hand, she caught the outstretched wrist of the guard sneaking up on her, twisting it then thrusting down in a move she had learned from one of the many classes Sister Yenael taught on dealing pain. Driven to his knees, the man cried out as several bones in his wrist popped. Ythnel rammed her knee into his lower jaw, snapping his head back violently. The guard's eyes lost focus, and he collapsed to the ground with a thud.

Ythnel backed away, trying to keep the other brutes within her field of vision. There was no way she could take all of them. They easily outweighed her by a couple of hundred pounds each. If even one of them were to get hold of her, she would not have the strength to break free. Running was just as futile. The throng of spectators formed a tight, living wall that would surely slow her down enough for one of the thugs to grab her before she could break through. If only she were stronger, then she might stand a chance.

She could give herself that chance with magic.

Ythnel knew she could call on Loviatar for aid, tapping into the Power to enhance her own strength enough that she might be able to defeat the Karanok guards. She would be vulnerable, though, while she uttered the prayer and gave herself over to the divine energy flowing from her goddess in response to the petition. It was a risk she would take.

Yanking out the small scourge she wore under her dress, Ythnel began to chant. While there were no visible signs that anything was happening, she could feel the Power begin to flow into her. The sensation was different for everyone. Some handmaidens had told her it felt like being immersed in a bath of ice. A maiden visiting from Calimshan said it was a fire burning from the inside out. For Ythnel, her skin stung from a thousand tiny whips as the divine magic coursed through her. She wanted to cry out with joy and scream in agony.

"The witch is casting a spell! Stop her!" The nobleman's shout echoed in the recesses of Ythnel's mind. From somewhere beyond the pain, she registered the movement of the guards as they closed in, but she stayed focused on the symbol held out in front of her. Any distraction now, before the prayer was complete, and the Power would slip away.

"Iuna!" With a cry, Prisus burst from the crowd. The commotion drew Ythnel's attention, and as she turned to look, her concentration broke, severing the link to Loviatar. Then something smashed into the back of Ythnel's head, and darkness enveloped her.

THE PRIESTS

The street was empty save for the light of the full moon shining down from a crisp and cloudless winter's night sky. Therescales stood in the shadows cast by a two-story building, his dark, hooded cloak aiding his thin frame to blend with the pools of blackness. Across the street lay his target, a large warehouse used by a local importer of exotic items to store his wares.

Satisfied no one else was around, Therescales intoned the Draconic words that accompanied the motions his hands were now making. With each syllable and sweep, his face began to change. The blond strands that barely covered his scalp became thick white curls. Skin that was once pulled tight over jaw and cheekbones now sagged and wrinkled.

Pockmarks appeared all over his beaklike nose, which flattened as the spell completed. In a matter of seconds, he was the spitting image of his mentor, the man who taught him this minor illusion.

Therescales picked the disguise not only for its irony, but because he never tired of the looks on the others' faces. It was like they had seen a ghost. Just the memory of their widened eyes and startled gasps brought a smirk to his lips as he crossed the street.

Stopping before the entrance, Therescales nervously played with the heavy gold ring on the middle finger of his right hand. He felt somewhat naked without his bracers and dagger, though the protection offered by the enchanted armbands would do him little good in this situation, and the weapon would only arouse suspicions. No, it was the shielding the ring provided that was important. Without it, his mind would be an open book to any with the means and desire to flip through its pages. Were that to happen, he would be as good as dead.

The thought sent a shiver down his spine. It wasn't the first time he considered the consequences, but there was no turning back; he was already in too deep. Fortunately, the rewards promised should he succeed made the dangers an acceptable part of the bargain. Therescales opened the door and stepped into the warehouse.

The interior of the building had been partitioned off so that Therescales now stood in a lantern-lit showroom that was only a fraction of the warehouse's square footage. Shelves of dark wood lined the walls at various heights, and marble pedestals dotted the floor. Upon these were displayed crafts and trinkets from all across Faerûn: ivory carvings by Cormyrean artisans, carpets from Tethyr, lamps of multicolored glass made in Neverwinter, Thayan artwork, and other items of less recognizable origin but certainly no less value. Therescales walked through the gallery, making a show of examining each and every piece. From the corner of his eye, he watched a small, balding man sorting through a pile of papers at a desk by a door in the far wall. He didn't recognize the clerk; it was always someone different, so that was hardly surprising. Therescales worked his way closer, getting to within a few arm's lengths of the desk, when the clerk finally finished his task and looked up.

"I'm sorry, but all sales are by appointment only." The man scowled. If Therescales had not seen his initial, startled reaction, he would have thought the clerk truly frustrated by the interruption.

"That's quite all right," Therescales replied confidently. "I was referred by a shadowy sage whose symbol is a black staff." He smiled and waited.

The clerk became still for a moment, and Therescales could practically hear the clockwork gears turning in his head. Recognition blossomed on the little man's face, and he walked over to the nearby door. He pulled a key from a pouch on his belt and inserted it into the doorknob. With a twist, the lock was undone, and the clerk pushed the door open.

"I hope you find what you're looking for."

Therescales quickly moved past the man and through the doorway. Beyond it waited the rest of the warehouse. The vast space was unlit save by moonbeams that fell through two skylights spaced evenly along the length of the roof. Crates and barrels stacked at various heights formed a maze of shadowy towers. Therescales gazed out into the mysterious landscape, suddenly hesitant. He gave a small jump as the door slammed shut behind him, taking with it the light that had spilled from the showroom. Once his eyes adjusted, he crept into the maze.

Silence blanketed the warehouse while Therescales searched for the mark that would identify his quarry. Even though much of the inventory had been rearranged since his last visit, he moved unerringly to the location mapped in his memory. Soon he stood before a large, seven-foot-high, rectangular crate. Dropping to a crouch, Therescales examined the bottom of the box. In the lower right-hand corner he found what he was looking for: a blue-white, eight-pointed star stamped on the wood.

With his eyes closed, Therescales reached forward, extending his arm beyond the point where the crate should have begun. He groped around the floor until his hand came into contact with cold metal. Gripping the metal tightly, he opened his eyes to see his arm cut off at the elbow by the side of the crate. Then the crate began to dissolve, leaving a wooden trapdoor in the warehouse floor and his hand wrapped around a metal ring bolted to the near edge of the wood.

A blast of warm air hit Therescales as he heaved the door open. Revealed in the soft red glow of some unseen light source was a flight of stairs leading down. Therescales descended, lowering the trapdoor behind himself.

At the base of the stairs, a narrow hall led a short distance to a pair of braziers standing waist high against a blank wall. Therescales grabbed a small pair of tongs that was hanging from a hook on a side of the brazier on the left. Using the tongs, he removed one of the glowing coals from the brazier. In the center of the wall, he used the coal to draw a Draconic sigil. Wherever the coal touched, it left a bright, burning mark in the wall. When he finished, Therescales replaced the tongs and moved back. The sigil flashed and was absorbed into the wall, leaving no trace it had ever been there. Therescales stood silently for a moment. His patience was rewarded as a thin line appeared on the wall a few inches from the ceiling. It stretched from the left brazier to the right then turned sharply and ran to the floor. Therescales stepped forward and gave a slight push, causing the section of wall to swing quietly inward.

Beyond the open portal lay the hidden library of the Mage Society. The square room was lined with shelves of books. Small orbs of blue-white light hovered at the ends of the shelves. There were several people in the library. Some browsed the collection of tomes, the orbs darting to their sides to provide a light over their shoulders. Others huddled in groups, talking in low voices. At Therescales' entrance, several of them looked in his direction and nodded in greeting. He frowned at the lack of startled expressions. Perhaps it was time to switch disguises. What would they think if he arrived looking like one of the Karanoks?

The wall closed behind Therescales, and he decided to take a seat in one of the vacant chairs nearby. Slumping in the low-backed, cushioned chair, he pressed his fingers together in a steeple and watched the room's occupants. Everyone used the Art to hide their features. With such a concentration of arcane energies, Therescales had always wondered how these society meetings had escaped detection. It wasn't until he became a full member that he learned a powerful abjuration had been cast over the building, masking magical auras and preventing attempts to divine the location.

So, rather than study faces, Therescales focused on mannerisms, cataloguing and storing them, trying to match them with people he had encountered before. Did the way that old crone batted her eyes when she laughed remind him of a certain young merchant's wife? Or was that one-eyed man in the corner tapping his chin in the same nervous habit Therescales had witnessed in the patriarch of a minor noble house?

A door opened in the wall to the right of where Therescales had entered, and three more figures emerged. All three wore hooded robes that shadowed their faces and long, flowing sleeves that covered their hands. The shiny black material reflected light from the orbs, creating a rippling effect across the voluminous garments as the three moved through the library.

"Brethren, let us begin," the lead figure announced in a gravelly voice obviously altered by magic. That would be Brother Hawk. The other two would be Brother Boar and Brother Crocodile, but the only way to tell them apart would be by their voices. The combination of cloaks and magic kept the identities of the Three secret.

Everyone fell in behind them as they crossed the library to another door opposite the secret entrance and into a grand, circular chamber. Murals depicting various uses of the Art covered the walls. A long oak table filled the center of the room; three miniature candelabras set atop it provided illumination. The society filed in, taking their places among the twenty chairs around the table. The Three sat at the head. Therescales noted that nearly half the chairs were empty.

Conversations died down, and everyone turned to face the Three.

"May Mystra guard us in our endeavors," Brother Hawk began. The rest echoed the mantra.

"May Azuth bless our efforts," the robed figure to

the right continued in a voice unnaturally deep, identifying him as Brother Crocodile. Again, it was echoed by the assembly.

"May we bring magic back to Luthcheq," the figure on the left, who could only be Brother Boar, concluded in a thick slur that was somehow still intelligible, and the statement was repeated in unison by all. With the litany finished, Brother Hawk stood.

"It is good to see you all again, brethren. There is much to discuss this night. Luthcheq has come to a crossroads. I can feel it, and I know you can, too. There are pressures from too many directions—something is about to crack."

"Could be us," a man across the table from Therescales, with a bushy mustache that hid his mouth, said dryly. A few chuckles arose from others.

"That is certainly a possibility, Brother Fox," Hawk said, no hint of humor in his voice. "But if we chose to act, rather than timidly discuss our situation, then we take our fate into our own hands." This brought murmurs of approval and dissent from several.

"Point of order!" Brother Crocodile cut through the growing din. "Point of order. There is old business to discuss first, Brother Hawk." Hawk nodded and took his seat.

"Sister Rat, report."

A woman at the far end of the table, with a long, pointy nose and buckteeth, stood. "Uh, yes. As you know, the Karanoks continue to increase local commerce taxes. My contacts tell me that not only are many merchants ready to pack up shop and leave, but with a little, uh, encouragement, an armed revolt could be triggered." With a quick grin, Sister Rat concluded and took her seat. Excited whispers filled the air.

"Thank you," Brother Crocodile said. "Brother Frog."

"I have been unable to discover more from my contacts at the palace." The man to Therescales' right rose. Several large warts protruded from his chin, nose, and forehead. At mention of the palace, Therescales' eyebrows arched, and his heart beat a little faster. "While I can confirm that Saestra Karanok has been responsible for an increase in burnings at the stake over the past few tendays, I cannot identify with any certainty that the victims were known practitioners of the Art. It is possible the Karanoks are now targeting those that merely sympathize with magic-users . . . or are political enemies." Many looks of concern flashed across the faces of the members, and some nodded thoughtfully at this grim news. "That is all I have, Brother Crocodile." Frog took his seat.

"Very well," Brother Crocodile acknowledged in his deep voice. "On to new items."

"Just a moment," Therescales said, standing.

"Yes, Brother Asp."

"What about my suggestion to seek help from a wizard outside Luthcheq? An alliance with the Red Wizards or the Simbul would surely give us the strength we need to topple the Karanoks."

Therescales looked around the table for support. Many refused to meet his gaze or glared back.

"I couldn't have asked for a better segue into the new item I wanted to bring up for discussion tonight," said Brother Hawk. He was standing again, and he motioned for Therescales to take his seat.

Therescales gave a half-bow and sat down.

"Brothers, I have made contact with a foreign ally, a wizard, who wishes to aid us in our struggle against the Karanoks." Brother Hawk could not keep the excitement from his voice.

There was stunned silence for a moment; then everyone began shouting at once. Therescales' mind raced with the ramifications of the announcement. This was not how things were supposed to have happened. When he had first suggested the idea of bringing in a powerful wizard to aid them, he never imagined one of the members would take it upon themselves to pursue this course of action. No, he was supposed to be the one who announced the discovery of a mysterious benefactor. He would be the one to arrange a meeting.

It would be a meeting that would ensnare the Mage Society and grant Therescales the power he was promised.

"Order! Order!" Brother Crocodile's voice roared. Immediate silence followed. "Please continue, Brother Hawk."

"I know this is sudden, and many of you felt there was more to discuss before a move was made, but as I said earlier, the longer we wait, the more control we relinquish over our fate.

"So, I made some discreet inquiries. Only yesterday did I receive word that a meeting could be arranged. It is my recommendation that we accept this invitation."

"Are you going to tell us who this wizard is?" Brother Fox inquired.

"I would," Brother Hawk paused for a moment, "if I knew who it was. I was contacted through a middle party." The words came out in a rush, and Therescales could see Hawk's shoulders slump. They both knew what was coming. Amid shocked gasps, Brother Deer jumped up.

"You want us to meet with someone who you've never seen or whose identity you can't confirm. How do we know it isn't a trap?"

"What about Brother Crocodile's suggestion to investigate the rumors of a hidden cache of artifacts buried in the ruins of Adder Swamp?" Others chimed in, and chaos erupted once more.

Therescales decided it was time to leave. He still had a report to make, and he needed some time to determine how best to turn this development to his advantage. In the commotion caused by heated arguments, Therescales slipped from his seat and slinked out of the room. If anyone questioned his disappearance when the society met again, he'd have a suitable excuse prepared.

Exiting through the trapdoor, Therescales made a snap decision not to leave the way he came in. No sense in having a witness to confirm his early departure. Nimbly, he scaled a stack of crates under one of the skylights. He leaped onto a rafter beam and pushed on the pane of glass with his hand. It was unlatched and swung open easily, but there was nothing to hold it. Grabbing the sill with his other hand, he lowered the glass so it rested on his knuckles. He pulled himself up and pushed his body between the sill and the skylight, grabbing the pane as he rolled out and lowering it back down gently without a sound.

At the edge of the roof, he paused. It was a long drop down. Fortunately, Therescales had memorized one of his most powerful spells before coming to the meeting tonight. He pulled a small loop of leather from a pocket on the inside of his cloak and waved his hand over it while uttering a few Draconic words. Then he stepped off the roof . . .

. . . and hovered in the air.

With a thought, he lowered himself to the ground. He returned the loop to his pocket and quickly moved south down the street toward the palace of the Karanoks. He stuck to the shadows, darting into doorways and alleys whenever a guard patrol walked by. It was not that he had anything to fear; it was just that old habits died hard. As an apprentice to Master Haraxius, he had spent the past ten years avoiding the guards when he ran errands smuggling various components or items in and out of the city for the old mage. Unbidden, the memory of the last errand he had ever run for Haraxius pushed forward in his mind.

A gull screamed, and Therescales flinched, nearly dropping the purse full of coin. He smiled sheepishly at the dockhand who snatched the purse from him and shoved the package into Therescales' chest with a sneer then walked away. Therescales stood in the middle of the pier for a moment, clutching the soft bundle.

"Is everything all right?"

Therescales started at the voice. He turned toward the tap on his shoulder and came face to face with a pair of the harbormaster's guards. Remembering the package clasped to his chest, he slipped it behind his back.

"Oh, yes, officers. I was just on my way. Have a good evening." He bobbed then strode off.

The crowds on the wharf were starting to thin with the setting sun. Therescales hurried through the streets, anxiously looking over his shoulder to see if he was being followed. If he were caught with what was wrapped in the burlap he carried, it would mean his death. He was proud that Master Haraxius trusted him with these supply runs, but Therescales wondered if the risks were worth it. Why didn't they just leave Luthcheq and go somewhere wizards were tolerated or even worshiped?

Therescales tucked the package under his arm and picked up the pace. He was supposed to be back before dark. There was another meeting of the Mage Society tonight. This would be the second time Master Haraxius brought him along to the clandestine gatherings. Therescales had no idea there were so many practitioners of the Art in the city. He didn't know who any of them were—they all went by animal names, and Master Haraxius said most of them used magic to disguise themselves. Therescales wondered what his name would be once he was fully initiated.

A crowd was forming as Therescales approached the street Master Haraxius's house was on. He shouldered his way through, intent on reaching the safety of home. However, when he was almost clear, he froze.

A large group of men were leaving the building. The white **K** of House Karanok with a burning branch above it was emblazoned on their uniforms. They were led by a middle-aged man with black, curly hair that contrasted sharply with the pale skin of his square face. In their midst, bound and gagged, was Haraxius, barely able to keep his feet. One eye was swollen shut, and the side of his face was bloodied.

Therescales backed into the crowd, a surge of panic-driven bile climbing up his throat. He barely made it to a side street before he pitched the contents of his stomach. He sat on the curb until the wave of nausea and dizziness passed, only to be replaced by despair. It was difficult to hold back sobs as he rested his head in his hands.

How had this happened? Everyone knew that the Karanoks had started raiding the homes of suspected wizards, and Master Haraxius had always stressed the need for caution and secrecy. Yet it seemed the Karanoks had discovered Master Haraxius's secret regardless of the precautions he had taken. Now they were dragging him off to be tried and executed.

Therescales' head was starting to clear, and the crowd was dispersing. He knew if he tried to enter the house now, someone would spot him and turn him in to the Karanoks. With nowhere to go and no idea what to do, Therescales started walking.

Twilight fell while Therescales still wandered the streets aimlessly. He considered going to the Mage Society meeting by himself. Surely they had already heard of Master Haraxius's capture and would help. He remembered the location of the warehouse where they met, but what would he do once there? He didn't know any of the passwords. Master Haraxius had not yet shared those secrets with him. If only there were some way he could prove to them who he was, they would let him in.

Perhaps he could show them something that only Master Haraxius would have. Yes, that was it. They would have to grant him entry then.

With a plan firmly in mind, Therescales made his way back to Master Haraxius's house. He clung to the shadows, dashing from doorway to alley while keeping an eye peeled for passing patrols. It was just after midnight when he finally reached the house. He stood across the street, watching for several minutes. There were no guards standing outside or movement inside. In the silence, his heart pounded like the hooves of horses at a chariot race. Knots began to form in Therescales' stomach as fear and doubt ate away at his resolve.

Finally, when waiting any longer meant never

going, he darted across the street. He fumbled through his pockets for the key, but as his hand pressed against the knob, the door creaked open. At that moment, Therescales almost fled. Yet, with eyes wide and mouth dry, he stepped inside.

Light from the waxing moon shone only a few feet past the entry, forcing Therescales to feel his way through the dark. He had lived in this house for the past two years, though, and Master Haraxius had kept everything in the same place since Therescales had first arrived. It would be a simple matter to navigate around any obstacles as he moved toward his mentor's private study.

Therescales turned to his left and entered the living room. It was sparsely furnished—Master Haraxius did not do a lot of entertaining—and Therescales took long, swift strides with confidence.

Halfway through the room, something smacked Therescales in the shin and he grunted in pain.

"Well, what do we have here?"

A light flared in front of Therescales. He closed his eyes and brought up a hand to further protect them from the sudden brilliance.

"Looks like Lord Jaerios was right." A new voice answered the first from behind Therescales. "The 'prentice 'as returned to 'is master's 'ouse."

Squinting in the light, Therescales could make out a figure sitting in a chair to his right. He held a lantern in one hand, and his legs were propped up on an ottoman. A spear lay across his lap. Therescales had run into the outstretched shaft of the weapon.

Panicking, Therescales dashed for the front door but was grabbed from behind. He struggled but could not break the grip of the arms encircling him. The man in the chair got up and stood in front of him, leering. Something struck Therescales in the stomach, and all the air *whooshed* out of his lungs. He looked up in time to see the shaft of the spear streaking toward the side of his face.

Therescales awoke stiff and sore. The side of his face throbbed where he had been struck by the spear shaft. His shoulders ached, and he could feel something biting into his wrists. He tried to move his hands, hoping to lessen the pain, only to discover they were bound. Awareness began to creep back through the fog of his mind. He realized he was on his knees, leaning forward with his arms pulled behind him and wrapped around a wooden pole. With effort, he rocked back onto the balls of his feet and tried to rise. His footing was unstable—he was standing on a pile of chopped logs—and it took a few attempts before he was standing. He leaned back against the pole, drawing ragged breaths as a result of the exertion.

"Ah, our other guest has finally joined us."

The resonant voice drew Therescales' eyes up and across the room to a balcony where five figures stood, three men and two women. They all wore sleeveless robes of white and gold circlets in their hair.

"Where am I?" Therescales, still a little groggy, asked no one in particular.

"You stand in the Burning Room." The same voice that had first spoken answered. Therescales could see that it belonged to a middle-aged man on the right, the same man he had seen escorting Master Haraxius. It had to be Lord Jaerios Karanok. "You have been found guilty of vile acts of wizardry."

"Bah," spat someone to Therescales' right. He turned to see his master, Haraxius, standing next to him, bound to another pole. "There is nothing vile about the Art. Rather, it is you and this—" A guard strode up onto the small stone platform on which Therescales and Haraxius were held and punched the old man in the mouth with a mailed fist, silencing the outburst.

"The sentence for this crime," Lord Jaerios continued, "is death by burning. Guards, bring in the witchweed." Two pairs of guards each carried in a basket of dried leaves between them and began dumping the contents on top of the wood piles then spreading them around the feet of the prisoners.

Therescales struggled against his bonds, desperate to be free, but it was no use. This couldn't be happening to him! His mind raced wildly to find some way of escape, some solution that would save him.

"Wait!" He screamed. "Don't do this. I don't want to die!"

All five faces were as compassionate as stone. "You should have thought of that before you became involved with the arcane, young man."

"If you let me live, I will tell you everything I know!"

"We want nothing to do with your filthy knowledge."

"But I know of a secret group of wizards that meets here in the city!" Therescales blurted out.

"No!" Haraxius gasped, horror on his face. "Don't do it, boy." Therescales ignored him.

The elderly man in the center of the group whispered something to Jaerios. He seemed resistant to the old one's counsel but finally relented with a nod.

"Do you swear to renounce all that is arcane?"

Therescales nodded vigorously, but Jaerios did not appear to notice or care what the answer was. Two guards moved forward and released Therescales then led him away.

"You treacherous snake!" Haraxius screamed as Therescales exited. The crackling of flames joined his old master's shrieks and coughs; then all was consumed in a roaring bonfire.

Jaerios Karanok sat in the plush, high-backed chair behind his desk, his fingers drumming on the polished wood of the chair's arm and a scowl darkening his face. Therescales was late. It was bad enough Jaerios had to associate himself with a wizard, but to be kept waiting by one was unacceptable. He shifted in his velvet night robe and let his eyes wander around the study once more: the dark wood-paneled walls, the shelves lined with books containing treatises on various subjects, the lit candelabra that cast a soft yellow glow onto the marble bust sculpted in his likeness. Perhaps the worm needed a reminder of his fate should he fail.

A knock at the door announced the arrival of the spy.

"Come in."

The door swung in, and Therescales entered the study. Jaerios remained silent, sternly staring at Therescales. The man didn't even flinch but moved casually over to the bust, ran his finger along the nose, and pretended to find dust on it.

"Have a seat," Jaerios offered, his voice full of impatience. Normally, he enjoyed these little sparring matches, but today had been a long day, and Jaerios wanted nothing more than to retire to his bedchamber. Perhaps Therescales detected the difference; he quickly accepted one of the two chairs in front of the desk. "You have news? Something good, I hope. Perhaps the identities of the other members of your little society?"

"Now, now, let's not let our greed rush things," Therescales smiled roguishly and waggled his finger. Jaerios snarled. He was in no mood to play. "I thought we agreed that taking them all in one fell swoop would expend fewer resources. Remember the plan?"

"Yes, your plan." Jaerios edged his voice with a hint of warning. He didn't like being reminded that he had agreed to a plan Therescales had come up with. "Have you convinced your friends that they should seek help? Or are they still arguing over the risk of exposing themselves? Such a timid bunch."

"Actually. . . ." Therescales paused, and Jaerios narrowed his eyes at the hesitation. The man was trying to figure out what to say next. Was he hiding something or simply afraid? "It seems they have taken it upon themselves to seek aid. One of the Three has already made contact with a wizard who is willing to help."

"How is this good news?" Jaerios roared. Anger flared red-hot inside of him. Jaerios wanted to reach across the table and throttle the incompetent fool, but the thought of touching something defiled by contact with the arcane was too revolting. "I don't know why I've kept you around. Perhaps I should have the guards prepare the Burning Room." Jaerios fixed Therescales with a look that promised death.

"I thought you might feel that way." Therescales sat there, unmoved by the threat. Was that a smile tugging at the corner of his mouth? "You're overreacting. We can still salvage the situation."

"You presume too much!" Jaerios exploded. He would not be talked to in this way by a wizard! "I have not waited this long, endured this abomination, only to throw it all away because of your ineptitude." Jaerios made his way around the desk to stand over Therescales. "Now I will be forced to raid your society's little hideout, profaning the city with the magic that they will inevitably use in defense."

"I assure you, Lord Jaerios, that will not be necessary." Therescales no longer slouched in the chair but sat upright against the back, the smug smile gone from his face. Jaerios smirked and leaned back on the edge of his desk. This was how these meetings should go.

"We can still proceed with the trap, my lord," Therescales continued. "It seems that this ally wishes to remain anonymous. Contact was made through a third party. As you mentioned, many of the members are leery of someone they do not know. I can still come forward with my—our fake meeting." Therescales visibly relaxed as he finished. Jaerios had to admit the plan still appeared feasible. Damn! He wasn't sure it wouldn't have been more satisfying to finally just burn the treacherous wizard at the stake.

"Very well. I can't say as I'm pleased with your handling of this, though." Jaerios watched Therescales for some sign of doubt or fear. The man was becoming too sure of himself. "Should you fail me again, I will see you burn." Therescales winced and tried to cover it with a small bow. He stood and moved to the study's door but paused before opening it.

"Oh, by the way, there is an informant in the palace. You might want to keep your eye on anyone who's been asking questions about Saestra's nocturnal activities." Flashing a roguish grin, Therescales slipped out of the room.

Jaerios ground his teeth. The man had the nerve to toss that information out as though it were a trifle that had just occurred to him. Jaerios knocked the chair Therescales had been sitting in onto its back.

"By Entropy, how long must I suffer the taint of these mages!" A wave of rage crashed over Jaerios, and he allowed himself to be swept up in it. There was power in such anger, such righteous anger. It was a gift from Entropy for faithful service. That was what his daughter had said when the priests first began to perform wonders and signs during their worship services. He remained skeptical, even after his own ability appeared.

The power continued to build within him. The sensation was still so new. He exalted in it but was frightened as well. It was too much like magic, and he had sworn long ago that he would not replace one form of corruption with another. The ends did not justify the means.

Jaerios's blood boiled in his veins. Pain threatened to eclipse anger. He focused on the tipped chair, envisioning Therescales still sitting in it. A loud, ringing noise filled the room, and the chair shattered into tiny splinters. Jaerios sagged against the desk. His bodyguard peeked his head in but, seeing his master unhurt, quickly ducked back out.

Sighing, Jaerios stood up and brushed the wood flakes from his robe. Feeling somewhat satisfied, he hoped he could now get a good night's sleep. As he left the study, he instructed his bodyguard to fetch a servant to clean up the mess then headed down the hall toward his bedchamber. The rest of it would wait until tomorrow.

THE **P**RIESTS

The knock on the door startled Ythnel. It was late. Her birthday party had lasted longer than expected, but some of the older sisters finally paired off with their male counterparts after most of the wine had been consumed, signaling the end of the public festivities. Ythnel had retreated to her room and prepared for bed. She wasn't expecting any visitors.

Pushing herself up from the kneeling position she had assumed, Ythnel walked the three steps from her bed to the door and opened it up just enough to peek outside. When she saw who it was, she quickly swung it open the rest of the way.

"Headmistress, I thought you were with ... I'm sorry, I was just beginning my evening prayers," Ythnel stammered, her face flushing.

"Follow me," Headmistress Yenael simply said then turned and walked back down the hall. Ythnel wavered for a moment but realized there was no time to put on something over her linen shift and hurried after.

As they passed the closed doors of the other initiates' quarters, Ythnel's mind wandered with the possibilities of where they were going and what would happen once they got there. She was pretty sure she hadn't done anything wrong or at least nothing serious enough to warrant a late-night visit from the headmistress herself.

Maybe this is a surprise birthday present, she thought. Or maybe she was being taken to the ceremony that would ordain her as a handmaiden. It would make her the youngest initiate the manor had ever raised to the position. It was not a likely possibility, given how much Headmistress Yenael was always hounding her, but that didn't mean it couldn't happen. In fact, now that she thought about it, perhaps the headmistress merely saw her potential and was trying to push her toward it as quickly as possible.

They made their way silently down a flight of steps at the end of the hall. Smoky torches sputtered in black iron sconces every few feet. Even though Ythnel had never been down here, she knew where they were going. Every initiate knew about the lowest level of the manor and what went on in those rooms. Ythnel shivered and not just from the cold stone under her bare feet. She heard the moans and cries echoing up from below before they even reached the bottom of the stairs.

A floor of packed dirt ran the length of the hallway.

There were iron-banded doors of thick, rough wood set every ten feet in damp, rock walls that glistened in the torchlight. Each door had a small, barred window, but Headmistress Yenael kept them moving swiftly enough that Ythnel thankfully couldn't see inside any of the rooms to discern what was happening or who it was happening to. She had a good idea, nonetheless.

The headmistress stopped at an open door at the far end of the hall and ushered Ythnel inside. Ythnel bit her lip and hesitated, trying to brace herself for what she might see. Headmistress Yenael's face darkened, and she grabbed Ythnel's arm and shoved her in.

The room was hardly any bigger than Ythnel's quarters. A torch sat in a sconce on the wall just to the right of the doorway. In the far corner stood a brazier of glowing coals with a poker shoved in amidst them, its tip bright orange. On the wall to Ythnel's left were several metal pegs bored into the stone. Whips of various kinds hung from them, coiled and waiting. Finally, Ythnel let her eyes stray to the center of the room. There, bent over a bench, his wrists and ankles bound by manacles anchored to the floor, was Oredas, one of the few male clerics serving at the manor. Oredas's back was exposed. His muscles rippled under sweaty skin as he shifted position slightly. Headmistress Yenael entered, closing the door behind herself.

"I remember when I was brought down here for the first time on my thirteenth birthday," the headmistress said fondly. She considered the row of hanging whips for a moment before choosing one that ended in three tongues, each about six inches long. A single small, smooth, steel bead was fastened at the end of each tongue. "There comes a time in every woman's life when classroom lectures no longer suffice. You must turn theory into application. Loviatar demands service through action, not endless discussion." She dropped the coil to the floor and lazily twisted the foot-long handle, causing the whip to slither in the dirt.

"I don't understand, Headmistress," Ythnel lied, afraid that she understood all too well. It had been one thing to sit in class and discuss the need for pain and suffering and to study the best ways to inflict it. Ythnel agreed that pain purified the soul, and shielding others from suffering only made them weak and unprepared for the tortures the world would subject them to. Yet, suddenly faced with hurting someone, she doubted she could do it, that she *should* do it.

"That's all right," Headmistress Yenael reassured. "You have much yet to learn still. Tonight is just your first step toward using what you have been taught." She smiled and moved behind Oredas. "I will show you how it is done. Then it will be your turn." The headmistress brought her right forearm up, perpendicular to the floor, the whip handle held loosely in her fist. With a flick of her wrist, the three feet of plaited leather leaped back and snapped forward, connecting with Oredas's flesh. Ythnel jumped at the sharp crack. Oredas merely grunted.

"There are many kinds of whips, Ythnel, and it is important to learn the purpose for each and how to use them." The headmistress struck with the whip again, leaving another set of welts on Oredas's back. "It's just as important to know how much pain your subject can take." When the whip hit this time, it broke the skin, eliciting a moan from Oredas. Blood began to seep from the wound. Ythnel felt a flash of heat accompanied by a wave of dizziness. She was sure her knees would buckle at any moment.

Headmistress Yenael returned the whip to its peg and reached for another that hung from a loop at the end of its handle. The stock was braided with leather that divided into nine different tongues at the end. Each strip was punctured with bits of glass, metal, and bone.

"This is a scourge. It is the preferred instrument of suffering for all those who follow Loviatar. It also requires the most skill to use effectively. If you're careless, you can easily kill your subject."

Ythnel watched with horror as the headmistress slapped the scourge against Oredas's right side then raked it across his back. The glass, metal, and bone caught the flesh and tore chunks of it away, leaving jagged stripes of blood. Oredas could not hold back his cries. She repeated this from the other side then dragged the scourge down his back from shoulder to waist a few times.

"There are signs to watch for in your subject to make sure you don't go too far. The rise and fall of the ribs," the headmistress pointed, "indicates that they are still breathing." Ythnel looked at the limp form of Oredas and felt bile rise in her throat. Was that bone she saw peeking out as his sides expanded with each shallow, labored breath? "Tensing of the muscles as the scourge hits means the subject is conscious." Oredas jerked slightly as Headmistress Yenael lashed him once more.

"When the subject reaches the threshold between life and death, it is time for Loviatar's Mercy. Not for the purpose of relief from pain and suffering, as some gods instruct their lackeys, but so they can endure more." The headmistress chanted a request in the tongue of devils, her free hand moving over Oredas's torn back. As her voice grew stronger, a harsh red glow enveloped her hand. Wherever it passed, blood flowed back into wounds and flesh mended. With each stripe that disappeared, the red glow deepened, until it was black as the Abyss and Oredas's back was whole. Headmistress Yenael ended the chant, and the glow around her hand faded. She stood and faced Ythnel.

"Now it is your turn." She thrust the stock of the scourge at Ythnel.

Ythnel stumbled backward until she pressed against the hard stone wall. "No." Her heart had climbed into her throat, and she could feel knots forming in her stomach.

"What did you say?" The headmistress's eyes narrowed.

"I-I mean, shouldn't we wait? Brother Oredas probably needs more time to recover." Ythnel knew she was walking dangerous ground, but she had to find some way out.

"Brother Oredas is fine. You saw me heal him. Besides, he is serving his goddess. Nothing could make him happier. Right, Oredas?"

"Yes, Headmistress." Oredas turned his head to peer up at the two of them. Ythnel could see the glint of fervor in his eyes. "Please do not be afraid for me, little one. I would suffer a thousand beatings for the name of Loviatar and the advance of her cause. Come, take your turn. I am honored to be your first subject."

"You see. Everything is all right. Now, take the scourge." Headmistress Yenael's voice was stern and insistent.

"No. I can't." Ythnel could feel the tears welling up.

"If you do not beat Oredas, you will take his place," the headmistress said through bared teeth. "I had high hopes for you, Ythnel. Do not make me regret—"

Ythnel shook her head then succumbed to the sobs she had been holding back, sliding down the wall to curl into a ball on the floor. Rough hands grabbed her, and she looked up to see Brother Oredas sneering at her. He ripped the shift from her body before pushing her down over the bench and clamping the manacles over her wrists and ankles. Then her sobs became screams.

Awakening with a jerk, Ythnel moaned as fire replaced the dull aches pervading her muscles. She went limp, swaying with the chains that suspended her by wrists and ankles above the floor, her head slightly higher than her feet. The burning died down quickly, though the occasional tug still brought a wince.

How long had she been hanging here? The hours were lost in a haze of pain.

Pain. Yes, the pain could tell her. Ythnel let her thoughts go and stopped trying to mentally over-come the pain. Instead she sought it out, measured and weighed it. Extended exposure to pain dulled the senses, lessened the intensity of the pain. The more sharply pain was felt, the more recent it was.

Pain still screamed down the nerves of her arms every time the chains rubbed against the raw flesh of her wrists. Her shoulder sockets throbbed in time with her heartbeat. There were some minor stings on her stomach, back, and thighs, but they were easy to ignore if she didn't squirm too much.

She hadn't been here more than a day.

Where is here?

The question came right on the heels of her diag-nosis. She tried to think back. There had been an incident in the market. Which market? Was she still in Thay, or somewhere else? A local lord had arrested her, accused her of witchcraft, so it wasn't Thay.

Iuna! The girl had gotten her into this. She had been hired as Iuna's governess. In Luthcheq!

Ythnel flailed again, this time in anger as it all came back to her. Pain exploded everywhere, serving only to fuel her rage. The chains rattled violently as she thrashed, but their hold on her remained secure. She screamed in frustration; her parched throat protested the abuse with a racking cough that left flecks of blood on her lips. Her fury spent, Ythnel sagged in defeat.

"My, my, that was quite a display."

Ythnel's head snapped up at the sultry voice. Through pain-blurred vision, she tried to discern who else was in the room. Dark shapes separated themselves from the walls by the orange glow of torchlight. With each blink, the forms distinguished themselves. A long, wooden table with manacles bolted down at each end materialized to her left. An iron box lay several feet in front of her, its lid open to reveal spikes covering the interior surface. Movement on her right caught Ythnel's eye, and she swung her head around, squinting. A young woman, perhaps only a few years older than Ythnel, stood there in a lacy, sleeveless gown of dark purple that accentuated her pale skin and did nothing to hide her voluptuous curves. Luxurious brunette tresses that fell to the small of her back framed a soft face dominated by violet eyes glowing with a light all their own.

"Who are you?" Ythnel croaked. The woman smiled sympathetically and glided over to Ythnel from her place at the base of a staircase that led down into the room. She stopped an arm's length away; the scent of lavender washed over Ythnel.

"I am Saestra." She reached out a slim hand to

stroke Ythnel's cheek. Ythnel pulled back, bringing a momentary frown to Saestra's full lips. "I only wish to end your suffering. I know how cruel my brother can be."

"My suffering pleases Loviatar. Accepting your offer would be a sign of weakness in Her eyes. I will not disgrace myself in such a manner."

"Interesting. Then what if I told you I could offer you immortality." Saestra brought her mouth in close to Ythnel's ear. "Just think of having an eternity to bring pain and suffering to the world in your goddess's name," she whispered, her breath tickling Ythnel's neck.

Saestra withdrew, and Ythnel shuddered as those violet orbs locked onto hers. Something was not right. How could this woman make such promises? Why would she even be talking to someone her family had imprisoned? Did she think Ythnel innocent? No, there was more behind Saestra's soft words, a trap that Ythnel was certain would cost her more than any punishment the Karanoks could inflict. Yet the longer she gazed into Saestra's eyes, the harder it became to resist the idea.

"I-I am not interested in your gift." Ythnel sighed, finally finding the will to look away.

"Very well." Disappointment was heavy in Saestra's voice. A smooth scraping sound brought Ythnel's head back up to see Saestra drawing a long, thin dagger from a sheath at her belt. "I suppose I will just take what I need and send your soul to meet its fate in the afterlife." Saestra lunged at Ythnel with the dagger. Ythnel twisted to her left, dipping her right shoulder to protect her chest. The dagger plunged into her back, sinking into the shoulder blade before Saestra yanked it out.

"What are you doing?"

Saestra whirled, hissing like some feral beast, to face the source of the booming voice. Ythnel could barely lift her head to see a figure descending the stairs. The wound on her back was suspiciously numb, and the lack of sensation seemed to be spreading. It was getting harder to move; the muscles in her arms and back felt like jelly.

"I was simply introducing myself to your guest, Naeros, my dear." Saestra had regained her composure. She brought the dagger up to her lips, licked the blood from its tip, and returned it to its sheath with a casual smile. Naeros raised a questioning eyebrow but said nothing.

"If the introductions are finished, I suggest you leave," he said finally. "She is my prisoner. I do not need you interfering."

"She is all yours." Saestra glided past Naeros to the foot of the stairs and paused. "Oh," she said, turning back to her brother, "it might interest you to know that your new plaything is a Loviatan. Have a good night." With a lilting laugh, she floated up the steps and disappeared.

"I apologize for that." A pair of dark leather boots came into view on the floor in front of Ythnel. Her head had become too heavy for her to lift any higher. The numbness had nearly spread throughout her entire body. "If anyone around here is to be inflicting pain upon you, it is me. My, my, but she did leave a nasty little mark, didn't she."

Ythnel felt a tug on her scalp, and her head suddenly jerked up.

"You will look at me when I speak to you!" The snarl on Naeros's face quickly calmed to a mocking smile. "So, you are a Loviatan? You know, I considered joining the church. I've been told I have a knack for making others suffer. Father would have nothing of the sort, of course. What do you think?" He swept his arm out to encompass the room and its various devices of torture.

"It takes more than a room full of toys to make one worthy of serving the Maiden of Pain." Ythnel's tongue felt like a lead weight. It was difficult to get the words out. "In Her eyes, you are nothing but a clumsy child playing at—"

"Silence!" Something struck the side of Ythnel's face—Naeros's fist, she guessed. She hardly felt it. He let go of her hair, and her head fell once more. Naeros's boots moved away, and Ythnel could hear the echo of them crossing the stone floor then swiftly returning. Her head was jerked up again, and she found the glowing tip of a hot iron brand inches from her face.

"Let's play." Naeros's voice dripped with malevolence. He released Ythnel's head and slid around to her side. Ythnel heard the sizzle of the hot iron. The smell of burnt flesh soon followed. "I'm going to show you the meaning of pain," Naeros taunted. "You're blessed goddess could learn a thing or two from me. Don't be ashamed to cry, I won't think less of you."

Ythnel started to laugh, a soft, breathy chuckle. She couldn't feel a thing.

"What's so funny?" Naeros demanded. He snatched her by the hair and studied her face. Ythnel couldn't move her lips to speak, so she just kept laughing. "Stop that!" Naeros struck her in the face. Her head lolled to the side, free of Naeros's grasp. She could taste blood. She laughed again. Naeros stalked off for a moment. His return was accompanied by a squeaking like old, rusty wagon wheels. Again, Ythnel's head was raised, allowing her to see a wooden cart next to Naeros, laden with various blades.

"I'm not sure if you're aware of this, but apparently I've acquired a nickname from the fair citizens of this great city. They call me 'the Marker.' Do you know why?" He considered the blades on the cart, finally choosing a knife with a jagged, two-inch-long blade. "I suppose it's because I like to leave my guests with a little something to remember me by. Now all I have to do is decide what would be an appropriate symbol of our relationship.

"I know, since you won't cry for me, how about I just make you bleed where those tears should be." Naeros pressed the knife on the flesh just under Ythnel's right eye, near the bridge of her nose. "Now don't scream too loudly, or you'll mess up my concentration." Naeros drew the blade down the side of Ythnel's nose, ending at the edge of the nostril. Ythnel felt only a slight tugging. Naeros's brow furrowed in puzzlement. His lips pinched, and he made a second cut from the outer edge of Ythnel's eye, down her cheek, all the way to her jaw.

Ythnel began to laugh again.

"Impossible." Naeros's face flushed, and he began to tremble. With a bellow, he assailed Ythnel, pummeling her until her vision went black.

THE PRIESTS

Ythnel floated in a sea of endless black. There was no horizon, no edge to the blackness. It was all around her, enveloping her, insulating her. Beyond the blackness was pain. It pushed against the buffer, sought to puncture the blackness, to drain the sea away until she was left standing there naked and helpless. Ythnel wished it would go away. She was tired of pain. She was afraid of it.

Fear intensifies pain, Headmistress Yenael's voice echoed through the blackness. *It creates anticipation, an expectation in the mind. Fear is a tool. Use it.*

Ythnel ignored the words. Pain was beating harder against the barrier. She tried to bury herself deeper in the blackness. Her heart raced with fear.

Fear.

A handmaiden was not supposed to fear pain. Pain was the air she breathed, the lover she embraced. Pain was a thing to control, not fear. Fearing pain gave it control.

Slowly, Ythnel let the black fade away. Light appeared, grew, and brought with it pain. Ythnel opened her arms and welcomed it.

Calloused hands supported Ythnel and lifted her while other hands removed the manacles from around her wrists and ankles. Her right shoulder stung, and her face throbbed. Her left eye was swollen shut. Two lines of fire ran down her right cheek. Her feet touched the stone floor, but there was no strength in her legs. She sagged against the hands that held her and tried to focus on her surroundings. Her right eye fluttered open, and she saw two people standing before her.

"You walk a thin line, Naeros. You know Father wants to be notified immediately when one of them is captured." The woman speaking looked familiar to Ythnel. She wore a sleeveless white tunic over leather breeches. Dark, straight hair, streaked sparingly with white, hung past her shoulders and framed a lean, angular face. The front of the tunic was decorated with a thick, black embroidered circle. Her emphatic gestures drew Ythnel's attention to the corded muscles flexed along the woman's arms. "He was very upset when he learned you had one secreted away down here. Entropy demands swift judgment against those who transgress Her will."

"Father could not care less." Naeros sneered. "If I didn't know better, Kaestra, I'd say you barged in here hoping to claim some of the credit for capturing this witch by presenting her to Father yourself. Afraid that with our sister's recent successes, she may earn enough favor to replace you as high priestess?"

Kaestra's eyes widened, and her mouth moved as though she wanted to say something. If those eyes were violet instead of brown, and her curves a bit softer, Ythnel realized, Kaestra would bear a striking resemblance to Saestra. Then the impact of Naeros's words struck her. The three were siblings!

"I'm leaving, Naeros, and I'm taking the prisoner with me. I'd suggest you don't make an issue of this." Kaestra pinned her brother with a look that dared a response. Naeros simply stepped back with a bow. A smug smile spread across Kaestra's face, and she moved up the staircase. The guards followed behind quietly, dragging Ythnel along between them.

Outside the tower, Ythnel squinted in the harsh sunlight as the guards carried her to a waiting cart. The back of the cart was enclosed to form a solid box about five feet high, four feet across, and six feet deep. One of the guards opened the door, and the other shoved Ythnel inside, swinging the door shut behind himself as he entered after her. Sunlight spilled in through bars in the door, bathing Ythnel as she lay on the floor. She pulled herself up onto one of the benches that ran the length of each side while the guard sat staring at her from the other bench, fingering the cudgel hanging from his belt.

"Thanks for the help," Ythnel said, smiling weakly at her chaperone. The cart took off with a lurch, and she was forced to brace herself with her hands to keep from slipping off the bench. The guard chuckled.

Ythnel ground her teeth and held back a groan as the pain triggered by her sudden movement finally reached the area of her brain that registered those specific nerve impulses. The particular lesson from her training at the manor where she had learned that bit of information was one she would not soon forget. The sisters had somehow removed the top half of the skull of a goblin while it was still alive in order to point out how the brain and nervous system interacted. Ythnel remembered the goblin's pain region being relatively small, which meant it could endure a lot of pain before becoming incapacitated. This was one of the few times she wished she had a goblin's brain.

A person shouldn't have to endure this much pain for this long, she thought. There's no point because there's no time to heal, to harden. That is the purpose of pain—to make one stronger. She sighed, a long, slow exhalation. And as she emptied herself out, doubt crept in.

Why is this happening to me? When will it be over? Surely, Loviatar has some greater plan for me. I just need to have patience. Just a little longer.

It was a reassuring thought, one that she clung to with desperation. But in the back of Ythnel's mind, a frightened voice echoed.

I don't think I can wait much longer.

Preoccupied as she was, Ythnel did not realize they had stopped until the cart door swung open and a guard reached inside to drag her out. She stumbled onto the white stones that composed most of the roads in Luthcheq, her legs weak but able to support her. They were in a small courtyard adjacent to some sort of outbuilding behind a large, sprawling palace that Ythnel guessed was the Karanoks'. The well-tended grounds, an area easily equal to four city blocks in size, were cordoned off from the general populous by the same thick, towering walls that separated the city from the unsettled wilds.

The palace itself covered half the grounds. A

grand marble staircase rose up to a portico that surrounded the first level. A broad architrave decorated with relief sculpture marked the beginning of the second story, and a great dome capped the center of the structure.

Ythnel was led to a small door on the south side of the palace. Kaestra took a key from a pouch at her waist, turned it in the keyhole, pushed the door open, and walked in. The guards shoved Ythnel after her. She found herself in a dark tunnel. About thirty feet in front of her, Kaestra stood running her hand up a wall, as if searching for something. Ythnel saw the wall swing inward to reveal the orange glow of torchlight in another room.

Two men stood at stiff attention next to a rough-hewn wood table with playing cards scattered across its top. Beyond them was a row of barred cells, all empty.

"We have a new prisoner, Corporal Urler," Kaestra said. "You know what to do with her."

"Yes, High Priestess." One of the dungeon guards hurriedly saluted then fumbled with the keys at his belt. He unlocked the section of bars that led into the row of cells and waved for Ythnel's escorts to follow him. The guard paused before one of the cells, a thoughtful look on his face, then nodded to himself and moved to the next one down. He opened that one and ushered the guards and Ythnel inside. Two sets of manacles, bolted into the wall, were fastened to Ythnel's hands and feet. Their job done, the two escorts withdrew, and the guard with the keys stepped forward, a wad of cloth in his hand. He shoved the wad into Ythnel's mouth then tied a strip of leather around her head to hold it in place.

"Don't want you castin' none of yer magic while yer

waitin' for Lord Karanok." He smiled, revealing a few gaps in his teeth, then turned and left, slamming the bars closed behind himself.

Ythnel watched him walk back to Kaestra, who nodded and left, the two guards who accompanied her trailing behind. The other two guards sat back down at the table as soon as she was out of sight and resumed their card game.

The manacles prevented Ythnel from doing little more than shifting from side to side, but she was still able to move her head. She could see the entire dungeon through the bars of her cell. All the cells were the same damp, gray stone. And they were all empty.

Ythnel leaned back against the wall and closed her eyes. What was going to happen next? She knew wizards were executed, but she wasn't a wizard. Surely she would get a chance to prove it. But what if she didn't? She shook her head, trying to dislodge the thought. She pushed everything from her mind and imagined the sea of black filling the emptiness, drowning all worry and cares until finally she drifted in its comforting embrace once again.

Prisus sipped at his morning tea while Iuna sat across from him happily eating her bowl of oats and maple syrup. Her disposition had turned quite sunny following the arrest of Ythnel. As much as Prisus enjoyed his daughter when she was in these good moods, he knew he would have to find yet another replacement. There was just no way he could run his business and raise Iuna.

There was a knock at the front door. Prisus continued to drink his tea; Leco would answer. Seconds after the first knock came an insistent pounding.

"Prisus Saelis? This is the city guard! Open up immediately!"

Leco hurried past the dining room on his way to the front door. Prisus sat up straighter and set his tea down, his brow furrowed in concern. Iuna glanced at him questioningly, but he motioned for her to stay seated. Prisus could hear heated voices coming from the living room. He dabbed the corners of his mouth with a napkin then stood up. Leco appeared at the entry to the dining room.

"Master Saelis, there is a Captain—" A uniformed guard barged past Leco, cutting him off.

"Prisus Saelis? By order of House Karanok, you are hereby placed under arrest for the aiding and abetting of a witch."

"What?" Prisus's face paled at the charges. Several armed guards filed into the room and grabbed hold of Prisus and Iuna. Libia entered with a tray, saw the guards, and screamed. The tray slipped from her hands with a clatter as she crumpled to the floor.

"Papa, what is going on? We didn't do anything wrong," Iuna cried as the guards' hands closed around her arms and lifted her out of her seat.

"Don't worry, Iuna. This will all get sorted out," Prisus said as he was led out, trying hard to hide the strain in his own voice. As he entered the living room, he saw Leco being held by a couple of guards at the door; he had been dragged from the room while Prisus was being arrested. When Leco spotted him, he struggled violently against the men who restrained him. Somehow he slipped free and charged the guards escorting Prisus. Before he could reach them, though, one of the guards by the door recovered and knocked Leco's feet out from under him with a sweep of the shaft of his spear. Leco hit the floor with a groan but struggled to get up. The other guard stepped to Leco's side and kicked him twice in the side. Leco collapsed and lay still, though Prisus could still see him breathing.

The guards led Prisus and Iuna out into the courtyard, where an enclosed wagon waited, the door of iron bars at the rear hanging open. A guard stood at the back of the wagon like an usher. Another sat on the driver's bench, twisted around so he could watch the procession, a loaded crossbow set casually in his lap.

A bellow of rage echoed out across the courtyard. Prisus, one foot in the wagon, turned back toward the house to see Leco charging out the door after the last guard, a fireplace poker brandished above his head. He hadn't gone two steps when there was a loud twang and something flew through the air.

"No!" Prisus cried. Leco's bellow was cut off and reduced to strangled grunts. A crossbow bolt was sunk halfway up its shaft into his chest, a blotch of red slowly spreading across the front of his gray linen tunic. Leco took one more step before tumbling down the remaining stairs to lie in a motionless heap at their base.

"Get them out of here," the captain ordered, "and move that body back inside. I'll send somebody by to pick it up later." The door closed behind Iuna, and the wagon lurched into motion as Prisus watched his life disappear from view.

They were taken to the Karanoks' palace and escorted through a service entrance to a small waiting room on the first floor. A single table and some plain wooden chairs were the only furnishings. A solitary guard was left to watch over them. Iuna huddled next to Prisus while they waited. Every breath seemed like a candle, and with each one that passed, Prisus's nerves unraveled further. Finally, the door opened and a stern-looking woman with long, straight salt-and-pepper hair entered.

"My name is Kaestra Karanok," she said, wasting no time. "Do you know who I am?"

Prisus nearly cried. The fact that they were speaking directly with the high priestess of the church of Entropy did not bode well. He nodded in answer to her question.

"Good. You should know that there is a possibility you will be charged with aiding a known witch. Are you aware of the sentence for such a crime?" She continued without waiting for a response. "Burning at the stake." Prisus gulped, beads of sweat forming on his brow.

"But we didn't do anything," Iuna protested.

"Shut up!" Kaestra was right in Iuna's face. His daughter whimpered and tried to hide behind him.

"You seem to be a fine, upstanding citizen, Master Saelis." She paused, looking at him out of the corner of her eye. "I understand you own your own business. And you have a lovely little girl here." Kaestra reached out to stroke Iuna, but she ducked away. Kaestra's face hardened.

"You will be called to testify against the witch you brought into our city. If you cooperate, I may be able to petition my father for leniency on your behalf."

"O-of course, we'll cooperate," Prisus stammered, desperate to grasp at any chance of coming out of this situation intact.

"Good. You will wait here until summoned. Remember what's at stake here, Master Saelis." Kaestra smiled, but it did little to comfort Prisus. She stalked out of the room, leaving them alone with the guard.

Prisus patted Iuna, hoping to reassure her. He, on the other hand, felt only an empty pit growing in his stomach. He started to chew nervously on a fingernail. There was nothing else to do but wait.

"Hey! Wake up in there! It's time." The shouting was joined by a loud clanging. Ythnel opened her eyes to see the guard Kaestra called Corporal Urler banging on the bars of her cell with a cudgel. He grinned when he noticed her stirring. "Lord Karanok's ready ta see ya." He unlocked the cell and swung the door open for two other guards who entered and flanked her. Corporal Urler trailed them, the keys in his hand. At a nod from him, the other two grabbed Ythnel by the wrists and ankles while he unlocked her manacles. They yanked her to her feet then wrenched her arms behind her back. Corporal Urler circled round and clamped something to her wrists. The guards relaxed their hold, but her arms were still bound behind her.

"She's all yers, boys."

Ythnel was led out of the dungeon to a flight of stairs near the secret entrance they had brought her in by. It was an unpleasant climb. Her legs had not regained their full strength, and the muscles in her thighs were burning by the time she reached the top of the flight. She paused for a moment and got a shove in the back from the guard behind her.

"Keep moving," he grunted. Unable to respond because of the gag, Ythnel glared over her shoulder before continuing.

After the stairs, they followed a hallway that curved to the left. The lead guard opened a door at the end, and they all filed through into a grand hall with an arch-vaulted ceiling that ran the length of the palace. She got little more than a glance before the guards were pushing her toward a set of wood doors decorated with some sort of metal inlay. At a knock from one of the guards, they swung inward to reveal an immense audience chamber at least one hundred feet across and more than half that distance deep. A dais dominated the side of the room opposite the entrance. Five chairs sat upon the second and third tier of the raised platform, one slightly higher than the other four. All but one were occupied.

To Ythnel's far left sat Naeros, fidgeting in his chair until the man to the right of him laid a hand on his forearm. That man Ythnel had never seen before. A square jaw, blunt nose, and bushy eyebrows all fought for dominance under a mass of dark, curly hair held back by a thin circlet of gold. There was some resemblance to Naeros, but this face was older, both in years and wisdom. It could only be his father, Jaerios Karanok. That made the elderly man sitting in the middle chair above the others Maelos Karanok, and to the right of him sat Kaestra. The last chair was empty.

The guards halted a few feet from the bottom of the dais and took up flanking positions slightly behind Ythnel. Kaestra got up from her chair and stepped down to the main floor, stopping in front of Ythnel.

"You are here because an accusation of witchcraft has been brought against you," she said in a stiff and formal voice that echoed back louder than she had spoken. "Is there anything you would like to say before judgment is pronounced?" Ythnel nodded.

"Know this, then. Should you try to cast a spell once your gag is removed, you will be killed before you complete the first syllable." Kaestra waited, her eyes locked with Ythnel's. Ythnel did not waver, and Kaestra looked away first, motioning one of the guards to remove the gag.

"I am innocent," Ythnel croaked. It was the first time she had used her voice in . . . she wasn't sure how long.

"Innocent? Lies will not help your case. There were witnesses. Lord Naeros saw you cast a spell in the marketplace."

"No he didn't. In fact, your brother *and* your sister both know that I am a handmaiden of Loviatar."

The smug look on Kaestra's face vanished. Her eyes widened, her lips parted slightly, and she turned to look at Naeros. He returned the look with a shrug of his shoulders.

"No matter. My brother may not have seen your wizardry, but I have other witnesses." Kaestra waved at a guard standing near a door on the wall to Ythnel's right. The door was opened and two figures shuffled out. Their hair was matted and their clothes were in disarray, but Ythnel could still recognize Master Saelis and Iuna. They were escorted up to the front of the dais and halted a few feet from Ythnel. Kaestra strode over to stand before Iuna. She bent over and cupped the girl's face with her hand, lifting it up until their eyes met.

"You saw this witch casting spells, didn't you, little one?"

Iuna bit her lip and tried to turn her head to look at her father, but Kaestra kept their gazes locked.

"Uh-huh," Iuna mumbled.

"Speak louder, child."

"Yes," Iuna quavered. "I saw her casting a spell in—"

"She doesn't know what she's saying! Be quiet, Iuna,"

Master Saelis interrupted. "The woman is a Loviatan. I hired her as a governess. Do you think I would bring a wizard into this city, into my home? I know the penalty. I don't want to die. Please, you have to believe me. This is all a big mistake." Master Saelis's voice quickly rose in pitch as he spoke faster. "I don't want to die. If you don't believe me, you can search through her belongings. I'm sure you'll find something that verifies what I'm saying."

"Silence!" Lord Jaerios's voice boomed out as he rose from his seat. "I've had enough."

Kaestra looked questioningly at her father as he approached, but he dismissed her with a wave of his hand. She bowed out of the way and took her seat. He reached into his robe and produced something hidden in his fist.

"Is this yours?" He opened his hand to reveal Ythnel's scourge medallion. She nodded, a wave of relief washing over her. They knew who she really was. Now they'd have to set her free.

Lord Jaerios closed his fist and tucked the medallion back into his robe. Ythnel looked up to see his face twisted in contempt.

"The cult of Loviatar and its practices are as degenerate and corrupt as those of wizardry. I will not have it in this city, and those I find involved in it I will execute." He returned to his seat.

"I order all three of you to be burned at the stake," Lord Jaerios pronounced. Master Saelis moaned, and Ythnel's heart sank. She could see a smirk forming on Kaestra's lips.

"But I didn't do anything wrong," Iuna wailed. "I tried to tell Daddy to get rid of her, and . . . and I turned her in. It's not fair."

Maelos Karanok leaned forward in his seat and

whispered something to his son, who nodded.

"You are correct, child. You did your best to root out this disease and should be rewarded. For your efforts, I will spare your life. You shall be made a slave to the Temple of Entropy, and attend to my daughter personally."

Kaestra beamed.

Lord Jaerios stood and helped his father down the dais, signaling the hearing was over. Naeros followed them out while Kaestra gave instructions to the guards to deliver Iuna. Master Saelis was brought alongside Ythnel, and the two of them were escorted back out of the chamber. They passed by Lord Jaerios in the hall, who had stopped to talk with a palace servant.

"Find Therescales, and bring him to my study," he told the young boy. "Tell him I have a change in the plan that should take care of the mages once and for all." The servant scampered off out of Ythnel's sight as the guards led her and Master Saelis back down into the dungeon.

There was a young woman behind the desk when Therescales entered the warehouse this time. There were no antiques either. In their place were racks of weapons: swords, maces, axes, and some exotic-looking things that Therescales wasn't even sure how to use, though he imagined it would probably be quite painful if he found himself on the wrong end of one of them. They all appeared to be of fine craftsmanship, many with intricately decorated hilts. One particular dagger, with a gem embedded in its pommel, caught Therescales' eye, but he was not here to shop.

"A fine piece of steel, imported all the way from the Moonshaes. I'm sure you'll find its balance to be near perfect." The young woman had come up on Therescales unaware—a sign of how nervous he was. One misstep and he could burn at the stake—or worse if he gave himself away to the mages.

"Actually, I'm interested in a black staff. It was once owned by a shadowy sage who carved symbols all over it."

The hungry light in the woman's eyes dimmed, and her shoulders slumped as she realized she would not be making a sale.

"Yes, of course. If you'll follow me, I believe you'll find what you're looking for over here." She led him to the door behind her desk and unlocked it with a key from her belt pouch. Therescales strode through as soon as it was open.

The illusionary box was in the same place. Therescales descended into the secret passage and inscribed the burning rune to open the hidden door. The others were already filing in to the meeting area, so Therescales slipped into place at the rear of the line.

"It's about time you showed up," the mage in front of him whispered over her shoulder. The hood she wore hid her profile. "Especially considering you were the one who called this meeting."

He ignored the comment as the mages took their seats around the table. Therescales was pleased to see everyone present. An expectant silence hung over the room until Brother Hawk cleared his throat.

"You called the gathering, Brother Asp. Please tell us what was so urgent that you risked our discovery with another meeting so soon after our last."

Therescales blinked at the lack of formality, unsure of what it meant. He glanced at the faces around him, trying to detect if he had somehow been found out. It was rare that councils were ever held this close together, but every member had the right to request one at any time.

Should they be on to him, though, he was ready. He had procured a scroll of invisibility and cast the spell on his dagger, which now hung unseen on his belt. He had also imbibed a potion just before entering the warehouse that would protect his mind from controlling enchantments.

Unfortunately, the various disguises made it almost impossible to accurately read anyone's expression. With no recourse but to press on, Therescales stood. He had rehearsed what to say a thousand times before tonight. He sent a silent prayer to Cyric that they would believe him.

"Brothers, I apologize for the inconvenience, but know that I would not have done so if I did not think the news I have to share was of vital importance." He paused for a moment to be sure he had everyone's attention. "I have learned from a source in the palace that the wizard Brother Hawk was prepared to meet with has been captured and will be publicly executed at dawn, two days hence." Murmurs and gasps sprung up as soon as he finished.

"I've heard nothing of the sort from my contact," Brother Frog bellowed, springing up immediately.

"I'm not surprised, seeing as how *your* contact couldn't even confirm whether or not the victims of Saestra Karanok were even wizards." Therescales raised an eyebrow, and Frog frowned but sat down.

"How do you know it's even Brother Hawk's ally?" Sister Rat's voice trembled. Therescales turned his head slightly to look at her but watched Brother Hawk from the corner of his eye. This was the catch in the plan. No one knew where Hawk's wizard was from, except maybe Hawk himself. Therescales had been forced to make an educated guess, hope that Hawk did know, and that the guess was right. If he was wrong, at best Hawk would simply reveal that the Karanoks had the wrong person, and the bait would be impotent. Then Therescales would have to find some way to keep Jaerios from burning him at the stake.

Or Hawk could suspect Therescales, and he would find himself at the mercy of the mages.

Therescales trusted he held the right cards, however. There were only so many wizards with the resources and motivation to aid an overthrow of the Karanoks. It was time to play his hand.

"My informant told me that a squad of House Karanok guards had stumbled upon the wizard's camp while patrolling the road up to Mordulkin. It appeared that the wizard had been on his way down from there and was waiting to meet someone." From the periphery, Therescales saw Brother Hawk's shoulder's sag. He forced himself not to smile as triumph welled in his chest.

Therescales took his seat, and everyone looked to Brother Hawk. The leader of the mages stood slowly and leaned on the table.

"Brothers, it appears that Brother Asp's information is correct." The concession was met with more murmurs and gasps. "Please, I'm not finished." Brother Hawk motioned for silence. "In light of this development, we need to immediately begin planning a rescue."

Cries of protest and shock erupted. Therescales was not surprised. He knew the bait wouldn't be taken readily by all. He waited to see how Brother Hawk would do his work for him.

"Order, order! You will be quiet," Brother Crocodile roared.

"I know this isn't how we planned things to progress, but if we can't be flexible, then we're no better than the Karanoks."

"Flexible has nothing to do with it," Brother Fox retorted. "Attacking the Karanoks is suicide."

"It would not be a full-fledged assault. We could hit them on the way to the execution yards. Please, you must see that this is the only way. If we do not at least try, how can we show future allies that we are even worth supporting?" Stone silence met Brother Hawk's plea, and he sat back with a sigh. Therescales decided to risk a little push.

"I call for a vote."

"A vote has been called," Brother Boar declared in his slurred voice. "According to our bylaws, a majority is required to act upon the proposal before us. As arbiter of the vote, I am not allowed to cast my own ballot unless a tie must be broken. I will call out your name, and you will answer 'aye' if in favor of a rescue attempt or 'nay' if against. I will start to my right. Brother Hawk?"

"Aye."

"Brother Crocodile?"

"Aye."

"Brother Chameleon?"

"Nay."

"Brother Fox?"

"Nay."

"Brother Frog?"

"Aye."

"Sister Rat?"

"Nay."

"Brother Tortoise?"

"Nay."

"Brother Raven?"

"Aye."

"Brother Asp?"

Therescales couldn't help the grin this time. "Aye."

"The 'ayes' have it."

"Yes!" Brother Hawk shouted, pounding the table with his fist. He stood once again. "I know that those who voted against this action will act honorably and fully support your comrades. Now here is what I suggest." He nodded to Therescales as he began to outline his plan for the rescue. Therescales just sat back and carefully took note of it all.

THE PRIESTS

Heralds from House Karanok had made the rounds through the city yesterday, proclaiming a public execution the following dawn of a foreign wizard. Even though the winter sky was still the gray of diffused morning light, crowds lined the boulevard that ran from Karanok Palace to the execution yards, squeezed together as much for warmth as for the hope of a better view. As the first rays of sun bounced off the marble dome of the palace, a drum roll cadence echoed down the grand staircase that led from the two great bronze doors to the courtyard. Gasps from the crowd announced the appearance of two guards in ceremonial bronze breastplates, shields, and helmets with horsehair plumes, all buffed to a mirror shine. They stood stiff and silent at the top of the stairs then rapped the butts of their spears against the floor before making their way down.

The guards were followed by a pair of clerics dressed in flowing robes of white, swinging censers from which wafted brownish green smoke. Behind the clerics came two pairs of guards dressed in similar ceremonial armor. Shackled between each pair were the condemned: a woman in rags, her dark hair shaved on one side, her face swollen and bruised; and a skinny man with thin, blond hair, his eyes staring off somewhere distant as he stumbled along. Another set of censer-bearing clerics created a buffer between the prisoners and a series of enclosed sedan chairs that undoubtedly carried the members of the Karanok family behind their lowered curtains. Bringing up the rear of the procession were a dozen crossbow-wielding guards, scanning the crowd as they moved out of the courtyard and down the boulevard.

Brother Hawk frowned. Already they encountered a variable they hadn't planned for. Which of the two was the wizard? Brother Frog's contact in the palace had been killed before a description could be obtained.

Brow furrowed, Hawk pushed his way through the crowd, trying to keep pace with the parade. The five other mages followed him, weaving through the rear ranks of spectators. They all wore heavy, hooded cloaks of drab wool pulled tight about them. No one gave them a second glance. The chill air was reason enough to bundle up; being able to hide your face was an added bonus. It had been decided not to use magic for disguises, as the spells would be a beacon announcing their presence to any divinations. That also meant no wands, rings, or staves. So they were left with the spells each had spent the past day preparing. It was an all-or-nothing gamble with the odds stacked high against them. Now with two prisoners to rescue, those odds doubled. There was no way around it, however. They could not take the chance of grabbing the wrong one.

The mages reached the ruins of the Old Wizard's Tower ahead of the parade. No one remembered the name of the former tenant, or at least no one ever spoke it aloud. The tumbled stone, now covered with creepers and other overgrowth, was once a great, white tower that rivaled the current residence of Naeros Karanok. It was also the site of the first enforcement of the Karanoks' law against magic. In the middle of the night, guards from House Karanok had invaded the tower. Explosions echoed across the city, and flashes lit the darkness as various wards and protections were triggered, but the Karanoks had numbers on their side. Outmanned and overwhelmed, the owner of the tower chose to destroy the structure and all the secrets held within rather than turn it over to the rulers of Luthcheq. The rubble was left untouched as a reminder of the fate awaiting those who practiced the forbidden.

Brother Hawk scanned the surrounding buildings as his comrades took their places scattered amongst the crowd. The remaining mages should have been in position since the night before. He peered into dark windows and studied rooftops, trying to catch a glimpse of movement, a sign that all was ready. The rooftops were still, and the windows peered back like the empty sockets of a skull.

Nothing to do but wait, Brother Hawk told himself.

Sections of the crowd were heckling the prisoners as they neared. Rotten vegetables pelted the pair sporadically. Hawk stood on his toes and craned his neck. They were just a few yards away now. He recalled the arcane words that would trigger his spell, holding them until the attack began.

The clerics at the front of the procession had drawn even with Brother Hawk's position. He started to cough as smoke from the swinging censers drifted past him. Brother Hawk put his hand over his face to keep from drawing attention then panicked as he felt the spell slipping from his memory. He closed his eyes to concentrate and fixed the incantation firmly in his mind.

When he opened his eyes, the prisoners had already gone past.

Fear gripped Brother Hawk. Why hadn't the hidden mages attacked? He looked around and met the scared and confused faces of his co-conspirators on the ground. Quickly, they all congregated at the rear of the crowd.

"What's going on, Brother Hawk?" Sister Rat's eyes were darting wildly.

"I don't know. Something's happened."

"Yeah, something bad," Brother Frog retorted. "We've failed. I say we call this thing off."

"No!" Brother Hawk nearly shouted. "No, we can't give up yet. There's still a chance to save them. If we don't, we can forget about anyone else offering to help overthrow the Karanoks."

"Do you have a plan?" Brother Crocodile asked. Brother Hawk was relieved that not everyone was ready to run.

"I'll think of something." Brother Hawk moved off before the others could protest. He didn't bother to look over his shoulder as he tailed the procession. Even if they didn't follow, he was going to see this through. He was tired of living in fear in the city he grew up in. He was tired of talking about doing something. It was time to change things.

The sun had finally crested the east city wall when they reached the execution yard. It was rumored that the yard had once been a beautiful public garden with rare flora that drew visitors from around the Realms. The Karanoks changed that in their quest to rid Luthcheq of magic.

The crowd filed in behind the procession, under the watchful gaze of two round towers that guarded an opening in the twenty-foot-high inner wall that separated the city from the triangular field of trampled dirt. On the west and south side, the yard was fenced in by the thirty-five-foot-high walls that surrounded the entire city. At each point of the triangle were the larger towers that flanked the sections of the outer walls. Armed guards patrolled the battlements.

A large, undecorated stone platform ran the length of the south wall. Here the procession diverged with the prisoners and their escort moving to the left, while the Karanoks in their sedan chairs veered to the right. Both groups climbed the stairs at either end of the platform. As the prisoners were bound by their shackles to two wooden poles that rose from a great log pyre built in the center of the platform, the sedan chairs were lowered and the curtains pulled back.

With a sharp intake of breath, Brother Hawk froze in the middle of the milling throng. Gathered together on the platform were the four most powerful members of House Karanok: old Maelos, the family patriarch; Jaerios, true ruler of the city; his son, Naeros; and Kaestra, high priestess of Entropy. With one well-placed fireball, Brother Hawk could reduce the family's control over the city to a pile of ash.

The inner struggle lasted for only a moment. It was tempting, but Brother Hawk knew there were enough

Karanok cousins spread across the land that the vacuum would be quickly filled.

"There's no more time." Brother Crocodile touched Brother Hawk on the shoulder. "What do we do?"

"We need a diversion."

Ythnel sagged against the wooden pole, closed her eyes, and let the weariness wash over her. The din of the gathering spectators faded as her consciousness drifted in the darkness of her mind. She had endured all that the Karanoks had put her through for naught. There had been no point to her suffering, no greater purpose. That had been the hardest blow.

Now she was going to die, and she didn't care. If there was no reason for all that she had gone through, then nothing mattered.

Something brushed lightly against her feet. From the rustling sound that accompanied the touch, Ythnel guessed it was witchweed leaves. Even though they knew she was not a wizard, they still went through with the charade. It was pointless.

A voice cried out from somewhere to Ythnel's right, and the crowd grew silent.

"Citizens of Luthcheq, your presence here is a testimony to your zeal in the war against the corruption that is sown by the use of magic. Entropy is pleased." It was the cold, hard voice of Kaestra Karanok. Cheers met her declaration, but they seemed halfhearted at best.

A scream from the crowd snapped Ythnel's eyes open. Across the yard by the two towers guarding the entrance, a large, black globe, perhaps ten feet in diameter, materialized out of the air; arcs of deep purple energy cascaded across its surface. All heads turned; all eyes fixed upon it.

"You see." Kaestra's voice was filled with fervor. "Entropy has come to witness the death of this witch and her servant. Bring the torches." Two guards started forward, burning brands in their hands.

The brands sputtered then erupted in huge clouds of billowing smoke.

A ball of fire streaked from the back of the crowd, blossoming as it neared the platform and exploding upon impact amidst the gathered Karanok crossbowmen. Several small darts of different-colored energy flew from various parts of the crowd to strike the guards now spilling out of the towers and send them tumbling over the battlements to the ground below.

Ythnel squinted, trying to peer through the smoke from burning bodies and sputtering brands, but her eyes were full of tears. From what little she did see, it appeared the yard was in utter chaos. The panicked crowd was running about like stampeding cattle, caught between the burning platform and the manifestation of Entropy. The Karanoks and their remaining entourage were fleeing the platform, only to get pushed back by the press of trapped spectators.

The sound of someone muttering nearby caught Ythnel's ear, and she twisted around to look but could see no one amid the smoke.

"Who's there?"

She was answered by a sudden coughing fit then a curse. Still no one was visible. The muttering started again a few moments later. Ythnel concentrated on the source, trying to pinpoint its location. Something about the muttering was familiar. She couldn't decipher what was being said, but it reminded her of a prayer chant.

That was it! Someone was casting a spell.

In that instant of realization, a figure wrapped in a hooded cloak appeared before her, and her bonds unlatched and fell to the ground.

"My name is Brother Hawk. I am here to free you," the man said, pulling back his hood to reveal a stern face with a set jaw, a tousled mane of black hair, and dark eyes that held a mixture of fear and determination. He reached out a hand to help Ythnel down.

"Please, don't leave me. You have to help me, too." The plea came from the prisoner on the other pole. Ythnel hesitated, her eyes locking with the man who was still bound. She had forgotten about Prisus, her former master.

"There is nothing we can do," hissed Brother Hawk to Ythnel. "I have used what spells I had to free you. Hurry, we have to get out of here."

Ythnel looked away, taking Brother Hawk's hand and climbing down from the pyre. Once down, however, she stopped.

"We have to try." She let go of Brother Hawk's hand and rushed over to Prisus. She scanned the ground for something to use to break the metal cuffs, but there was nothing suitable. With a *thunk*, a crossbow bolt sank into the post just above Ythnel's head, and she looked up. A guard on the wall was reloading his weapon while keeping one eye on her. She froze, her mind suddenly going blank. The guard brought his crossbow back up and took aim.

Brother Hawk appeared between Ythnel and the guard. He murmured something as his hands moved in front of him. The guard fired at them, but the bolt bounced off an invisible disc of force inches before it reached Brother Hawk.

"Hurry!" he shouted.

"Maybe we can pull them off," Prisus cried over his shoulder. Ythnel took hold of one of the manacles while Prisus tried to pull his hand through. It only took a few seconds before Ythnel realized they would never go over his hands. She released the manacle she was holding, and Prisus looked up at her. When their eyes met, Ythnel could see the pleading in his gaze, but she shook her head and turned away. Brother Hawk started moving for the far side of the platform, and Ythnel followed.

"No!" Prisus wailed.

"The witch is escaping." Alerted by Prisus's cry of despair, Kaestra rushed the platform, calling to the guards on the battlements above. "Shoot them!"

Ythnel looked over her shoulder. Through the clearing smoke, she could see several guards training crossbows at them. A fireball erupted atop the wall, hurling burning bodies over the sides. A single guard remained standing. He aimed his crossbow and fired. With uncanny clarity, Ythnel watched the bolt fly through the smoky air toward her. She felt Brother Hawk grab her wrist and shout something. The air around her shimmered, distorting objects near her like a ripple in a pond. The ripple collapsed upon itself, upon her, and she was standing across the yard by the entrance to the city.

"I have her! Let's go," Hawk shouted. Several cloaked figures converged on Ythnel and Brother Hawk. Together they pushed their way through the churning mass of bodies.

"What about Sister Rat?" one of the figures asked.

"She'll hold the illusion as long as she can then catch up," Brother Hawk answered. "That was the plan."

They were passing through the entrance to the

yard when the giant black globe disappeared. No one would have noticed if not for the shouts of the guards up on the battlements. The group watched as Sister Rat's spell failed, and she ran toward them. A whistling filled the air. The sound ended with a *thud.* Sister Rat glanced down, surprise on her face. Blood welled around the protruding tip of a crossbow bolt that pierced her chest from behind. She took another step and collapsed.

"Run," Brother Hawk breathed. "Run."

Shock kept the group rooted in place despite Brother Hawk's urging. The man grabbed Ythnel by the wrist and dragged her past the towers guarding the entrance to the city. The rest of the group slowly came back to life and scrambled after their fleeing leader.

Directly across the street from the execution yard was a rectangular building that took up almost the entire block and served as stables for the nearby barracks. Releasing Ythnel's wrist, Brother Hawk began a chant, bringing his hands together, fingers spread apart like a fan. With a final word, a sheet of flames shot forth from Brother Hawk's fingertips to engulf the two guards that barred the way. Before the charred remains even hit the ground, Brother Hawk and Ythnel rushed into the building, gasping for breath.

Another guard was inside. He drew his sword and moved to block them from getting to the horses. Ythnel spotted a whip looped around a peg on the wall to her right. Keeping her eyes on the guard, she sidestepped to the wall, grabbed the whip, and in the same motion, sent it snapping out at the guard. It fell well short of the mark, but the threat was enough to make the guard rock back on his heels, halting his charge. Ythnel sent it lashing out again, and this time the whip wrapped itself around the guard's blade. Caught by surprise, the guard was unable to keep his grip on the sword as Ythnel yanked the whip back toward her, and the blade flew from his hand. He lunged for it, but Ythnel tripped him up with the whip, jerking his feet out from under him. Brother Hawk scooped up the sword and plunged it into the prone man's back just as the rest of the mages entered the stable.

"Grab a horse. We'll make for the South Gate." Brother Hawk announced. He turned to Ythnel. "Are you well enough to you ride on your own?"

Ythnel straightened and walked over to a stall. She swung the gate open and approached the horse. Stroking its forehead and neck, she calmed the animal's nervous snorts then heaved herself onto its back. With hands firmly gripping the horse's mane, Ythnel steered the animal out of the stall. Brother Hawk brought his mount up beside her, his eyes questioning. She kicked her heels into the horse's flanks and took off.

The others quickly caught up to her as they galloped east into town. Brother Hawk drew even and pointed to an upcoming intersection, indicating they would turn right. Ythnel rounded the corner first then quickly reined in her horse, causing it to snort and toss its head. Everyone else skidded to a halt behind her.

One hundred yards ahead of them was the South Gate. Between them and the huge wooden doors was a mass of armed soldiers who were already swinging them closed.

"We can't get through here," Ythnel said.

"Back into the city," Brother Hawk ordered. "We'll try the West Gate. It's the next closest. It might be better if we split up and meet again at the gate. You"—he pointed at Ythnel—"stay with me."

Brother Hawk wheeled his horse around and led the

way. They raced through a park block, tree branches slapping at them, and exited onto a wide street running north. Ythnel noticed the others had peeled off during the run through the park. She and Brother Hawk charged ahead without slowing. Pedestrians who found themselves in the path of the wild flight frantically dived aside. One man, crouched down playing dice with his fellows, oblivious to the approaching commotion, was bowled over when Ythnel's horse brushed by him.

The pair followed the street as it curved gradually to the west then urged their mounts faster as it straightened to the north once again. Brother Hawk shouted something at her, and Ythnel looked up to see a row of buildings that marked the street's end. Without slowing, Brother Hawk veered to the left and disappeared down a narrow lane. Ythnel tightened her grip on the horse's mane and followed but took the corner too wide and was pulled off the back of the horse by the force of the turn. Still grasping onto the mane firmly, she was dragged into several wicker baskets stacked under a storefront awning. The baskets went tumbling, spewing their contents across the lane, and the awning collapsed as Ythnel collided with one of the poles holding it up. The horse's mane was ripped from her hands.

Ythnel lay there dazed. For how long, she didn't know. A pair of hands grabbed her, and she flailed, thinking the Karanoks had caught up. She opened her eyes to see several figures backing away—not guards, just citizens, shopkeepers. Ythnel stood, and the world spun, forcing her to stumble back a step.

"Are you all right?"

She nodded, one hand on her head and the other stretched out to touch the wall of the nearby building and steady herself. A shout from the entrance to the lane drew everyone's attention. Ythnel swore as a squad of city guards appeared. Adrenaline pushing aside the fog in her head, she sprinted out the other end of the lane and into a mire of foot traffic. Ythnel shoved her way through, glancing back occasionally to check on the progress of the guards, who now stood at the mouth of the lane, scanning the crowd. One of them pointed in her direction and cried out. At the squad leader's orders, they fanned out into the crowd.

Ythnel surged ahead with renewed determination, fueled by a growing panic she could not stifle. She kept her head down in an effort to blend better with the slightly shorter Chessentans, but it also prevented her from tracking the progress of the guards. Blindly, she pressed forward.

"You, there! Stop!" The shout brought Ythnel's head back up, and she expected to see an armored figure closing from behind, but there were no guards near her. She cast a glance about, searching for the source of the command. She spotted it in front of her. Somehow, one of the guards had gotten ahead of her and was closing in on a horse and its rider wading its way through the river of people. It took a moment for Ythnel to realize the rider was one of the cloaked figures who had rescued her.

"Brother Hawk!" she shouted in warning, hoping the rider would react to the name, even though it was not his. She was rewarded as he twisted around, his hood falling back to reveal a shaved head and meaty jowls. He scanned the crowd, but did not appear to see her. However, on his sweep back, he saw the guard. His eyes widened, and he tried to urge the horse forward, but the mass of people packed tightly together impeded his flight. The guard was almost upon him.

Ythnel muttered the words of a prayer, calling upon Loviatar and requesting access to the Power. It coursed through her, and she began to shape it with gestures in the air before her. There was nothing to see, no physical manifestation, but Ythnel could feel it building inside her, filling her. She released it, channeling it toward the guard. In her mind's eye, she watched it weave through the crowd, swirl around the guard until it had fully enshrouded him, and settle atop him like a mantle.

The guard stopped and slowly turned around. Even though there were hundreds of bodies between them, Ythnel knew he was looking right at her. She could feel his eyes widen, his heart race, and his body begin to shake. Beads of sweat formed on his forehead and palms. He could not control his bodily functions. An unnatural fright was consuming him. With a shriek, the guard bolted in the other direction.

Ythnel started forward again, intent on reaching the rider. As she neared him, she saw his brow furrow while he watched the departing guard.

"That was me," she said as she came up alongside the horse. He looked down at her, puzzlement still on his face. Then recognition struck him. "Mind if I ride along. I seem to have lost my horse?" He nodded, and she accepted his hand up as he hoisted her onto the back of the horse.

Ythnel could now see that they were at the rear of the reassembled group. Brother Hawk was out in front, wading through the river of people walking up and down the street. The others were slowly pushing their way north as well. Ythnel felt her heart pounding as they moved through the crowd. This was taking too long. There were still guards searching for them, and word could reach the guards at the West Gate before they got there. The gate would be closed, and a hundred loaded crossbows would be waiting for them.

"Painbringer's touch!" Ythnel cursed out loud. Loviatar had freed her, even after she had let doubt shake her faith. She was not going to squander this second chance. She would get out. Ythnel dug her heels into the horse's flanks, and the animal leaped forward, trampling pedestrians as it surged ahead. Her fellow rider yelped but seemed at a loss as to how to stop the animal. Ythnel did not care. All that mattered was that she reach the gate.

They overtook the other riders and soon reached Brother Hawk just as he was turning left off the street onto another that led to the West Gate. Wagons, riders on horseback, and travelers on foot stood in a line waiting their turn to pass through the gate. There was no sign of alarm as the rest of the group caught up.

"There was no need for—" one of the riders began, waggling a finger at Ythnel, but looks from the others silenced him.

"All right, everyone. We're not out of this yet, but it appears that word hasn't reached this far yet," Brother Hawk said. "So let's just take deep breaths and—" There was a commotion at the front of the line, and guards began pouring out of the towers onto the wall. The thirty-foot-high, iron-reinforced wood doors of the West Gate groaned as they began to swing inward, cutting off the countryside beyond the city walls.

"Azuth's beard!" Brother Hawk said, his horse prancing in a circle. With a cry from its rider, the horse bolted down the line in a race to beat the closing gate. The remaining mages hesitated for only a breath. The doors were moving together too fast; there was no way they could make it. Something whooshed overhead, accompanied by a wave of heat, and Ythnel looked up to see a swirling mass of flames growing larger as it hurtled toward the gate. It rapidly overtook Brother Hawk and slammed into the gate doors with a thunderous boom, sending splinters of wood in all directions. Ythnel looked back to see one of her rescuers lower his hands. Then the other riders shot past her on their way out of the city.

As they approached the shattered gate, crossbow bolts began to rain down on the street from the battlements. People scattered, shrieking as missiles struck targets indiscriminately. The horses dodged and weaved as they carried their riders through the charred remains of the West Gate. Ythnel crouched low to avoid the many bolts flying through the air from all directions. Something brushed her shoulder, and she looked up to see a shaft stuck in her companion's head. The horse jumped over a large piece of debris from the gate, and he slid from the horse, almost pulling Ythnel along with him before she realized what was happening. She wrenched her arms free from around his waist at the last moment and grabbed onto the horse's mane as it galloped into open country.

She didn't slow down. She didn't stop. She didn't care. She was free.

Her horse let out a loud neigh and tumbled to the ground; Ythnel rolled free before it could land on her. She got to her feet and saw that horse was standing once again. Concerned about the cause of the spill, Ythnel made a cursory examination of the animal. She quickly found the crossbow bolt embedded in the horse's haunch. It would not be able to run any farther.

The other mages had already broken through the gate and where increasing the distance between themselves and the city with each breath. There was no one to come back and help Ythnel. She looked back to the gate, caught by indecision, and saw a lone rider galloping toward her. Instinctively, she knew it was the first of the city guards who pursued them.

Ythnel grabbed the shaft of the bolt in both hands and pulled. The horse let out a terrible shriek as the missile tore free, and it almost kicked Ythnel. Tossing the bolt aside, Ythnel laid her hands over the wound and said a quick prayer to Loviatar. When she removed her hands, there wasn't even a scar.

The mounted guard was almost upon her as she swung up onto her horse's back and spurred it into a gallop. She looked over her shoulder as she sped away and saw that he was still in pursuit and gaining. Ythnel urged her horse on, but it was at its limit already. Then the guard was right beside her. Before she could react, he punched her in the jaw with his mailed fist. Ythnel's vision flared white, and she almost fell from her horse, but somehow she managed to hold on. She tried to move away, but the guard followed her.

That's when she noticed the dagger hanging from his side.

She swung her horse into the guard's mount, surprising him. As he tried to maintain control, she grabbed his dagger and plunged it into his face. With a cry, he fell from his horse, and it veered away. Now all Ythnel had to do was catch up.

THE PRIESTS

CHAPTER 7

You're not even a wizard?"

They had finally come to a stop once the walls of Luthcheq were out of sight. Of the six people who had rescued her, only four remained. They all sat staring at her. She could see the disbelief and bitter disappointment that laced Brother Hawk's question mirrored in their eyes.

"Did you free the wrong one?" It was an accusation from a man with a thick mustache.

"No. You all heard Kaestra call her a witch." He nodded at Ythnel. "What I can't understand is why they would mistake you for one. Exposing you to witchweed smoke should have revealed the truth."

"They knew I was not a wizard." Ythnel met each and every one of their gazes unflinchingly.

"I was bait in a trap set for the Mage Society, which I take it you are all members of. Or should I say, were?" She gained some satisfaction when a couple of them cringed.

"That explains some things," Brother Hawk said, stroking his chin. "But if the Karanoks knew about our plans, that means we were betrayed from the inside."

"I did overhear Jaerios send for someone named Therescales to discuss the plan to set up the society," Ythnel volunteered.

"Fires of the Nine Hells!" The man with the thick mustache spat. "Brother Asp really was a snake. I'm starting to wonder if those rumors about his involvement in the capture of Haraxius weren't true."

"Now is not the time for such speculation, especially when there is nothing we can do to exact vengeance." Something smoldered in Brother Hawk's eyes. Ythnel guessed it might be the fires of revenge. "For now, we need to decide where to go. I suggest Mordulkin. As many of you may have guessed, our potential ally is from that city."

"Need I remind you that Mordulkin lies on the other side of the bay?" Another of the mages, his face lean and head shaved bald, spoke up. "That would require trekking around Luthcheq. I'm sure the Karanoks will have patrols swarming the countryside. Simply expelling us from the city will not be enough for them."

"Why not Cimbar?" the mustached mage suggested. "They are across the Adder River and are no friends of Luthcheq."

"That also means crossing Adder Swamp, Brother Fox," Brother Hawk said grimly. "I do not think we are prepared for that. I still say Mordulkin is our best hope. If we are careful, we can avoid patrols."

"Decide quickly," the fourth mage hissed. "I see riders." Everyone turned toward the direction he was pointing to see a plume of dust rising from back toward the city.

"Fires of the Nine Hells, indeed. Into the swamp! We'll ride for Cimbar." Brother Hawk spurred his horse into motion once more, galloping toward the borders of the Adder Swamp.

The grouped raced westward, but their pace eventually slowed to a canter to avoid exhausting the horses. There was a palpable shift in the mood of the group that accompanied the change from a frantic gallop to a more steady, even flight. Panic drained away and was replaced by silent reflection. Ythnel noticed it within herself. Where before her mind had been clear, focused only on escape, thoughts now began to filter in. An image of Prisus and Iuna, bound and being led into the audience chamber at the palace, floated to the front of her mind. It faded and was replaced by Prisus chained to a stake, wailing in despair as Ythnel walked away. She wondered where Iuna was and how Kaestra was treating her.

It was strange that she should be so concerned with the fate of the girl who had caused the whole mess. Iuna had been Ythnel's first responsibility upon leaving the temple, and she had failed miserably. But it was something more than guilt. There was a connection between them that Ythnel could not explain. She had sensed it that first night in the Saelis house, as she prayed to Loviatar. The girl needed Ythnel, needed the guidance she could provide.

"You look like you lost your best friend. Or lover, perhaps?"

Ythnel came out of her reverie and noticed the

mustached mage had fallen back to ride even with her. She hadn't caught what he had said and gave him a confused look.

"The man next to you on the platform back in the execution yard, was he your lover?"

"No," Ythnel shook her head. The man looked at her expectantly, but she didn't elaborate.

"Well, anyway, Brother Hawk asked me to come back here and check on you. He was worried you might be distracted; you're starting to fall behind."

Ythnel looked up. The next horse was easily a hundred yards away. She cast a glance back over her shoulder. The patrol from Luthcheq was getting closer. She could actually make out darker spots within the cloud of dust that was following them.

"Sorry. Thanks for the warning." She nudged her horse a bit faster. The mage nodded and matched her pace.

They rode in silence for a while, closing the gap with the rest of the group. When they finally caught back up, Ythnel decided to ask a question that had been nagging her.

"Why the animal names?"

"Hmm?"

"Why do you call each other by animal names?" she repeated.

"Oh, that. It was a way to protect our identities. We were a secret society, after all." A broad grin accompanied the mirth in his voice.

"I suppose there's really no point in it anymore; just hard to let go of some things." He brought his horse in close to Ythnel and extended his hand. "My name is Viulvos, formerly Brother Fox."

"I'm Ythnel." She accepted his hand with a brief smile. "Who are the others?"

"Well, the portly fellow in front of us is Brother Tortoise, who goes by the given name of Muctos. Our fearless leader, Brother Hawk, who you've already met, is known outside the society as Kestus. Riding behind him is Brother Crocodile. I don't know his real name, unfortunately. One of the safety precautions we took was to share our true identity with only two or three other members. That way, if one of us was captured, we couldn't reveal who everyone was."

Ythnel nodded. It sounded like a wise move.

"Hmm, it appears our pursuit is gaining on us." Viulvos's comment caused Ythnel to turn and look back. Sure enough, she could now make out several small shapes that resembled horses. "Perhaps we should increase the pace a little." Viulvos excused himself and rode back up to Kestus. After a brief council, Kestus spurred his horse faster and shouted for the others to do likewise.

At the edge of the swamp, Kestus brought them to a halt.

"We'll go single file, slow and cautious. Do not stray. The ground is just as dangerous as anything else." With that, he led them in.

Twisted, black-barked trees crowded together, competing for what little solid terrain there was. Even in winter, without their leaves, the branches of the trees were so intertwined that only small patches of sky were visible through the canopy. A perpetual haze floated up from the swamp floor, gases escaping in crude belches to warm the air, creating tepid, oily moisture that clung to everything. The wet bogs sucked at the horses' hooves, reluctant to let go.

Ythnel found herself once again at the rear of the line. She looked back quite often, though more from wariness of the sounds she heard than fear of seeing their pursuers suddenly appear. The noises of the swamp were strange to her. A rustle, the snap of a twig, a bird caw, or the hoarse cough of some beast echoed in such a way that she couldn't tell if it was a mile away or right behind her. She shivered at the eerie silences that hung between. It was nothing at all like the continuous bustle of the city.

Their path weaved through the trees, reminding Ythnel of the flight of a dazed housefly after it had been smacked with a roll of parchment. The terrain made it impossible to move in a straight line. Pockets of quicksand or deep pools of water were encountered every few yards, forcing the group to backtrack or alter their course many times. Tension within the group was palpable. As Kestus turned them around yet again to avoid a large expanse of water, it became too much. With a frustrated cry, the mage who Viulvos had named Muctos urged his horse into the stagnant mire.

"No, Brother Tortoise, don't!" Kestus shouted.

"I'm tired of all these detours! We're not making any progress. If we just cut across—" Muctos hollered back as his horse waded in up to its rider's calves.

"You don't know how deep it could get, Muctos. Now turn back before we have to come in there and pull you out."

Movement beyond Muctos caught Ythnel's eye. A shape as thick as her leg and longer than the horse dropped from a distant tree into the still water with barely a ripple. Unsure of what she was seeing, Ythnel moved her horse closer to the water and squinted. For several moments, the surface of the water was unbroken, save for the splashing made by Muctos's progress. Then Ythnel spotted what appeared to be a half-submerged log floating across the top of the water. Ythnel blinked and realized the log was not floating; it was slithering, slowly closing in on an unaware Muctos.

"Look out!" Ythnel warned, pointing at what she could now clearly see was a huge snake. Muctos's horse panicked and reared, dumping the mage into the swamp. The snake quickly switched targets, veering toward the floundering man. Three bolts of green light streaked across the swamp and slammed into the snake. It sank from view.

Muctos's horse had made it back to shore, but the mage was hindered by his cloak and was barely keeping his head above water.

"I should leave you to drown," Kestus spat as he started to walk his horse out to Muctos. He was still ten feet from the mage, when the snake reared up out of the water right behind Muctos with a demonic hiss. The floundering mage swiveled around to come face-to-face with the monstrous serpent and screamed.

Another barrage of green-colored arcane darts smote the snake in the face, almost tearing its head clear off. It hovered half out of the water for an instant before sliding back below the surface, a growing cloud of red under the water marking its location.

Kestus pulled a panicked Muctos onto the back of his horse and waded back ashore. Muctos slid of the horse and flopped onto his back, breathing hard, his soaked clothing clinging to him. "Thank you, Brother Hawk."

"Fool," Kestus rebuked. "Adder Swamp is so named because of the deadly snakes that infest it. Legend has it that their venom is so poisonous, the god-king Gilgeam nearly died when he was bitten by one while crossing the Adder River.

"Now get on your horse. I trust we'll have no more

side trips from anyone else after this."

Everyone rode in silence. It was unclear what time it was, as the swamp haze and tree branches obscured the sun overhead, but Ythnel guessed it must be close to highsun. Her belly was grumbling. She doubted there were any meals in the near future. There hadn't been any meals in the recent past, either, she realized. In fact, the last thing she could remember eating was morningfeast that first morning at Master Saelis's. Visions of grilled sausage and eggs danced unbidden in her head. Her stomach rumbled even louder.

"A bit hungry, are we?" Viulvos grinned over his shoulder at Ythnel. "Perhaps Muctos would be so kind as to catch us a big, fat, juicy snake we could roast over a fire."

"Ha, ha, very funny, Brother Fox." Muctos frowned from his new position at the end of the procession. Ythnel giggled.

"At least someone appreciates my humor," Viulvos said. He turned in his saddle so he was facing Ythnel and slowed his horse a bit, closing the distance between them. They rode together for a while without speaking. Ythnel could feel Viulvos watching her from the corner of his eye. Several times he appeared about to speak, but he turned away when she looked at him.

Finally, Ythnel's patience ran out. "What would you ask of me?"

"Heh, was I that obvious? Very well, I do admit to being curious about a few things. You said you weren't a wizard, but you are a Thayan?"

Ythnel nodded. "You can be one without the other."

"Right, right. I suppose you get that a lot." Viulvos smiled apologetically. "Can I ask what brought you to Luthcheq? I wouldn't think someone from a country known for its wizards would consider a city prejudiced against the Art as a destination."

"I took a job as a governess."

"And the man you were with up on the platform, he was your employer?"

Ythnel nodded, suddenly unable to speak as a wave of emotion washed over her. Why had it all gone so wrong? Anger and sadness fought for control within her.

The play of emotions must have been visible on Ythnel's face because Viulvos said, "We don't have to talk about it if it is too painful."

"No, that's not it. I barely knew Master Saelis or Iuna. I'm more angry than anything, I guess."

"Iuna? She was the girl you were caring for?"

"Mm-hmm. And the one who started this whole mess."

"Really? How so?" Viulvos was obviously intrigued; his eyebrow arched above his left eye.

"She accused me of witchcraft in front of Naeros Karanok."

"Oh, my, that would certainly cause problems. Why would she do that?"

"She was a spoiled brat and didn't like me." Ythnel didn't hold back the vitriol in her voice. "As I understand it, the family had gone through several governesses before me."

"So, did she have any proof? As zealous as the Karanoks are, I can't imagine them just sentencing you to death without something to support their claim."

"I cast a spell when Naeros tried to capture me."

"But I thought you said you weren't a wizard."

"I am not." Ythnel hesitated but decided to continue. Ever since she had left the manor, she had been met with strange looks and outright hatred whenever she told someone who she was. It had made her leery of telling others about her faith, but the thought that she might be growing ashamed of her beliefs was something she could not tolerate.

"I am a handmaiden of Loviatar." Ythnel tensed, waiting for the reaction.

"Interesting," Viulvos replied, stroking his mustache. "I heard that Jaerios Karanok forbade his son from joining the Loviatan faith, the state religion being what it is and all that. I bet he wasn't too pleased to learn about you."

"No, he was not," Ythnel said, a slight edge to her voice.

"My apologies, I did not mean to offend."

Ythnel dismissed it with a wave of her hand.

Viulvos opened his mouth, but was interrupted as his horse started prancing around and neighing nervously.

"What's going on?" Ythnel looked up to see all the horses acting skittishly. The riders eventually got them under control and came together. They were on a flat expanse of firm ground between a scattering of the twisted, rough-barked trees, with a small hillock covered in some unidentifiable vegetation sitting on the west side. Ythnel realized an eerie silence had settled over the swamp. All was quiet but for a slight breeze that rustled through the grasses and leaves on the hillock, creating a strange ripple effect across its face. The hairs on the back of Ythnel's neck went stiff and straight, and a shiver ran down her spine. She glanced around, alert for the sudden appearance of the source of the sense of impending doom that was spreading through her, but the only things visible were the black-barked swamp trees that surrounded them like unmoving sentinels.

Something tickled in the back of Ythnel's mind. She swept back across the clearing, taking in the wind-tousled vegetation of the hillock and the still branches of the trees.

The trees weren't moving. There was no wind.

The hillock reared up, supported by thick vines, and opened a maw filled with teeth-like rows of thorns and sharp branches. It lunged forward on the leg-like vines while leafy limbs whipped out from its side.

"Look out!" Ythnel screamed, but it was too late. One of the limbs knocked Viulvos from his saddle. Another wrapped around the startled horse, which barely got out a neigh of terror as it was lifted into the air. Time seemed transfixed, the scene frozen for a heartbeat before rushing back into chaotic and grisly motion.

"Brother Fox, get out of there!" Kestus bellowed. The fallen mage lay stunned on the ground, staring as his mount disappeared into the mouth of the plant monster. Muctos's horse bolted, taking its startled rider with it. As it reached the edge of the clearing, it passed under a low branch of one of the swamp trees, which caught a helpless Muctos full in the chest, ripping him right off the horse's back and slamming him to the ground. He lay there, motionless, while the horse ran off into the swamp.

"Brother Crocodile, get Brother Tortoise," Kestus ordered as he struggled to get his mount back under control. "Ythnel, grab Brother Fox."

Brother Crocodile rode over to where Muctos had fallen. He was forced to dismount but kept one hand wrapped in the horse's mane. It was not enough. As soon as his feet touched the ground, the horse spun away, wrenching the hairs from Brother Crocodile's grasp. The mage tried to chase after the animal but gave up as it faded from view. He turned back to bend over Muctos's still form.

Ythnel dug her heels into her horse's ribs, steering her reluctant mount closer to Viulvos, who was finally scrambling to his feet. She reached out a hand to pull him up, but he was jerked away by another leafy tentacle. He screamed as he was lifted up into the air, dangling by his ankle.

Frantic neighing drew Ythnel's attention to her right. Kestus's mount was bucking, its eyes wide enough that the whites showed all the way around. The mage was thrown to the muddy dirt of the swamp, but the animal kept bucking, a lather starting to form around its lips. Its momentum carried it smashing into a tree. Ythnel heard the crunch of bone as its head bashed into a thick branch, and the horse collapsed to the ground.

Kestus had picked himself up by the time Ythnel looked back. He tossed something on the ground in front of himself then sprinkled a handful of dust over the object while chanting. A sphere of flame appeared before him, quickly growing to a diameter of five feet. Kestus pointed at the monster, and the sphere rolled toward its target, striking the side of ambulatory plant and bouncing away. The vegetation blackened and shriveled where the sphere touched, but the living greenery failed to catch fire, perhaps protected by the swamp muck that coated it. Ythnel heard Kestus curse.

A cry from Brother Crocodile pulled Ythnel around once more. The plant creature's other tentacle was groping for the mages. Brother Crocodile had managed to pull Muctos back, putting the tree between them and the threatening limb. Ythnel could see his mouth moving and watched as Brother Crocodile pointed a finger at the tentacle. A thin ray of ice-blue shot out from his fingertip and struck the tentacle, frosting the vegetation. The monster jerked back its limb then lashed out. Brother Crocodile ducked as the tentacle swept across and slammed into the tree with enough force to shake loose several branches.

Desperation and panic threatened to overwhelm Ythnel. Nothing they did seemed to affect the plant creature. Their attacks were little more than distractions to its feeding. Kestus slammed the flaming sphere into the monster yet again, but it had the same lack of effect as before. In fact, the spot where he had first struck had turned green again, filling out with new growth. Ythnel helplessly watched Viulvos flail wildly as he was lowered into the monster's waiting jaws. She turned away, but she could still hear the crunch of bone and the suddenly cut-off screams as the plant monster ingested the mage.

"We have to get out of here!" Ythnel screamed. Kestus looked at her grimly but nodded. He sent the sphere at the creature once more before turning to run. Ythnel glanced back to see Brother Crocodile helping Muctos up and supporting him as they tried to flee. The plant monster's tentacles were snaking after them, however, and Ythnel knew they wouldn't make it.

Exerting all the skill and strength she could, Ythnel forced her horse to charge between the escaping mages and the tentacles. Sensing a new target, the monster turned to grab at the approaching animal. As the two leafy limbs wrapped around the horse's neck and its haunches, Ythnel leaped from its back. She tumbled to the ground and rolled to her feet. Swinging under Muctos's other side to aid Brother Crocodile, Ythnel looked back to see the plant monster lift the horse into the air, grab on with another tentacle, and pull it in two.

❧ ❧ ❧ ❧ ❧

At a signal from her scout, Kaestra brought the patrol to a halt. All seven guards fingered their crossbows and cast furtive glances around the clearing where they had stopped. Kaestra slid off her mount and walked over to where the scout crouched. She hoped he had found something that would indicate they were closing in on their quarry. The idea of traipsing about in the swamp after dark was not especially appealing to her. It felt as if her skin were covered in layers of slime so thick she could peel it off with a knife, and the sooner she could return home, the sooner she could take a bath.

"What have you discovered?" Kaestra finished tugging off her riding gloves and tucked them behind her belt.

"It appears there was some sort of battle here. There are two sets of hoofprints leading off in different directions."

"So, our fugitives have split up?"

"No. There are a group of footprints heading north together. I think they're on foot now."

"Hmm, that should make it easier to catch up with them. But how does that indicate there was a battle?"

"It doesn't. It's these strange scorch marks that make me think there was a battle." The scout rose and pointed to a pair of scorched paths leading from the middle of the clearing to a hillock on the west end of the clearing.

"What I can't figure out," he continued, tracing the paths to their endpoints, "is what they were fighting."

"Was anyone killed? Injured?" Kaestra followed the scout, eager to hear that one or more of their prey had been eliminated from the hunt.

"Well, there is some blood on the ground." The scout stooped yet again, fingering some dark, sticky fluid spread across a few dried leaves.

One of the guards yelled something behind Kaestra, and she turned to look, only to see him pointing in her direction. She swung her head back, and her eyes widened as she witnessed the scout struggling furiously against a vine twice as thick as her forearm that had wrapped around his midsection. It lifted him up into the air, and Kaestra saw that the vine extended out from the hillock.

Another vine lashed out from the opposite side of the hillock. With lightning speed, it whipped around Kaestra's upper torso, pinning her arms to her sides. As it lifted her, too, into the air, she watched the front of the hillock split open to reveal a gaping maw of thorns and jagged branches.

"Guards, do something! I command you! Shoot it!" Kaestra screamed. A couple of the men fired their crossbows, but the bolts just disappeared under the layers of vegetation that covered the monster.

With a sickening crunch, the plant monster impaled the scout on its wooden teeth. The monster withdrew its tentacle then tossed its head. The body of the scout was thrown into the air and swallowed whole.

Kaestra knew her turn was next if she didn't do something fast. She couldn't think of any spells she had prayed for that would affect a living mound of vines, grasses, and shrubs. However, she could still use one of those spells, twisting it from its original purpose to directly channel the Power of Entropy instead.

Calling upon her goddess, Kaestra recited the words to the prayer, slightly altering the intonation of certain syllables. Still able to bend her arms at the elbow, she brought her right hand up. A black haze began to form in the center of her palm then spread until it encased her entire hand. She exalted in the blessing of her goddess, the ability to hold pure chaos, anathema to all living things.

Smiling with confidence, Kaestra pressed her entropic hand against the vine that held her. Instantly it withered away, breaking the monster's grip on her. She dropped to the ground, rolling away from the creature and springing to her feet.

Without hesitation, she ran to her horse and leaped into the saddle. Her men were already turning their horses, spurring them away from the clearing, back the way they had come. Kaestra let them go. They would pay for their cowardice once they returned to Luthcheq, but she was done with the swamp. Father wouldn't be happy that they returned empty-handed, but even if the mages had survived whatever that monster was, she doubted they would make it through the night. There were things far worse than snakes and living plants that dwelt in Adder Swamp.

THE PRIESTS

Jaerios lounged in the velvet-cushioned chair, his fingers steepled before him, as he gazed down upon the line of prisoners being led in. The balcony overlooking the Burning Room was one of his favorite places in the palace. It was a metaphor for the divine appointment that had been bestowed upon the Karanoks, and the family's elevation above those who practiced abomination. From its height, judgment was meted out upon those who had joined themselves to the arcane, while the purity of the judges was maintained by preventing contact with the guilty.

It was time to pass judgment.

The guards escorted the first of the prisoners to a tall alcove that resembled a cylinder with the front cross-section removed. At the base of the alcove, a pile of wood surrounded a blackened pole the width of a tree trunk. The pole rose almost to the top of the alcove, ending just below a metal grill that would allow smoke to be drawn up through it then expelled from the mouth of a grotesquely stylized humanoid face. Finally it was permitted to drift out a chimney in the ceiling that led to the outside.

"I shouldn't be here. This is a mistake. She wasn't a witch," the prisoner mumbled as the guards shackled his ankles and wrists to the pole. The acoustics of the Burning Room carried the plea to Jaerios's ears, but he had long since stopped hearing the cries for mercy, as well as the screams of pain that inevitably followed.

Another prisoner was being marched to the next alcove, but Jaerios waved them off. There were enough alcoves for all five of the condemned to be judged at once, but Jaerios preferred to let them watch the fate of the one before them as additional punishment. The pair of guards who had brought the first prisoner carried in a basket of witchweed and dumped it at the feet of the chained man.

"She's a Loviatan, I tell you, not a wizard!" the prisoner screamed as a guard set a torch to the dried leaves and tinder. "You have to believe meeeee!"

Jaerios sensed someone behind him and turned his head from the shrieking and writhing to see his daughter standing in the archway that led to the balcony. He had been informed during dinner that she had returned. From her cleaned robes and damp hair, it appeared she had freshened up first before coming to the palace.

"Come. Come, Kaestra." She hesitated before entering and sat stiffly when he offered the seat next to him.

"How did your patrol fare?" From the sullen set of her jaw, he was fairly sure he already new the answer.

"I lost them, Father. We were ambushed by a tendriculos. The guards fled, and my scout was killed.

"We tracked them to that same clearing, and there was blood along with other signs of a fight, so I'm sure they encountered the same creature. If there were any survivors, they fled deeper into the swamp. We can consider them as good as dead." She looked at him, a question in her eyes. He leaned back in his chair, considering the news. From the corner of his vision, he saw his daughter wet her lips with the tip of her tongue. Good. It was important that she feared failure, feared failing him.

Kaestra had always done her best to please him, however. She had earned the position of high priestess and worked diligently in her duties, though of late, she seemed more interested in the divine abilities that Entropy had recently begun to grant rather than their crusade against the arcane. He was going to have to say something to her about that eventually. Putting the cart before the horse only created more work for those driving the cart.

But now was not the time for such discussions. Now was a time to enjoy the fruits of their labors. The city was finally cleansed. The information Therescales provided had allowed the family's forces to lie in wait for the members of the Mage Society who were to position themselves on the rooftops along the procession route to the execution yard. Those who were captured now waited their turn below, watching the poor fool who had hired the cleric of Loviatar burn for his mistake. It was mildly frustrating that the rest escaped, but they were no longer infesting Luthcheq, and that was what mattered most.

"Yes, you're probably right," Jaerios turned back toward his daughter and let the smile that had been growing in his heart spread across his face. "Wizards and their ilk are weak; easy prey once you remove them from their sanctums. I'm sure the swamp will take care of them. A tendriculos, did you say?" Kaestra relaxed visibly, and Jaerios turned back to the proceedings of the Burning Room.

"You've done well, daughter. Let's celebrate this victory by watching those who sought to defile our city receive their just fate.

"Guards," Jaerios ordered, raising his voice slightly to be heard above the crackling fire that continued to consume the blackened husk still standing in its midst. "Dispose of the remains and bring forth the next prisoner."

Ythnel stumbled over something sticking up out of the ground. It could have been a root or a stone; in the fading light, small pools of shadow obscured most of the ground. She would have sprawled face-first, but Brother Crocodile caught her up by the arm and steadied her.

"Kestus, we have to stop. We're lost, and wandering around in the dark isn't going to change that. When the sun comes up in the morning, we can—"

"In the morning, we could all be dead," Kestus said, his voice strained with frustration.

"We could die tonight by stepping in quicksand because we can't see a foot in front of us." Brother Crocodile tried to reason with him.

"Or we could trip over a rock and break our necks," Ythnel chimed in sarcastically.

Kestus sighed and turned back to the others.

"You're right. I'm sorry. It's foolish to push on." He looked around them for a moment, as though coming to a decision. "This spot is as good as any. We'll rest around this tree." He pointed to a thick, gnarled trunk with black, corrugated bark. "I'll set up a few wards that should give us ample warning if anything comes too close."

As Kestus strode off to set his alarms, Ythnel plopped down onto the soggy ground and leaned back against the base of the tree. The rough ridges irritated the raw skin around the knife wound on her shoulder. The linen dress she had been wearing was little more than rags now and did nothing to protect her from direct contact with the elements. She shifted so that most of her weight was on the other shoulder, but the position was just as uncomfortable as the bark bit into her bruised muscles.

"Those are some nasty wounds," Muctos commented as he ungracefully lowered himself next to Ythnel. "You're a cleric, right. Why don't you heal yourself?"

"Loviatans seek to embrace pain, not avoid it." Ythnel grunted as she shifted once more. "The Maiden of Pain doles out mercy sparingly, and frowns upon those who are too quick to seek escape from suffering when endurance will suffice."

"That sounds like you're reading straight from your creed book." Muctos raised his hand and smiled wearily at Ythnel. "Hold on, I'm not trying to start a fight. I was under the impression that Loviatans dealt suffering and pain to others, not themselves."

"No one is exempt from the torments of this life," Ythnel replied. "By understanding pain, I become a better instrument in teaching others how to endure it."

"Understanding is one thing, but I don't see the point of running yourself into the ground. How is that serving your goddess?"

Muctos's words reverberated in Ythnel's head, echoing back the doubts she had entertained while in the hands of the Karanoks. Why was she subjecting herself to needless suffering? Had she not proven herself able to endure? Would it not be appropriate to let herself heal now?

Somewhere in the back of her mind, Ythnel wondered if perhaps she should continue to suffer as penance for her earlier lack of faith. However, even Headmistress Yenael had said that there was a time to relent and give kindnesses.

"You're right," Ythnel said slowly, still unsure of the decision she had reached. One thing she did know was that she needed to be by herself right now. Pushing herself up off the ground, Ythnel walked a few yards away from the tree.

"So, you know my name."

Ythnel started at Kestus's voice and turned her head to see him approaching. "Yes. Viulvos told me." Her voice caught at the dead mage's name, and she saw Kestus's face harden for a moment.

"I suppose it doesn't matter now, anyway," Kestus said with a shrug. "Don't go too far. I've set wards about forty feet out, so if you go beyond that, you'll trigger them unless you say *'ssorpa.'*"

With only the barest nod to acknowledge she had heard the mage, Ythnel changed direction, deciding to go where Kestus had come from. The thick night air closed behind her like a heavy curtain while the chirps and hisses of the swamp rushed in to carry her off to another world. She glanced over her shoulder, suddenly afraid she had wandered too far, but she could still see Kestus's back as he approached the two dark forms of the other mages huddled around a tree.

"*Ssorpa*," she whispered, just in case.

Feeling sufficiently isolated, Ythnel knelt down on the spongy turf, crossing her arms over her chest and placing her hands on opposite shoulders. She drew a deep breath and released it slowly. With another breath, she closed her eyes and prayed. As the words left her lips, tiny lashes began to sting Ythnel, indication that Loviatar was pouring out the Power to her. The stings flared into a wave of burning, a cleansing fire that scorched away all the aches and pains and soreness in its path. In its wake, Ythnel was renewed.

She opened her eyes with a gasp and was almost surprised not to see burnt husks in the place of trees, with a layer of ash covering everything. Ythnel rubbed her shoulders, trying to get out that last little bit of ache. Her fingertips brushed across a small patch of hard, smooth skin just above her right shoulder blade. Curious, she moved her hand to her cheek and traced two rough lines running down from the corners of her right eye. Loviatar had left her the scars to remember the pain she had endured.

Ythnel stood, ready to return to the others. She was tired, and with the edge taken off her injuries by the healing, perhaps she could get an hour or two of rest before they had to move on. She took a step, and a thought surged from seemingly nowhere to stop her in her tracks.

Pray.

It had likely been days since Ythnel had last performed her nightly ritual of prayer to Loviatar. She had lost all sense time while in Naeros's care and hadn't thought to ask the mages what day it was.

Going more than even a day without praying was unwise. The ritual strengthened the link Ythnel shared with her goddess and bolstered her faith.

Ythnel hesitated for a moment as she realized she didn't have her scourge medallion. The symbol served as the focus of her prayers, and a conduit through which she could channel the Power. It was an integral part of being a Loviatan, and Ythnel, her dress hanging in tatters that barely concealed her flesh, felt naked for the first time, knowing the medallion was not hanging around her neck.

Do not let your medallion become a crutch, Headmistress Yenael's voice called out from Ythnel's memories. *It is only one means of focus. Anything can be used as a representation of your faith in the Willing Whip.*

Ythnel scanned her surroundings. It didn't take long for her to find what she needed. She strode over to one of the rough-barked trees nearby. Standing on her toes, Ythnel reached up and grabbed one of the bare branches. She tested several of the thin offshoots, bending them this way and that until she found a suitable one of the right length. She twisted the piece off near its base and came away with a switch just shy of a foot long.

Kneeling once more, Ythnel began her chant, the rhythms punctuated with a swat of the stick over her shoulder or around her side. Each small sting brought euphoria, a sense of closeness to her goddess that made her swell inside. The connection continued to grow stronger, and Ythnel felt herself being pulled away somehow, detaching from her physical body and slowly drifting higher and higher.

The sun shone brightly upon the white stones of the courtyard. Ythnel thought she recognized the buildings that surrounded her, crammed together so they looked as though they were simply one expansive unit. The flat roofs reflected the light in such a way that all the edges of the structures were blurred, even when Ythnel squinted.

Gazing at the stairs in front of her that lead to a nondescript wooden door, Ythnel realized she was standing before the entrance to Master Saelis's home. Somehow, she was back in Luthcheq. The thought did not disturb her and quickly flitted away. It seemed as natural as the eerie silence she now noticed: in the center of a bustling city of tens of thousands, not a sound carried in the air or echoed off the buildings.

Ythnel turned the handle, opened the door, and stepped inside without hesitation.

"Master Saelis? Iuna?" Even before the echoes of her call died out, Ythnel new the house was empty except for herself and the furniture. She glanced around the living room. Everything looked as she remembered, except that all the edges seemed fuzzy. Ythnel blinked a few times and rubbed her eyes, thinking they were still adjusting from the brilliance outside. She looked again, but nothing had changed . . .

. . . besides the fact that she was no longer alone in the house.

Headmistress Yenael stood by the marble fireplace in her buffed leather bodysuit, tapping her palm with the handle of a scourge. Next to her hung Naeros Karanok in nothing but his skin. Chains suspended him above the floor by wrist and ankle. When Ythnel eyes followed the chains up, she saw them disappear into a cloudy, black void that spread out to cover where the ceiling should have been.

"Show me."

Ythnel brought her eyes back down to see Headmistress Yenael holding the end of the scourge handle out to her. Only, it wasn't the headmistress's voice Ythnel had heard. It was Iuna's.

"I-I don't understand."

"Yes, you do." Headmistress Yenael's lips moved, but the voice was definitely that of the little girl Ythnel had been hired to care for. "It is your turn, now, Ythnel. Take the scourge. Do not disappoint me."

Ythnel didn't move. It was as if she were thirteen again, back in the dungeons below the manor in Bezantur. The same emotions, the same doubts, threatened to overwhelm her.

No, this was different, she told herself. This time pain and suffering was deserved. This time she wanted to do it.

Ythnel reached for the scourge, and it instantly appeared in her hand. She flexed her grip on the handle, feeling the comfort of its weight, the precision of its balance. She bounced it lightly, untangling the leather tongues. Moving to Naeros's side, Ythnel bent over so her lips brushed against his ear.

"Let's play." She flicked her wrist, and the scourge shot out like lightning. Naeros screamed.

The constant ringing of a hand bell brought Ythnel's eyes open with a flutter. She was on her knees, her arms clutched to her chest, rocking back and forth from the waist up. She stopped, disoriented, and tried to get her bearings. Movement in the gloom ahead of her coalesced into the charging form of a large crocodile nearly twenty feet long. Its clawed fleet churned up the bog as it ran toward her. The fog in her mind instantly became crystal clarity. She rocked back on her heels, scooting on her hands and feet in a frantic scramble to get out of the path of the monstrosity that was closing on her, its toothy maw snapping in anticipation. With a hiss, it made a lunge at her, but Ythnel rolled to her left, came to her feet, and sprinted back toward the mages.

"Wake up! Wake up!" she screamed as she ran. She could see they were already stirring, probably alerted by the alarms Kestus had set. As Ythnel reached them, more scaly, gray-green shapes came slithering out of the murk. Their long, pointy snouts and ridged backs tapered into powerful tails that whipped side to side as they stalked closer.

"We have to get out of here," Ythnel ordered. She helped the groggy mages stand and pushed them along ahead of her, away from the approaching crocodiles. "I'll try to slow them down a little." Focusing on the switch she still held, Ythnel called out to Loviatar for aid. "Willing Whip, send us help."

The air between Ythnel and the pursuing crocodiles began to shimmer. Motes of red light appeared and separated into three different groupings a few inches above the ground. The motes collected until each group was about three feet high; then they began to stretch out and merge. When all the motes in one group had finally merged into a single globe, they faded away to reveal a fiendish-looking rat the size of a dog. Their eyes glowed red and their black, bristly hair stood on end like quills.

Before Ythnel could utter a command, the three summoned rats launched themselves at the nearest crocodile. One rat was snatched in midair by the monster and crushed with a squeak in the reptile's powerful jaws. However, as the crocodile tried to swallow the rat, it disappeared in a cloud of red motes that winked out one by one.

The remaining two rats landed on the back of the crocodile, their claws and teeth seeking purchase amongst the scaly bumps. The crocodile tried to shake them loose, but they were firmly attached. The huge reptile roared in frustration, and his call was answered by two more crocodiles that appeared out of the mists to flank him. With deadly efficiency, the two crocs picked the rats off their fellow's back, flinging them up into the air and catching them in open mouths. Red motes floated away when their mouths snapped shut.

Ythnel was stunned. The rats' losing the battle was not astonishing. She hadn't expected them to actually defeat any of the crocodiles; they had been meant only to delay the giant reptiles long enough for Ythnel and the mages to escape. What surprised her, and sent a chill down her spine, was the intelligence the crocodiles had exhibited in dispatching the rats. Even now, she thought she could see the gleam of something unnatural in their eyes.

Now was not the time to ponder the source of that intelligence, however. Ythnel turned to follow the mages and ran right into their backs.

"What are you doing?" Ythnel looked up and saw three more of the giant crocodiles approaching. They were surrounded. "Painbringer's touch! What do we do now?"

"Let me handle this." Brother Crocodile stepped away from the group, and the crocodiles paused, their heads turning to follow. The tall, lanky mage shuddered and let out a low moan. Ythnel gasped as his nose and chin began to stretch out and widen. His hands and feet bent into wicked claws, while his arms and legs retracted until they were little more than thick stumps protruding from his torso. The mage's skin mottled, turning from smooth pink to bumpy green. His entire body swelled, the weight seeming to drive him to the ground. As he landed on all fours, a ridged tail grew from his rear, extending more than three feet long.

"A werecrocodile," Kestus breathed. "So the stories are true."

"What do we do now?" Muctos asked, looking to Kestus.

Before he could answer, the crocodiles began hissing and coughing at each other. One charged Brother Crocodile, its mouth agape, but the former mage did not back down. He snapped his jaws inches from the challenger's snout. With a warbling chirp, the challenger backed away, its snout lifted in the air, signaling its surrender. Brother Crocodile turned to Ythnel and the mages and transformed back into a man.

"Do not be alarmed. These are my brothers." He looked at each of them, searching. As if on cue, the crocodile that had challenged Brother Crocodile reared up on its hind legs. Its snout began to shorten, and the color of its scales shifted from dark green to pale pink, the rough, bumpy hide becoming smooth. Eyes that were on the side of the head swam to the middle. Arms and legs lengthened, while the tail shrank until it disappeared entirely. In seconds, a lanky, naked man with a thin face dominated by a long nose and chin stood where the scaly monster once was.

Kestus turned to Brother Crocodile. "Who are you?" Kestus asked.

"My name is Kohtakah. I am the Royal Sorcerer to Lord Mulkammu, High Priest of Sebek."

"What is going to happen to us?" Ythnel asked.

"My brothers and I will escort you to our city. I promise you will not be harmed."

"Why should we believe you?" Kestus sneered.

"I can understand how you feel. This must seem like I am betraying you, but I am not."

"And how is this not a betrayal? You infiltrated us, and now you are handing us over to be taken as prisoners."

"No, that is not how it is. I was sent to find help for my people. You will be honored as heroes. You must trust me. Everything will turn out fine."

"What if we refuse?" Kestus asked.

Kohtakah sighed. "I'm afraid you do not have that choice."

THE PRIESTS

Morning brought dull, gray skies and a chill wind that rattled gnarled branches and swirled the fog covering the surface of the brackish ankle-high water that Ythnel and the mages trudged through. Steered by the werecrocodiles, they had left behind the bogs and now traveled directly across an expanse of liquid filth. Ythnel's skin had stopped crawling at the oily touch of the water hours ago; extended exposure to the cold had numbed her from the calves down.

A small splash to her left reminded her that the two werecrocodiles in human form were not their only escort. Occasionally, she caught glimpses of two bumps, each about the size of an authokh, floating just above the waterline, but usually ripples were the only sign that their captors' brethren were keeping pace.

A wave of nausea rolled up from Ythnel's stomach, and her legs suddenly grew weak. She stumbled into the water face-first but caught herself on her hands and knees before falling fully in. Muctos, who had been marching behind her, stooped to help her up, but she pushed him away.

"What's going on?" The werecrocodile who had been at the rear strode up to Ythnel.

"I'm hungry," Ythnel said, her head still hanging down. "I haven't eaten in ... I don't know how long. I'm not going anywhere until I get some food." She slowly raised her head, defiance in her eyes. Muctos was looking at her with eyes wide. He mouthed something, but she couldn't understand.

"You wait here." The werecrocodile moved to speak with Kohtakah, the mage they had known as Brother Crocodile, at the front of the group.

"What are you up to?" Muctos asked in a harsh whisper. Before Ythnel could answer, the werecrocodile returned.

"We don't stop until we get to the city. You"—He indicated Muctos.—"carry her." The heavyset mage frowned but helped Ythnel up then turned and offered her his back. She hopped on, looping her arms around his shoulders as he hooked his arms under her knees. The march resumed.

For the next few hours, Ythnel was passed between the mages; her weight was too much of a burden for any one of them to carry for too long. It slowed the group's progress until finally Kohtakah brought them to a halt. As though responding to some unseen signal, one of the submerged werecrocodiles reared up in a spray of water and transformed into its human shape. Kohtakah pointed at Ythnel, and the other took her from Muctos, slinging her over its shoulder so that she had a perfect view of his naked rear.

When the sky began to darken once again, the group found themselves at the edge of the river. Here the current was stronger, the water not as murky. Ythnel could see groupings of trees that marked the far bank several hundred yards away. To the north, an island sat in the mouth of the river. The island was covered in half-sunken ruins. Pillars of dried mud-brick leaned precariously, threatening to topple over and disappear beneath the surface of the swamp. With the crumbling archways and broken walls, it looked to Ythnel like a long-neglected graveyard.

"Is *this* your city?" Muctos asked.

"Yes," Kohtakah said, either missing or ignoring the obvious incredulity that laced the mage's question. "We will cross the river here." The werecrocodile that was carrying Ythnel set her down and proceeded to change back into his reptile form. As the transformation completed, he slithered into the water.

"How? I don't see any boats or ferries," Muctos noted. "You aren't expecting us to swim across, are you?" Ythnel hoped not. Even in the sluggish current, she knew she didn't have the strength and would likely get swept out into the bay.

"No. You will ride on our backs." Kohtakah made his own transformation and entered the water, where he was joined by three other floating reptilian forms.

The three captives looked to each other. At least one other of the werecrocodiles still stood guard in human form; who knew how many were lurking just beneath the surface of the swamp, ready to take them in a flurry of scales and teeth. Ythnel was in no shape to run. Besides, if the creatures had wanted to kill them, there had been plenty of opportunities before now. With a shrug, she stood up and waded out to one of the werecrocodiles. It swung around, and Ythnel clambered on, lying across the uncomfortable collection of hard lumps. The mages hesitated for a moment before following suit. Once everyone was loaded, the werecrocodiles pushed out into the river, letting the current take them. Ythnel could feel the powerful strokes of the creature's tail from where she was positioned, guiding them toward a point of the island where the river split.

When they were about one hundred feet from the bank of the island, Ythnel spotted movement amongst the nearest ruins. At first, she dismissed it as more werecrocodiles, but as they got closer, she caught glimpses of furry shapes with thin, whiplike tails moving in and out of the shadows on two legs. Whatever they were, the werecrocodiles did not want to meet them, for they began to shift course farther downriver. When the creatures on the island realized they had been spotted, a cry went up, and several of them came out into the open. It was then that Ythnel saw they were some sort of humanoid rat. She wondered if perhaps they were related to the werecrocodiles. The ratmen all carried bows and had them pulled taut, aiming at the werecrocodiles and their passengers. As the group passed by, the ratmen let fly, sending a hail of arrows across the river. Ythnel instinctively clutched at the werecrocodile she was riding, trying to flatten herself as much as possible as the deadly shafts plunked into the water around her. She looked around to see if any of the others had been hit, but a sharp hiss brought her gaze snapping back to find an arrow embedded in the shoulder of her escort, inches from her hand.

The werecrocodile shuddered and pitched violently, rolling onto its back and throwing Ythnel into the water. She struggled to the surface, coughing and spitting out a mouthful of river. Disoriented, Ythnel thrashed in momentary panic before realizing she could keep herself above water easily by treading in the lazy current. She searched for the others, spotting them just as they rounded the far side of the island and disappeared from view. Somehow, Ythnel had drifted down the west branch of the river after being tossed from the werecrocodile, while the rest of the group continued down the east branch. She waited for one the werecrocodiles to reappear and reclaim her, but no one came.

A commotion to her left drew her attention back to the near bank of the island, only a few yards away. Several of the ratmen had gathered and were pointing at her, chattering excitedly. It seemed someone had noticed her separation from the group.

One of the creatures appeared with a jumble of ropes in hand. It twirled them over its head, finally releasing it after building up enough momentum. As the ropes flew out across the river toward Ythnel, they expanded into a weighted net. Dread filled her as the net descended over her, the weights dragging her down under the water. With a sharp tug, the net closed around her, and Ythnel felt herself being pulled toward the bank.

This was not happening, she screamed to herself. Frustration and rage rose as she once again found herself at someone else's mercy. But her struggling only served to entwine the net tighter around her. Just as she thought her lungs would explode, she broke the surface and was soon lying in a tangled, muddy pile at the feet of the ratmen. While several arrowheads were pointed threateningly at her, one of the ratmen unwrapped Ythnel from the net.

"Why were you with the werecrocodiles? Who are you?"

"My name is Ythnel. I was a prisoner, along with my friends."

"Why did they capture you?"

"Probably for food." A ratman holding a bow chuckled.

"I'm feeling a little hungry, myself," another called out.

"No! No, they were taking us to their city because we are wizards," Ythnel protested. Several of the ratmen hissed, but Ythnel wasn't sure if it was in response to the werecrocodiles' claim to the city or that she and her friends were wizards.

"You will come with us," the ratman who had netted her commanded. He motioned for her to stand and led the group into the ruins.

They moved steadily inland, weaving through abandoned towers and half-built dwellings. From the many piles of unused materials that still lay at the base of some of the structures, Ythnel was beginning to think the city had more likely been left uncompleted rather than succumbing to time and the elements.

"Where are we going?" Ythnel sidestepped a two-foot-long rat that scurried from the shadows of a doorway to glare at her with undisguised malevolence.

"We are taking you to our village."

"So you share this island with the werecrocodiles? Did you build all this? Or were you here first?"

"Yes, the werecrocodiles built this, but we were here first. The werecrocodiles came from the east and tried to re-create their home, using the power of their god to enslave us. Something happened not long ago, and their god disappeared. We rose up and fought them, eventually freeing ourselves.

"They no longer try to build; the territory each side controls keeps shifting. For now, they occupy the north half of the island, while we live on the south."

Ythnel nodded at the ratman's reply. Its mention of the disappearance of the werecrocodiles' god stirred an early memory from her childhood at the manor. The temple had been filled with panicked sisters and hushed whispers that Loviatar had abandoned her followers, been cast out of the planes, or had even been killed. In time, things had returned to normal, but Ythnel now wondered if perhaps these two events were somehow related.

Unfortunately, her curiosity would have to go unsatisfied. There were more immediate concerns to deal with.

They reached the ratmen's village just before nightfall. In the fading light, Ythnel began to notice lean-tos erected against unfinished walls. Midden heaps inhabited several of the roofless buildings they passed, assailing Ythnel's nose with their ever-present stench. A crowd of onlookers began to form behind the group, following them as they neared what Ythnel guessed to be the center of the camp. The growing entourage consisted of males and females, most in the rat form of her escorts, but there were one or two who appeared human. So, they are werecreatures as well, Ythnel concluded.

The wererats stopped before a building whose walls completely enclosed its interior. What appeared to be a curtain of hide hung in the doorway, and a thatch roof sat atop the walls. The lead wererat entered the dwelling while everyone else waited outside. The area in front of the building was well trod and muddy. A pot of something unwholesome-smelling stewed atop a small cook fire nearby. Ythnel's stomach gurgled at the thought of food, unconcerned with how unappealing whatever was being served might be.

The hide curtain was pushed back and out strode a striking older man with Ythnel's wererat captor in tow. While the man's shirt, breeches, and boots were patched and sullied, he carried himself with an air of confidence and a twinkle of cunning in his deep blue eyes that seemed out of place in the middle of a swamp. A thin mustache, touched with the same gray that streaked his fading hair, did little to separate the man's sharp nose from his broad grin. He stopped before Ythnel, covering her thoroughly with his eyes while the other wererat whispered in his ear. Nodding, the man raised his hand, and the wererat stepped back with a slight bow.

"So I understand you were part of a group of wizards recently captured by the werecrocodiles. You're very fortunate that some of my men were able to rescue you." The man spoke with disarming friendliness and concern.

"It was my impression your men would have been just as happy to eat me," Ythnel scoffed.

"Ah, I'm sure it was just a poor attempt at humor." He smiled. "Unfortunately, hunger is a common epidemic amongst my people, thanks to the werecrocodiles. Making light of it is often our only relief."

Ythnel took a second look at the crowd gathered around her and noticed how gaunt many of the figures were. Skin was stretched taut, and many faces had hollow cheeks and dark circles around the eyes. The way they all looked at her made her suddenly very uncomfortable.

"What do the werecrocodiles have to do with your going hungry?" Ythnel asked.

"They constantly patrol the waters around this

island, attacking us when we try to cross. It makes it difficult to hunt or forage; there's nothing left on the island to support either us or the werecrocodiles."

"So how have you survived?"

"Raids mostly. The werecrocodiles are overconfident and sloppy. It's easy enough to slip past their pickets with an appropriate diversion. Occasionally, we make it across the river and can ... trade with passing caravans." The man's hesitation gave Ythnel the idea that the trades were probably one-sided.

"Enough business," the man declared suddenly. "I would imagine you are tired from your ordeal. Please, accept what hospitality we can offer." He waved his hand in a grandiose gesture that encompassed the surrounding ruins and midden heaps.

"That is quite generous," Ythnel said, trying hard to keep the skepticism from her voice. "I don't even know your name."

"Ah, where are my manners. I am Torgyn." He bowed. As he straightened, he looked at her expectantly.

"I, uh, am Ythnel."

"Well met, Ythnel. Join me for a bite to eat?" He motioned her toward a table made of stacked mud bricks and crossbeams. When they sat, a pair of plates were brought to them. The "meal" presented to her made Ythnel's stomach turn. Rotten vegetable matter and bones, which were covered as much with maggots as meat, were piled on the plates. The stench was more than enough to cause her to gag. She daintily picked through the refuse, earning snickers from the assembled wererats. Torgyn was watching her intently.

Ythnel wondered if this was some sort of test. Would they kill her if she refused to eat it? Even as hungry as she was, she knew she couldn't force herself to eat the putrid dish in front of her.

That's when it occurred to her that she wouldn't have to. Overcome by hunger as she prayed last night, Ythnel had requested a seldom-used orison she had learned early in her days at the manor and eventually forgotten. She began to chant while holding her hands just above the plate and channeled a small burst of Power. With a smile, she picked up a chunk of meat, brushed the maggots off of it, and took a bite. The overwhelming odor of decay was gone. The texture was a bit gamey, and she tried not to think of what it might have been before the wererats killed it. She just enjoyed the feeling of something in her belly.

"A useful spell," Torgyn remarked, "but not very effective in a fight." He grabbed a handful of the rotten food on his plate and shoveled it into his mouth.

"An empty stomach is as much a distraction in a fight as having a strap on your armor unbuckled. It is a weakness that your enemy can exploit," Ythnel replied.

"Very true," Torgyn said, his mouth still half-full. "Purifying food is not really a concern of ours."

"And what is your concern?"

"The werecrocodiles. Therefore, I'm very interested in what they would want with some wizards. I'd also like to know what you and your wizard friends were doing in Adder Swamp to begin with." Torgyn smiled, but there was a wicked cunning behind it that put Ythnel on guard. She chewed slowly to give herself time to think. There really wasn't anything to gain by lying to the wererats. She doubted they would return her to the Karanoks, and it was possible that there was a way to play the conflict between the two groups of werecreatures to her advantage.

However, she would have to be careful to avoid mentioning the revelation that Brother Crocodile was really a werecrocodile. Even the slightest indication that there was some sort of connection between her and the werecrocodiles could result in the wererats turning on her.

"My friends are members of an underground society attempting to overthrow House Karanok." Ythnel took Torgyn's raised eyebrow to mean he at least knew of Luthcheq's ruling family. "After rescuing me from the Karanoks, we fled to the swamp. That is why we are here.

"I have no idea what the werecrocodiles want with us. They captured us last evening, as we were sleeping."

"I think I know: magic. They used magic once to enslave us. It would give them the advantage should they be able to wield such power again." He seemed to mutter this last to himself, but he kept his eyes on Ythnel. "They knew you had magic. The question, though, is how did they know?"

Ythnel's mind raced for an answer that would not involve Brother Crocodile. "On several occasions when we first entered the swamp, we had to use magic to fight off creatures that attacked us. Perhaps they witnessed one of those encounters." Ythnel held her breath as she waited for Torgyn's reaction.

"Perhaps," he said, nodding thoughtfully. "So it would appear that Lord Mulkammu finally has his wizards. This time, though, it seems we would have a wizard of our own with which to fight back." The man's eyes narrowed shrewdly. "It appears that your rescue was just as fortunate for us as it was for you."

They had rounded the island, following the west fork of the Adder River until it finally spilled out into the Bay of Chessenta, before anyone noticed that Ythnel was lost. A wounded werecrocodile had finally caught up to Kohtakah, whom Kestus rode, a broken arrow shaft protruding from its left shoulder. The group immediately headed for the island shore, and once beached, the werecrocodiles transformed into their human shapes. The wounded werecrocodile reported he had been hit by the wererat volley and had thrown the woman while trying to dislodge the missile. By the time he had resurfaced, she was gone.

"The woman is of no real concern," Kohtakah shrugged off the news of Ythnel's disappearance. "We still have the two wizards." He tentatively examined the other's festering wound, Kestus noted, taking extra care not to touch the arrowhead. "We need to get you back to the city to have this removed."

The group marched along the northern edge of the island, heading east. That side of the island was covered with the same mud-brick structures Ythnel had pointed out earlier, but they were more often in some semblance of completion. Squat, square buildings were huddled together in what could have passed for city blocks had they been connected by cobblestone streets rather than channels of muddy water.

Small points of flickering light began to appear in the distance as night fell, indications that the group was finally nearing the werecrocodile community. The mages were led past lit dwellings toward a towering pyramid that appeared to be the center of the village. The entrance was guarded by only a pair of sputtering torches set in sconces on either side. Kohtakah knocked then waited a moment before pushing the door open and ushering the group inside.

The first to enter, Kestus gazed about the grand chamber. Braziers of dried mud, sinuous crocodiles carved in shallow relief around the bowls, held glowing coals that cast a soft red light against the inner walls of the pyramid. At the far end of the chamber, a great chair of dark wood rested at the base of a dais upon which sat a nondescript altar. Standing over the altar with its face toward the chamber entrance was the immense statue of an athletic man whose horned crocodile head disappeared into the shadows of the ceiling, some twenty feet above them.

A gong sounded from somewhere at the back of the chamber, and a near-giant of a man with a jutting chin and shaved head strode out from some hidden doorway behind the dais. He wore a sleeveless leather tunic that ended just above the knee, exposing corded muscles on his arms and thick calves. A fur-lined cape hung around his shoulders, billowing slightly in his wake as he made his way to the great chair. When he had seated himself, Kohtakah stepped forward and bent on one knee before him.

"Lord Mulkammu, your servant has returned from the human city with great news. I have brought wizards with me."

"Kohtakah, it is indeed a blessing to see you after so long." Mulkammu's grim face transformed into a warm smile for the Royal Sorcerer. "We had feared that perhaps you were lost, but to hear that your mission was instead a success ... praise Sebek!"

"Yes, Lord Mulkammu, though I regret that I could not bring more help. It seems the rulers of the city seek to eradicate magic and its practitioners. These two are the last members of a group that had operated in secret but were recently discovered and forced to flee. Shamshur's"—He indicated the werecrocodile behind him who had carried Muctos.—"patrol came across us as we sought to escape from further pursuit."

"Hmm, that is indeed unfortunate. But you are unhurt? And your pursuers?" He looked between Kohtakah and Shamshur.

"We lost them in the swamp, my lord," Kohtakah responded.

"Hanat was hurt, my lord," Shamshur said, stepping forward. "We were attacked by the vermin slaves. One of their cursed silver arrows struck him, forcing him to buck the female prisoner he was carrying. The wound is not grave, but he needs immediate tending."

Mulkammu raised an eyebrow at the mention of the woman and looked at Kohtakah. "Explain."

"My apologies, Lord Mulkammu. The woman is nothing, bait that was used to trap the wizards."

"Then why bring her along?"

"She is a cleric of a Faerûnian goddess—"

"So she has magic?"

Kohtakah nodded.

"Sebek's smile! Magic cannot be allowed to stay in the hands of the slaves." Anger flashed across Mulkammu's face, but his expression quickly returned to its former stony calm. "First things first, though." He signaled with his hand, and the gong sounded again. This time two men in simple, flowing white robes emerged from the same hidden doorway in the rear of the chamber. They moved silently to Hanat and made a cursory examination of his shoulder, pulling at the edges of the wound for a better look. Hanat gritted his teeth as skin and dried blood separated.

One of the men departed but returned swiftly pushing a handcart with a black leather satchel and a lantern sitting on top. He retrieved a set of tongs from the satchel and handed it to the other white-robed man.

Then he lit the lantern and held it up high enough so it cast its light over the wound. The man with the tongs delved into the wound with the instrument, took hold of something, and yanked. Hanat moaned and swayed on his feet, but Shamshur quickly slid up behind him to provide support. While the man with the lantern set the light source down and began bandaging Hanat's shoulder, the man with the tongs moved to the cart and started cleaning up. Kestus could see a bloody arrowhead lying next to the tongs atop the cart.

"You have done well, Kohtakah," Lord Mulkammu said, rising from his throne. "Let us see to our guests. Then we will make plans to retrieve the woman from the wererats. Shamshur, you and your men may go." Shamshur bowed and turned to follow the rest of his patrol back outside, leaving the two mages with Lord Mulkammu and Kohtakah.

Once the others had left, Mulkammu greeted the mages with a toothy grin that was unnervingly predatory. "Welcome, my friends."

"You have an odd way of treating friends," Kestus said, stepping forward. "Kohtakah said we would be honored as heroes."

"Did he?" Mulkammu faced Kestus. "I make no apologies for the way in which you were brought here. Dire circumstances call for dire actions."

"And what would those circumstances be?"

"Why, nothing less than the continued existence of my people."

"Is that why you sent Brother—Kohtakah to infiltrate us?"

"Yes, though his instructions were not that specific. He was merely to seek out individuals who could be of use to us."

"Wizards, you mean." Kestus did not like the

undertones of this conversation. Mulkammu was hiding something. "Why do you need wizards?"

"That requires a bit of explanation. In fact, it may be easier to show you than tell. Please, follow me." He turned and began walking toward the back of the chamber. Kestus looked at Muctos and shrugged. The man seemed unconcerned with whether they were following him or not. There was no one between them and the door out. Of course, Kestus was sure they wouldn't get far before they were caught again, and their treatment then might not be as hospitable. Taking quick strides, Kestus and Muctos hastened after Mulkammu. Kohtakah brought up the rear.

The lord of the werecrocodiles led them through a small anteroom off the main temple chamber and down a flight of stairs. The stone of the lower level was damp. The waters of the swamp had found a way inside the pyramid. Kestus wrinkled his nose at the musty scent of decay that permeated the air. The group stopped before a great stone door set in the wall and framed by a pair of smoky torches. Symbols that Kestus thought might represent words in the Mulhorandi language were carved across the surface of the closed portal.

"When we were driven from our homeland more than two hundred years ago," Mulkammu began, "my people settled here. Blessed by our god, Sebek, lord of the crocodiles, our forefathers began construction of this city. It was a slow process that involved expanding the borders of this swamp, as well as the raising of the buildings that would serve as our homes.

"The task was a tremendous one, and so our fathers, in their foresight and wisdom, enlisted the aid of some of the lesser beings that already inhabited the region. Together, they continued their work, believing that Sebek was smiling upon them.

"Then, when I was just a boy, Sebek disappeared.

"My father, who was high priest of Sebek, no longer felt the presence of the Smiling Death; his prayers went unanswered, and the items of Power we had brought with us from our homeland no longer functioned. Our workers, jealous all these years of our success, took advantage of our predicament and tried to destroy us. But we prevailed, though my father was killed by their assassins.

"It has been a brutal struggle, and we have suffered, as you could probably see from the state of our city. Sebek has returned, though the connection to him is much weaker than it was before, and many of our artifacts remain useless. I became high priest in my father's place and have tried to lead my people as best I can."

"You have our sympathies, Lord Mulkammu," Kestus said, trying to keep the impatience from his voice, "but I don't see why you need us."

"The answer to that lies behind this door. This is the vault in which our artifacts are kept. Because of the weakened connection to Sebek, I do not possess the ability to use them. To be honest, I'm not even sure what some of them are capable of. Without them, however, my people will never rise to the greatness they once held. So you will learn what they are and how to use them." Mulkammu turned and faced the vault door. Muttering in some language Kestus did not recognize, the werecrocodile lord began tracing the symbols that had been etched in the stone. Each symbol he touched glowed a soft, dark green. When he had finished, the vault door slowly swung open with the harsh sound of stone grinding against stone to reveal a room half hidden by shadows. Mulkammu removed one of the torches from its sconce on the wall and walked in.

To Kestus, the room seemed more of a storage closet than a vault. A short, square wooden rack to his left held a staff of dark, twisted wood and what looked like a scepter. What could be a couple of wands rested on a flimsy table in the middle of the vault. Mulkammu lit a candelabrum with the torch then stepped out to return the burning brand to its holding place. The flickering light danced off an opaque black orb that Kestus had not noticed before. Set by itself on a shelf along the back wall, it rested on what appeared to be braces made from withered tree branches.

"You have an interesting collection," Kestus remarked, "but I'm not sure we can help you. If these are divine artifacts, they will not be attuned to the Weave, generally speaking, but will draw their energy from the patron deity of whoever crafted them. Our magic would have little effect on them. And without the proper tools or our spellbooks, I doubt we'll even be able to identify the items' properties. I'm surprised Kohtakah hasn't already explained this to you. Perhaps if you had approached us more openly, before our hand was forced by the Karanoks, we could have worked something out.

"As it is, we need to be on our way. There is much that needs to be done if we are to have any chance of freeing Luthcheq."

"You are not going anywhere!" Mulkammu's face darkened for a moment, his mouth tightening as his brow furrowed. A touch from Kohtakah seemed to relax him. "I can understand your hesitancy. Let me provide a little incentive, then, to motivate you. If there is nothing you can do with the artifacts, then your special skills are useless to us. You become ordinary humans.

"We eat ordinary humans," he said with a devilish smile.

Kestus didn't back down. He had nothing to lose. "And if you did, you would be right back where you started. Didn't you hear what Kohtakah said? There are no more wizards in Luthcheq. No one will be coming near this place. You'll all rot here, caught up in your little war!"

Mulkammu was seething, and Kestus was sure the werecrocodile would hit him, or worse.

"My lord, please." Kohtakah stepped between them, his back to Kestus. He steered Mulkammu out of the vault, where the two spoke in hushed voices. After a few moments of heated discussion, Mulkammu approached, Kohtakah in tow.

"It seems my Royal Sorcerer has spent too much time amongst you," Mulkammu sneered with disgust "He feels some sort of loyalty toward you and has prevailed upon me to consider an ... alternate form of persuasion.

"If you succeed in discovering the secrets of our artifacts, I will let each of you choose one of them, though I can veto any choice. Would that be satisfactory?"

Kestus could tell it was struggle for Mulkammu to speak those words. "Those terms are agreeable." In fact, the situation was more than Kestus could hope for.

"I'll leave you to get started, then. Kohtakah will aid you. Someone will come down to check on your progress every few hours. Should you fail, however, know that I will kill you and eat you myself.

"Now, if you'll excuse me, I have a raid to plan. Good night." With a flourish of his cape, Mulkammu spun around and strode back up the stairs, leaving the three alone.

"How do we get out of this?" Muctos finally asked after moments of stunned silence.

"We do what he says," Kestus replied. He moved around the table to stand in front of the black orb.

"What? You said it yourself. We don't have any means of researching, by magic or tome. Our spells are exhausted, and without spellbooks, we're not going to get very far."

"I may be able to help with that," Kohtakah said.

The two mages looked at their former brother. Kestus had almost forgotten about him.

"Why should we trust you?"

"You have no reason. But know this, if you fail, if we fail, Mulkammu will kill me as well."

Kestus let the revelation hang in the air. The hurt of Kohtakah's betrayal ran deep, and he was not ready to let go of it so quickly. He would be a fool, however, to refuse any aid.

"How can you help?" he asked finally.

"I have some old tomes, passed down by my predecessors. Their knowledge of the Art is written within those pages. There are many spells recorded in them, some of which may be of use to us. Unfortunately, because of the innate nature of my abilities, I have not been able to learn all of them. I imagine the same would not hold true for you."

"Where are these books?" Kestus could not keep the excitement from his voice.

"They are in my quarters. I will go fetch them." Kohtakah turned to leave but paused. He must have seen the look of doubt on Kestus's face because he said, "Trust me, Brother Hawk. I will return." Kestus nodded, and Kohtakah bounded up the stairs then disappeared.

THE **RIESTS**

CHAPTER 10

Ythnel sat in the hovel she had been escorted to by the wererats after her meal with Torgyn, their leader. Night had fallen, the half-moon obscured by building clouds, but Ythnel could still see the silhouette of her "escort" through the gaps in the walls. For all the smiles and reassurances Torgyn offered, Ythnel knew she was more prisoner than guest in the wererats' camp.

She performed her evening prayers with a leather strap acquired from her guard, finding comfort in the familiar chants and the slaps on her skin. It was the only stability she had left, a last link to her former life now buried by the chaos of these past few days. The memories of the events that had swallowed her up since arriving in Luthcheq tried to break through her mediation and shatter the peace she had surrounded herself with, but her focus was too great, her connection with her goddess too strong, and they were forced back to the shadowy corners of her mind.

When her prayers were finished, Ythnel rocked back on her heels and brushed the mud off her knees. She stood and stretched, her cramped and aching muscles protesting the activity with painful reminders that they were still quite sore and bruised. Restless, Ythnel paced the small interior but had to stop as the constant turning threatened to dizzy her. She leaned against the one corner of the hovel's walls that wasn't missing any bricks and stared out into the darkening night.

The memories crowded their way to the front of her mind.

Ythnel let them come but on her terms, channeling them like the waters of a rushing river, controlling the speed and direction by which they traveled as she sifted through them. She held no anger toward Prisus or Iuna, and she felt no guilt over what had happened to them. Nor did she wallow in self-pity as she remembered the betrayal and abuse she had suffered. She had gone through those fires and come out tempered steel, a finely honed weapon. Those images, those experiences, now served to strengthen her resolve. It was time to wield her sharpened edges in retribution.

Perhaps that was why she had really been sent to Luthcheq. Ythnel recalled the dream she had just the other night in the swamp. If nothing else, she knew it was a portent of revenge against the Karanoks. There was more to it, though, but what that was, was unclear to Ythnel.

She continued to muse over the idea of paying back the Karanoks for all that had been done to her.

However, she kept coming back to the reasons she had come to Luthcheq. If she were meant to take down the ruling family, why have her placed as a governess to a middle-class merchant? Why not have her inserted into the palace or some other noble house? Why not have her make contact immediately with the Mage Society? The only reason that made any sense was because she was meant to meet Prisus Saelis.

Or she was meant to meet Iuna.

Ythnel nearly gasped as the thought occurred to her. Why hadn't she made the connection before? Even though it had been Yenael standing next to Naeros in her dream, handing her the scourge, it had been Iuna's voice that asked her to show her. It had been Iuna who she was originally sent to teach. Iuna was the young girl who had lost her mother—a mother who had once been a Loviatan.

The impact of the revelation jolted Ythnel and threatened to overwhelm her. She was meant not just to help raise Iuna, but to bring the girl into the faith. She had been put in the perfect position to do so but had failed. The fact that Iuna was ultimately the source of all the troubles Ythnel now found herself in did little to console her. After all, she was an adult and a handmaiden. She should have had more control of the situation.

Ythnel nearly fell to her knees to beg for forgiveness, but she realized that was not what Loviatar wanted, nor was it what she expected. No, what was needed was for Ythnel to figure out some way to fix what had happened, to find Iuna again and fulfill the purpose for which she had been sent.

That meant her first order of business was to get away from the wererats. Ythnel peered outside again. The wind was picking up, and the stars and moon were almost completely hidden by a roiling blackness that Ythnel guessed were storm clouds. Movement in the shadows across from her hut revealed the location of her keeper. She wasn't sure if wererats could see in the dark better than normal humans, but that really didn't matter. She had another plan for escaping.

Kneeling down in the mud, Ythnel began to inscribe the symbol of her faith, drawing a scourge in the wet, earthen floor. The prayer she was going to incant required the use of a focus in order to call the Power she needed from Loviatar. Ythnel moved her hands over the symbol in time with the chant. The air above the symbol shimmered, and Ythnel could feel the Power flowing into her. She closed her eyes in concentration and directed the divine energy into the space between her hands, shaping it with her will until it conformed to the purpose for which she had summoned it. When Ythnel opened her eyes, a ghostly scourge hovered in the air before her.

She stood and moved to the doorway of the hut. She stuck her head out and called to the wererat that was assigned to guard her. However, the wind had picked up enough that Ythnel's words were carried away. She raised her voice and tried again. The wererat must have heard her this time because Ythnel saw a form detach itself from the shadows and approach. She tensed, prepared to send her spirit weapon hurtling at the wererat as soon as it was within range.

When the wererat was only twenty feet away, a sinister hiss issued from the darkness nearby, and both Ythnel and the wererat turned their heads together in an effort find the source of the sound. The action was unnecessary. A twenty-foot-long mass of scales, claws, and teeth hurtled out of the night, tackling the wererat and carrying the pair of combatants back into the night with its momentum. Ythnel heard the rustling of their struggle and cries of pain. Then she realized she could hear similar cries echoing through the night, punctuated by the howls of the rising wind.

Thick drops of rain splattering against her face freed Ythnel from her shock at the unexpectedness and speed of the attack. Her first instinct was to take advantage of the situation and run off into the night, but she quickly realized that would not be the best solution. Where would she go? She had no idea where she was or where to go. Left to her own devices, it was more than likely she would just wander in circles or stumble into yet another hazard. She needed a guide.

She needed Kestus.

It was the obvious answer. Not only could he help her get out of the swamp, but he would also surely return with her to Luthcheq. He had his own reasons for wanting revenge on the Karanoks. She just hoped he was still alive.

No, she knew he was still alive. Brother Crocodile had indicated that the werecrocodiles needed the wizards. It was just a matter of finding them and freeing them.

Torgyn had said the werecrocodiles inhabited the north side of the island. Unfortunately, Ythnel had no idea which way north was.

There was movement in the shadows at the edge of Ythnel's vision, and she realized she could no longer afford to stand in one place. She slinked out of the hut and was bathed in a pale blue light. Startled, she turned to see the spirit scourge hovering behind her. As much as the illumination helped her to see, it was also a beacon pinpointing her location for anyone interested. With a thought, she dismissed the weapon and was swallowed by the darkness.

While her eyes adjusted, Ythnel considered her options. It took less time to list her choices than her eyes needed to get accustomed to the darkness. She needed to leave the wererats and make her way to the werecrocodiles' side of the island. The only way to do that was to follow somebody, and as there were werecrocodiles close by, they would be the likely candidates. However, that meant finding one of the many pockets of fighting without getting caught. She hoped the werecrocodiles would eventually break off the attack to return home, and she could trail behind far enough that they wouldn't detect her but close enough that she wouldn't lose sight of them.

Ythnel nearly laughed at the ludicrous idea. It was an impossible task. She was no thief who could creep stealthily about the shadows, avoiding notice. There had to be another way. She decided to wait it out. This was likely one of the many raids Torgyn talked about. Ythnel wasn't surprised the werecrocodiles performed them as well. Perhaps with her missing, the wererats might think she was taken by the werecrocodiles. Torgyn would probably order a counterattack, desperate to get her back, and when the camp emptied out, she could leave. It would then be a simple matter to make her way to the shore of the island and work her way around until she came to the area controlled by the werecrocodiles.

She crept into another ruin only a few buildings away from her original holding place and crouched down. The sounds of fighting still rang out in the night, but with the rain and wind, it was impossible to tell how close they were or from which direction they came. Eventually, though, the frequency of the clashes Ythnel heard lessened. Then they ceased all together.

Voices and lights approached moments later. Ythnel

pressed herself against the wall and tried to breathe as quietly as possible. Her heart was pounding in her chest, throat, and ears. One of the voices she was able to identify easily.

"Do we know for certain that they took her?" Torgyn demanded.

"We found Saumbeth a few yards away. He was killed by a werecrocodile. I think it's pretty obvious they were after her."

"I don't care what you think," Torgyn snarled. "For all we know, she could have slipped away while they fought."

"I guess that's possible," the other voice offered meekly, "but there's no way to know for sure. The rain has obliterated any tracks." There was a stretch of uncomfortable silence. Ythnel was afraid that they had started searching the surrounding buildings for her, but the quiet was broken finally by Torgyn swearing.

"I suppose there is no choice but to go after the werecrocodiles. We can't chance that they have taken her. Gather everyone together. We will get our wizard back, or we will kill her before the werecrocodiles can make use of her!"

Several cheers rose in response; then Ythnel heard several pairs of feet sloshing off in the mud, and the lights faded away. She waited several more minutes and was rewarded by another great shout that erupted somewhere off in the night, signaling the departure of the wererat forces. After a few more minutes, Ythnel eased herself from her hiding place. She stood in the crumbling doorway of the building and strained her senses, but it was impossible separate anything from the gusting winds and heavy downpour that filled the night.

In that instant of realization, Ythnel changed her mind. There was no chance she could hope to find her way in these conditions. It could take her several hours of wandering before she found the shoreline, and she still would have to guess which direction to follow. The wererat attack that she hoped to use as a diversion would likely be over long before she could reach the ruins inhabited by the werecrocodiles, let alone find the mages.

She decided she would follow the wererats instead.

Ythnel headed in the direction she thought she heard the last shouts from the wererats. She dashed from building to building, relying on the weather to hide her sufficiently from any eyes that might still be watching. When she could finally see the bobbing torches carried by the wererats, she slowed, careful to keep well back from any rearguard.

Between the hypnotic dance of the distant torchlight weaving through the unending ruins that covered the island, lack of sleep, and the cold rain that had soaked Ythnel to the bone, the trek became mind-numbing. She was moving without thinking, mentally asleep. So it was that Ythnel continued for several steps before she noticed that the points of light ahead of her were quickly winking out one by one. She froze as the last one vanished, plunging the area back into total darkness. Her first thought was that they had spotted her. Panic washed over her as she imagined the wererats circling around in the pitch black to surround her. She didn't dare move, afraid the slightest sound would give her location away.

Then the clash of arms sounded somewhere ahead, followed by cries of alarm, and Ythnel realized that she hadn't been discovered. The wererats had put out their lights because they were close to the werecrocodiles' settlement and hadn't wanted to give themselves away to any sentries that might be posted. Ythnel let go of the breath she had not noticed she was holding. She could follow the sounds of battle easily enough now to find her way. The hard part would be finding the mages and getting back out.

Iuna's brisk pace slowed considerably as she neared the door. She stood before the plain, brass-banded wood door and hesitated. Mistress Kaestra would be angry if she were late, but she desperately wanted to be anywhere besides here. Last night was still fresh in her mind, aided by the bruises and welts she still felt, which had been given to her by Mistress Kaestra for her disobedience. Iuna shivered before reaching up to knock on the door.

"Come in," the stern voice she'd already begun to fear called from the other side. Iuna opened the door, entered timidly, and gave a curtsy.

"Where are your manners, child? Close the door."

Iuna jumped and turned back to the door, closing it. Tonight was already starting off badly.

"Come over here." Mistress Kaestra sat at her desk, scribing something. She wore a sleeveless gown of simple white, with a small black circle over her left breast. Her salt-and-pepper hair was pulled back into a bun, making her harsh, angular face even starker. Piles of parchment covered her desk, and several stacks of books lay on the surrounding floor. Iuna moved silently to stand before her.

"I'm finished with my meal. You may remove the dishes." Mistress Kaestra indicated a platter set on a nearby chair. Iuna could see a half-eaten serving of meat and vegetables covering the thick, ceramic plate that rested there. "When you're done with that," Mistress Kaestra continued, "you can start moving the piles of finished parchment back to the library, and bring me some more blank pages.

"And need I remind you," she added as Iuna started to walk away, "to be very careful? These writings are to become the tenets of our faith. I was chosen by Entropy to pen them. It is the reason she has blessed me with the powers I have: a testimony to the validity of the words I record." Iuna nodded solemnly, noting the strange gleam that flashed in Mistress Kaestra's eyes as she spoke.

Mistress Kaestra went back to her writing, seemingly dismissing Iuna from her thoughts as though she were no longer there. Iuna approached the chair with the platter and bent over to grasp it. Made of wrought silver with delicately inscribed lines that called to mind blooming flowers, it reminded Iuna of the tableware Libia used to carry from the kitchen to the dining room back home.

Distracted by memories, Iuna paid little heed to where she was stepping, and her foot caught on the base of one of the stacks of books as she turned. Iuna hopped forward, trying to regain her balance, but she was unable to compensate for the additional weight of the platter and fell forward. When she crashed to the ground, the dishes went flying off the silver tray with a clatter. The ceramic plate flipped end over end, spraying the remnants of food it held across a pile of freshly inked parchment.

"You clumsy imbecile!" Mistress Kaestra shrieked. She stood up behind her desk, bristling, her face a mask of unrestrained rage.

"I'm ... I'm sorry, Mistress. I'll clean it up right away. It'll be—"

"You will touch nothing. I cannot believe your incompetence. I thought having you as a personal slave would be of some benefit, but it is obvious Father was just being generous rather than sending you to the stake. You are useless. I am going to have to waste precious time training you, it seems. And your first lesson will be to learn the consequences of failure." She came around the desk so fast that Iuna barely had time to get up on her hands and knees. Mistress Kaestra picked her up by the collar of her brown, woolen robe and slapped her. Sparkles of light danced before Iuna's eyes, and she staggered backward when Mistress Kaestra released her.

Her rage was not quenched so easily.

"Ruined! Do you know how long it took me to write this?" She stared at the stained parchment then turned back to Iuna and punched her in the stomach. Air whooshed out of Iuna's lungs, and she doubled over.

"I'm sorry, Mistress," she cried. Tears welled in her eyes, and she started to sob. This wasn't how it was supposed to have turned out, Iuna thought as she gasped for breath. They were just supposed to take the governess and leave Papa and her alone. Instead Papa was dead now. Mistress Kaestra had almost gloated about it when she told Iuna last night.

Mistress Kaestra's fist slammed into the side of Iuna's head, and she fell to the floor. She lay there, curled up in a ball, whimpering. Mistress Kaestra stood over her, her chest heaving as she breathed heavily. Then her shadow moved away, but Iuna refused to open her eyes and look up. She wasn't sure she could even open the left one. She just wanted to sleep.

"When you're done feeling sorry for yourself," Mistress Kaestra's cold voice called out from somewhere distant, "you can get up and finish your chores." Iuna wondered what would happen if she didn't. It was hard to keep awake, and her thoughts were fuzzy. She wondered if she was dying. Perhaps that wouldn't be so bad. She had never paid much attention to any of the lessons on religion that her many governesses had tried to teach her, but she thought there was some sort of life after death. Maybe she would get to see Papa. That would be wonderful; it certainly would be better than life as a slave to Mistress Kaestra. Anything would be better than that. Why, Iuna thought as she slipped into unconsciousness, she'd even rather have that Ythnel woman as a governess again than live like this.

The wind picked up as the night wore on. It wrapped around the temple in howling gusts, winding its way from off the bay, deeper into the swamp. The steady patter of raindrops beating against the bricks created a soothing counter-rhythm to the rise and fall of the wind's cries. It made it hard to stay awake. Several times, Kestus watched his companions nod off, only to start awake when their heads drooped to their chests. He seemed to be rubbing his eyes as much as he was staring at the tome in front of him.

For hours they had been pouring over the spell-books Kohtakah brought. They were rich with arcane lore, and Kestus quickly began reading through the texts, more interested in spells that would free them than divinations that would unlock the secrets of the werecrocodiles' artifacts.

Kestus looked up from his studies to gaze at the werecrocodile. He noted the subtle shift in his own thinking. The man was no longer Brother Crocodile to him. The revelation in the swamp had turned him into a stranger, an unknown, no longer an ally. Doubt had crept in and displaced the trust that had once been there.

Had he ever really known him? It wasn't the first time Kestus pondered the question. At first it had been an angry response to his feelings of betrayal, but this time Kestus turned the query over in his mind, examining it from different angles. Secrecy had been an integral part of the functioning of the society back in Luthcheq. How much did he really know any of his fellow mages?

This is not the same, Kestus argued with himself. And yet, Kohtakah had never worked against the goals of the society. He hadn't been the one to betray them to the Karanoks. Kestus snarled soundlessly as an image of Therescales sitting silently at the table, listening to their plans to free Ythnel, flashed through his thoughts. Kestus swore once more to himself that that man would pay for his crimes.

"Sounds like quite the storm brewing outside." Muctos pushed back from the pages of the book lying in front of him and glanced nervously at the walls and ceiling of the vault.

"Been a while since we've had a real good one this winter," Kestus replied. He stretched, scratched his backside, and strolled over to the doorway, where he leaned against the jamb. He had barely crossed his arms over his chest when he jerked upright, twirled around, and strode back to the table.

"Someone's coming." The echoed sound of someone shuffling down the steps immediately followed his warning. Muctos and Kohtakah stopped what they were doing, and all three men peered ahead curiously.

A shadow appeared at the base of the stairs, growing in eerie coordination with the intensity of the wind outside. At the height of the howling crescendo, a man appeared. His receding hair was plastered to his scalp, and water dripped from his hooked nose. As the man entered the vault, Kestus could see tiny gashes laced his arms, and there were dark spots on his soaked tunic.

"The city is under attack," the man said in a rush between panting breaths. "Lord Mulkammu sent me down here to protect—" An arrowhead burst through the man's chest before he could finish. His eyes rolled back into his head, and he toppled to the dirt floor. Kestus watched him fall then looked up to see Ythnel standing at the base of the stairs, a bow held up in her left hand, her right hand still poised at her shoulder where she released the bowstring.

"Come on! We don't have much time," she shouted to them.

"Grab what you can," Kestus ordered immediately. Muctos scooped up some wands while Kestus grabbed the book he was studying and the black orb that had first caught his attention upon entering the vault. As he turned to leave, his eyes locked with Kohtakah's. The werecreature was just standing there, his brow furrowed as though he were locked in some sort of great internal struggle.

"Are you coming?" Kestus asked. Kohtakah's eyes widened, surprised perhaps that Kestus had assumed that he wouldn't try to stop them, let alone made the offer. Kestus was a bit taken aback himself, but it had been a gut reaction, and even now he knew he wouldn't take it back even if he had the chance.

"We need to go. Now," Ythnel insisted. It appeared that was enough to decide Kohtakah. He nodded at

Kestus and grabbed the staff of dark, twisted wood from where it rested on the rack against the left wall. Kestus followed, taking a torch from its sconce beside the vault door. Then they were running up the stairs and into the main chamber. Ythnel paused at the entrance to the temple, opening the door only partway and peering out into the night. Kestus came up next to her and glanced out.

"What's going on? What happened to you?"

"The wererats are attacking. There was a were-crocodile raid on their settlement. They think I was taken. I slipped away when the guard assigned to me was killed. I followed the wererats here.

"We have to move quickly, though. I don't think the attack will last much longer. The wererats are unorganized, and the werecrocodiles are stronger. We have to make it to the bay before they realize you're gone. Are you sure you trust him?" Ythnel jerked her head slightly in the direction of Kohtakah. Kestus nodded.

"All right, then. Follow me." Ythnel darted out into the darkness and the rain, leaving Kestus with his mouth open and more questions swirling in his head. He ran after Ythnel, the torch he carried hissing as droplets of water struck it. He could hear Muctos and Kohtakah sloshing through the muck after him, but he didn't risk looking back on the chance he might lose sight of the Loviatan's dim shape weaving through the buildings ahead. Occasionally, screams and shouts rose above the fury of the storm on their left or just ahead of them, pinpointing the clashes between the werecreatures.

The group turned a corner and ran right into the middle of one such clash.

The wererats had transformed into their hybrid ratmen forms and were clawing at the armored and better-armed humanoid werecrocodiles. Ythnel, several feet ahead of the mages, careened into the retreating backs of the wererats. They parted, a few of them tripping over her, and she stumbled into the outstretched arms of a stunned werecrocodile. Before anyone could react, in one motion she slammed her right elbow into the nose of the werecrocodile holding her, drew back the string of the bow she carried, and released the arrow she had nocked. It flew point blank into the face of the wererat right across form her, and as the dead body fell, transforming back into a human, she dived over it to rejoin Kestus and the others.

"That was impressive," Kestus breathed, helping Ythnel up.

"We should run," she said, herding them back the way they came. Sure enough, Kestus could see over Ythnel's shoulder that both groups of werecreatures were shaking off their momentary surprise and starting after them.

Kestus tossed his torch to Kohtakah, sidestepped Ythnel, and set down the items he was carrying.

"What are you doing?" she called back, pausing.

He was tired of running. He had never been the biggest or strongest kid growing up, and neither of his parents were fighters, so no one had taught him how to defend himself. His father's advice had been to run whenever Kestus found himself in a situation he couldn't handle.

While sound advice, following it had never sat quite right with Kestus. He hated being called a coward whenever he ran. More important, though, something inside of him wanted to stand up to the bullies. He longed for a different, better way.

Magic became that way for him.

He readily admitted he practiced the Art for the

power it gave him. Kestus had never been the scholarly type. It was not that he wasn't bright; he just didn't get excited by pouring over obscure writings, trying to uncover long-lost lore. He suffered the studying because it was necessary to gain the power.

Fortunately, he had just spent the past few hours engaged in such studying.

Kestus brought his hands up and cupped them around his mouth, forming a funnel that would amplify his voice. Wetting his lips with his tongue, he coughed out the single word he had read earlier from the book that now lay at his feet.

A circular ripple formed in the air inches from of his mouth. It expanded and pushed outward, followed by another circle, then another and another, until four concentric, circular ripples filled the entire street and were hurtling toward the werecreatures. When the first ripple hit, a loud *boom* was released, knocking several of the wererats to the mud. The following ripples produced similar results, until all the werecreatures lay on the ground. Blood trickled from the ears and noses of several of them.

Kestus scooped up the book and the orb and followed after his fleeing companions. They didn't get too far. A column of armored werecrocodiles was marching down the center of the avenue, heading straight for them. Kohtakah pointed to an empty street to their left, and they rushed for it. The column turned to follow. Muctos paused at the corner and fumbled a wand out of the bundle at his belt. He glanced at it for a moment before pointing it at the column and barking a harsh command. Lightning lanced out from its tip and raced through the column, turning the werecrocodiles into a mass of smoking, charred flesh.

"That was a dangerous risk," Kestus shouted at

Muctos when he finally caught up. "You had no idea what might have happened." Muctos smiled and pointed at the handle of the wand. Engraved in the metal was the Draconic word for lightning. Kestus laughed and patted his friend on the back.

Kohtakah was in the lead now, steering them through the maze of half-formed buildings. Shouts of alarm and brusque commands rose from all around. It was apparent that the tide was turning against the wererats. Their assault had been beaten back, and now the werecrocodiles were systematically hunting down any remaining enemies. Kestus worried that they would be caught in the slowly closing net as well.

They ducked down a narrow lane between two huts and came face-to-face with a group of ratmen slinking away through the shadows. Both groups stood facing each other, the tension palpable. The lead wererat noticed Ythnel, and its eyes narrowed.

"You," it hissed.

"Torgyn?"

"So you escaped. And are these your wizard friends?" An evil grin split his narrow muzzle. "You will come with us." He motioned for his comrades to surround them.

"No," Ythnel said firmly. She gripped a mace she had picked up from a fallen werecrocodile in her right hand. "We're leaving—by ourselves."

Torgyn snarled and lunged at her with the short sword he wielded. Ythnel took a step to the side and batted his blade down and away from her with the mace. Kohtakah spoke and a fan of flame shot from the splayed fingers of his hands to engulf two wererats that were trying to flank them on their right. The wererats dropped to the ground, thrashing in the mud until the flames were extinguished. Patches of missing fur exposed seared flesh; the two wererats scrambled backward and fled to cower in a corner nearby.

Ythnel and the wererat leader continued their duel while the mages kept the remaining wererats at bay. Torgyn slipped past Ythnel's guard, but the Loviatan brought her left forearm down, deflecting his sword from its intended target and receiving a nasty gash from her wrist to her elbow. She followed up with a blow to the shoulder of his sword arm. Kestus expected to hear the crunch of bone as the metal-studded head of the mace made contact, but there was only a soft thud. Torgyn grinned.

"Your simple weapon can't hurt me. You've caused me a lot of trouble. I've lost half my men coming after you. You're not worth that, not even four of you, but I can't let the werecrocodiles have you either. So I think instead of taking you prisoner, I'm just going to kill all of you." He advanced on Ythnel, his menacing look a promise of death. Emboldened by their leader's words, the other two wererats closed in as well.

Kestus heard someone speaking behind him and turned to see Muctos holding what looked like a wispy piece of thread between his finger and thumb. Kestus recognized the words his fellow mage was chanting and shouted at Kohtakah and Ythnel, who were standing in front of him.

"Duck!"

The pair dived to the muddy street as Muctos completed his incantation. The threadlike substance that he had been holding shot out in a stream toward the three wererats, expanding into thick webbing that entangled the werecreatures. The momentum of the spell forced them back, slamming them into the wall of a nearby building and pinning them there.

"I'll kill you, Ythnel!" Torgyn screamed as they ran past him. Kohtakah paused long enough to put the torch to the webbing and set it afire.

They continued to make their way through the werecrocodile city. Kohtakah led the way unerringly at a swift pace that soon had Kestus and Muctos panting for breath. As they crossed a large street, someone shouted out Kohtakah's name, and he stopped. The entire group turned to see Lord Mulkammu not a hundred feet away, with at least ten bowmen behind him.

"I am very disappointed, Royal Sorcerer. You put these humans before your own people. If you stop now, though, and return them to me, I will forgive you."

"I am sorry, my lord. I cannot do that. They have become as much my brothers as you."

"Then I label you a traitor, and you will die with your new 'brothers.' Archers, fire!" No sooner had the command been given than Kohtakah began to chant, his hands moving almost frantically in the air before him. The archers let loose their arrows. No one could move as the missiles flew toward them. Kohtakah was still casting, and Kestus couldn't help but wonder if this would be their end.

The wind suddenly picked up, rushing with a howl from all directions. Kestus's robe and hair whipped about him, forcing him to turn his head protectively. From the corner of his squinting eye, he watched for the arrow that would pierce his heart. It never happened. An invisible curtain of wind rushed up in front of the party, deflecting the arrows upward. None of them struck their intended target.

"Let's get out of here!" Kestus shouted. Ythnel and Muctos eagerly obeyed, but Kohtakah stood rooted in his spot, eyes locked with Mulkammu. Kestus grabbed him by the arm and dragged him along.

Finally, they broke from the ruins into some brush not far from the edge of the island. Ythnel paused for a moment, and the mages all bent over, their lungs heaving as they tried to replenish their supply of oxygen.

"Quiet," Ythnel said in a hoarse whisper.

Their labored breathing slowly subsided, leaving only the sound of the bay waters lapping at the shore, and the splash of raindrops. A rustle snapped all their heads to the right. Kestus signaled Kohtakah to hold the torch up high, and he took a step in the direction of the sound.

From out of the brush lunged a massive crocodile, its jaws snapping relentlessly at Kestus. The mage backpedaled, but he caught his heel on a root and tripped, stumbling backward to land on his rear. Both the orb and the book he was carrying went flying off into the night. He scooted away, his arms and legs flailing to keep out of range of the pursuing crocodile's crushing bite, but he was losing ground. Kohtakah threw the torch at the reptile's head, but the brand bounced harmlessly off its rough hide and landed in the mire, extinguished. Sure he was about to die, Kestus uttered a prayer to Mystra.

A buzzing sound rushed toward Kestus, and he threw his arm up defensively, bracing for whatever was about to happen. Through squinted eyes, he saw a swarm of black beetles fly between him and the charging crocodile. In an instant, the creature was entirely covered in dark, crawling carapaces. It began to thrash about, trying to dislodge the stinging and biting insects, its original prey all but forgotten. Kestus rolled to his feet and ran back to the others. Kohtakah was lowering the staff he had taken from the vault.

"Let's get out of here," Ythnel said, and they all jogged to the water's edge.

"There are some old fishing boats beached along here," Kohtakah offered. They moved along the bank, searching. It was hard to see in the darkness, but as they got closer, Kestus could make out the shape of a flat-bottomed skiff. There were no paddles, but Muctos found a couple of old planks lying nearby and tossed them in. Once everyone was aboard, Kestus pushed the boat out into the bay and hopped in.

THE PRIESTS

Out in the bay, the small craft and its occupants took the full brunt of the winter storm. Whipped by the fierce winds, the waves crashed over the sides of the boat until all four were soaked to the bone. The planks were quickly abandoned, and any hope of maneuvering through the tempest was lost. The group merely held onto the sides of the skiff for dear life. Tossed and turned about, Ythnel had no sense of where they were in the darkness.

The skiff suddenly rose on a cresting wave and was pitched over, tumbling the four into the chilling waters. Ythnel panicked, unable to tell which way was up, and let go of the breath she was holding. As the bubbles rose in front of her, she realized they would lead her back to the surface. She frantically kicked after them. She surged out of the depths with a gasp only to be pounded back under by another wave. Refusing to give up, Ythnel surfaced once more.

"Kestus—" Her shout was cut short as she swallowed a mouthful of water. She coughed it out and tried again. "Kestus! Muctos! Kohtakah! Anybody?" Ythnel squinted, hoping that something recognizable would materialize in the darkness. The gash in her arm stung from the salt water. Forcing herself to calm down, she whispered a prayer to Loviatar and touched the wound. The flesh wove itself back together, but Ythnel could feel a scar.

She returned to her scanning of the night. As she treaded water, surrounded by an unnerving silence, the waves rolling about her, Ythnel felt a terrifying sense of isolation creep into her heart. Panic began to rise again. She was out of her element and all alone.

"Kestus! Muctos!" This time, she thought she heard a voice calling and began to swim in the direction it came from. The cry sounded again, closer, and a large, dark shape appeared, drifting just ahead.

"Who's there?" she called out uncertainly.

"It's Muctos," came the excited reply. Ythnel thought she saw a waving arm, but in the blackness of the storm, she was still too far away to be sure. With a few more strokes, Ythnel reached the dark shape, and discovered it was Muctos clinging to the overturned skiff.

"Where are the others?"

"I don't know," Muctos sputtered. Ythnel called out their names again, and Muctos joined her in the attempt to locate the others. The wind was dying down, and the rain had been reduced to a light drizzle. With the storm's dissipation, the rolling swells were replaced by small whitecaps chopping the waters of the bay. The slow lightening of the sky signaled the approach of dawn. Ythnel scanned the horizon, hopeful to catch sight of their missing friends.

"Over there!" Muctos exclaimed and pointed off into the distance. "I think I see something. Kestus? Kohtakah?"

Ythnel looked where Muctos pointed. Someone was indeed swimming toward them. As the figure neared, Ythnel could make out the stern features of Kestus, his dark hair plastered against his scalp. The mage no longer had his cloak. Ythnel let go of a breath she hadn't realized she was holding when he finally reached the skiff.

"Where's . . . Kohtakah?" Kestus panted and leaned heavily against the side of the boat, trying to catch his breath.

"We haven't seen him yet," Ythnel answered.

Kestus nodded and said, "We need to get this boat turned back over."

"How?" Muctos asked.

"We should just be able to flip up one side."

They positioned themselves at the bow, middle, and stern. Together they heaved the edge up out of the water and tossed it away from them. With a small splash, the skiff was righted.

Ythnel swam over and pulled herself in, kicking to thrust herself high out of the water and over the side of the boat. She sat there for a second, exhausted but glad to be finally out of the water. An overwhelming feeling of safety and comfort swelled inside her, bringing her to the verge of tears. The boat rocked, startling Ythnel. She grabbed the sides of the skiff, bracing herself, when she realized it was only Kestus struggling to get in. With a deep breath, Ythnel calmed herself and moved to help him. Together, they dragged Muctos out of the water.

For a while, all three of them huddled quietly in the bottom of the boat, unable to do anything but shiver in the steady wind that blew across the bay. The clouds parted to reveal a bright winter sun that did little to warm them.

"We should look for Kohtakah," Muctos said between chattering teeth.

Kestus shook his head. "If he hasn't shown up by now, he's not going to," he said in a subdued voice. Muctos opened his mouth, but Kestus cut off any protest. "He could be anywhere out there. It would be useless to try and search for him. I'm sorry." Muctos frowned, clearly not pleased, but nodded. They continued to sit in silence, not willing to meet each others' eyes.

"We can't just sit here, or we'll die of hypothermia," Ythnel said finally. "We have to get moving. The only way we'll get warm and dry is by our own body heat."

"What do you suggest?" Muctos's tone overflowed with sarcasm. "I don't think running in place will work given our circumstances."

"No, but we could paddle. We need to get to shore anyway."

"And in what direction might that be?" Muctos's question dripped with undisguised scorn.

"That's enough, Muctos," Kestus growled. The portly mage scowled back but kept his mouth shut.

"I can still see land that way," Ythnel said, indicating a thin, dark line just visible on the horizon to their left. "From the position of the sun, I'd guess that's where we came from."

"Well, then, let's start paddling back," Muctos suggested.

"No," Kestus grunted. "If we go back, we'll risk recapture by the werecreatures or the Karanoks. We head east, to Mordulkin."

"What? That will take days," Muctos cried.

"Then we had better get started." Kestus leaned over the side of the skiff and started paddling with his cupped hands.

Progress was slow. For every hour they paddled, it seemed as though they moved only a few yards. Even taking turns to rest, Ythnel's arms quickly turned wooden, and feeling returned to her hands like a prickly fire only just before she had to dunk them back into the numbingly chill waters. By the end of the first day, Ythnel could see all of them were exhausted. They slept fitfully, huddled together at the bottom of the craft to protect themselves from the wind and share body heat.

Kohtakah was plunged into waters of the Bay of Chessenta like all the others as their little skiff was flipped by the raging sea. Unlike the others, though, he didn't panic. Water was a second home to him. He was a werecrocodile, after all.

Shedding his robes, he reoriented himself and, with a few strong kicks, broke the surface in a spray. It was dark, and the storm still tossed waves about the bay violently. He could not see any of the others.

Something bumped against Kohtakah's leg as he treaded water. A dark triangle broke the surface of the water ahead of him, and a sense of dread filled him. There were other predators besides crocodiles that inhabited the waters of the Bay of Chessenta, he knew. In his current form, he was extremely vulnerable to an attack. Fortunately, he had an alternate shape.

Kohtakah was born a werecrocodile, as many of his generation were. Unlike those who contracted the disease at some point in their lives, he had grown up with the ability. The years had given him mastery of the transformation. It didn't make it any less painful, though.

As his body temperature rose, Kohtakah could feel the blood boiling in his veins. Bones snapped and reformed, tendons broke away and reattached as his body reshaped itself. Kohtakah moaned in response to the pain. It would be over soon, though.

Kohtakah screamed as the mild pain in his right leg became the excruciating sensation of a hundred knives puncturing his flesh. A sharp tug pulled him under water. His scream became a bubbling roar as the transformation completed.

Specialized lids closed protectively over each eye, turning his vision murky. He could still see that the lower half of his right, rear leg was missing and a cloud of red was slowly drifting away from the wound. The change had partially healed the damage so that he was no longer in immediate danger of bleeding to death, but there was enough blood in the water that the scent would attract more sharks, or at least bring his current attacker back for more. He needed to get away from there. With a powerful flick of his tail, he went in search of his companions and their boat.

A dark, blurry shape came hurtling out of the depths, its jaws snapping on the empty water Kohtakah had just passed through. He whipped around and clamped onto the shark's tail as it passed, but the creature's momentum allowed it to yank free. As it swam away, Kohtakah estimated the shark was easily seventeen feet long, nearly as big as he was.

Sensing something behind him, Kohtakah banked to the side. He was too slow, though, and a second shark slammed into him, its jaws closing on his back. His thick hide protected him from any serious damage, and Kohtakah thrashed his body to free himself, taking a few of the shark's teeth with him.

He didn't stop there. With a sharp turn, Kohtakah came around the side of the shark and bit down hard on the animal's pectoral fin. His hold secure, he began to roll violently, twisting and tearing the shark's flesh until the fin pulled away. Fresh blood clouded the water as the shark swam away, its flight erratic as it slowly and uncontrollably descended into the murk. Kohtakah knew he wouldn't see it again.

That left its mate.

It came at Kohtakah head-on, its mouth open wide to reveal rows of serrated teeth several inches long. If he were still in humanoid form, he was sure the creature could easily have bitten him in half. As a crocodile, that was an entirely different matter.

Propelled by wide sweeps of his own tail, Kohtakah shot forward to meet the shark. At the last second, he angled up and grabbed the shark by the nose. His jaws locked in a death grip, Kohtakah spun once more, brutally shaking the shark until he felt the creature's head separate from its body. He released the carcass then and watched it sink into the depths.

A wave of exhaustion washed over him, carrying with it the burning pain from his missing leg. Even in the water, he tired quickly in this form; the heavy muscles of the crocodile sapped his energy faster than his human muscles would. He surfaced, inhaling air through his scaly nostrils to fill his lungs. The storm was abating, and the surface of the bay had calmed considerably. The skiff, however, was still nowhere in sight.

Kohtakah floated for a bit, letting the current take him with only the occasional flick of his tail for guidance and forward motion. His leg throbbed painfully, but he relegated it to a back corner of his mind while he considered his options. He could bide his time until dawn and set his course using the location of the sun. The real question was where to go.

Adder Swamp was out of the question. Lord Mulkammu had seen him with the fleeing mages and declared him a traitor. If he ever showed his face there again, it would be his death.

He could set off for one of the human cities. It would be difficult at first. He had no food, no coin, and now no clothes, but he was sure his sorcerous abilities would quickly find him employment.

He didn't relish the thought of being alone again, however. He remembered when he first came to Luthcheq, the isolation he felt. He recalled the fear and secrecy by which he had to live, not only because he was a werecreature amongst humans, but also because he was a wielder of the arcane who was seeking others who were the same. It was only after he had found the Mage Society that he once again felt as if he belonged.

That thought brought him to his third option. He could search for his friends. It was reassuring to think that he could still call them that. Kohtakah feared that they would consider it a betrayal when they learned he was a werecrocodile. He had been right, but somehow Kestus had overcome those initial feelings and welcomed him back.

Unfortunately, Kohtakah had no idea where the other three might be, or if they were even still alive. No, they live, he told himself, and if such were the case, that meant he had to try to find them.

His decision made, Kohtakah continued to drift, waiting for the sky to clear and the sun appear. The sky gradually brightened, and within a few hours, the sun was peeking over the horizon on Kohtakah's left. Orienting himself by it, he began to swim south, searching, until he spotted the shore. Then he made a lazy turn east and headed north, back out into the bay until he could no longer see the thick line behind him that indicated land.

Kohtakah continued the search pattern the entire day, steadily moving eastward hour by hour. Finally, as the sun began to set, he spotted a dark blot on the horizon. The wind had picked up, chopping the waters of the bay into little whitecaps. He was tired and at the end of his strength, slowed enough by his wound and the battle with the sharks that he was unable to catch any of the fast game fish that swam in the bay. He was sure the blot was his friends in their skiff or at least some other small vessel, and he called on what energy he still had to propel himself through the water closer and closer.

Finally, he was near enough to see the object was indeed the skiff. Night had fallen, however, and he could not see anybody inside. He swam right up to the side of the boat and bumped it with his snout. It made a solid thump, and he heard something stirring. Not wanting to scare his companions, Kohtakah dipped below the water and transformed back into his human shape, the pain momentarily eclipsing that from his lost leg. When he resurfaced a few feet away, he saw Muctos sitting up, looking out across the water.

"Muctos," he called, waving. "Over here." He saw the mage turn toward him and heard him gasp.

"Kohtakah? Hey, it's Kohtakah! Wake up." Muctos bent down and shook someone. Kestus sat up, followed by Ythnel. They were all alive! Muctos pointed toward where Kohtakah bobbed.

"How did—" Kestus started to say but shook his

head. "Are you all right? Can you swim over here?"

Kohtakah shook his head. "I'm hurt. I don't think I have anything left."

"Don't worry. Hold on. We'll come to you." The three started paddling with their hands. Kohtakah could tell they were exhausted, and he felt honored that they would push themselves further on his behalf. When they reached him, they pulled him into the boat.

"Your leg?" Ythnel gasped as he came fully out of the water.

She directed them to quickly turn him over onto his back. She took the mangled stump in both hands and started to pray. A dark and unholy light radiated from Ythnel's hand, and a momentary pang of fear raced through Kohtakah. Ythnel was a cleric of Loviatar, he remembered. Then a searing pain racked his body, and he stiffened. It was gone in a second, and he was left fully drained. He struggled to lift his head, unwilling to give in to sleep until he saw what was done. Ythnel removed her hands, the glow fading from them, and Kohtakah saw that the skin had closed over the open wound, leaving a fully healed knob just below his knee.

"Thank you," he breathed, closed his eyes, and drifted off to sleep.

When they awoke it was midmorning, and land was nowhere in sight. Kestus judged the current had likely carried them farther out into the bay. Once again using the sun, they oriented themselves east and started paddling. Ythnel's mouth was uncomfortably dry; her tongue felt heavy and swollen. She absently scooped a handful of water to her mouth, but spit it out before she swallowed. It was salt water, she reminded herself. They wouldn't be able to drink any of it. Rain would be the only fresh water available to them, and from the clear sky, Ythnel didn't think they would see any soon. The irony made her chuckle.

"What's so funny?" Muctos croaked from his resting place at the stern of the skiff.

"Nothing. I'm just thirsty."

"It'll get worse," Kestus said quietly as he paddled on the starboard side. "Keep your mouths closed to conserve spit." Ythnel nodded and went back to her own paddling.

There was still water as far as the eye could see when their third day in the boat began. Ythnel leaned against the side of the skiff, her arm hanging over the edge and into the water. Kestus sat across from her, staring into the east. Dark stubble had appeared on his face, and there was a hollow look in his eyes. The craft rocked gently in place; no one had the strength to paddle. Kohtakah seemed mostly healed from his encounter with the sharks, but the lack of water and food probably wasn't helping with his recovery. She was worried about Muctos, as well. He had been restless through the night, a sign, Ythnel thought, that he may be succumbing to dehydration quicker than everyone else. Ythnel leaned over and shook the still-sleeping form of Muctos.

"Wake up." Her voice was barely a whisper. Muctos stirred slightly and groaned, but he did not sit up.

"Let him lie," Kestus muttered. "What's the point, anyway? We're going to die."

"No," Ythnel blurted out. The mage's admission startled her, and she searched desperately for some way to prove him wrong. They had come this far, endured so much. She would not lose hope, not give up on Loviatar again. The dream Ythnel had in the swamp shoved its way to the front of her mind. She was sure it had been a message, another sign from the Maiden of Pain that she would endure through these trials. She had been promised revenge, and she meant to have it.

"I-I can purify water for us," she said excitedly, suddenly remembering the spell she had used amongst the wererats.

"What would we hold it in?" Kestus sneered. "And what would we do for food? Water won't provide the strength we need to keep paddling."

"We have to at least try." She turned to Muctos and yanked him up. The mage leaned against her, unable to support himself. "Muctos, I need you to scoop up some water with your hands." She leaned him against the side of the boat and helped him raise his arms. "Please, Muctos. I can't do this alone. I need you to hold the water. My hands have to be free to cast the spell. Please." He sat there, unmoving, his arms dangling in the water. Kestus laughed softly.

"Shut up!" Ythnel screamed. "It won't end this way. I won't let it. There has to be some way to collect the water." She tried to think, but Kestus kept laughing. "I said shut up!" She lashed out at the mage, her face twisted in rage. The blow snapped his head to the left, and he slid sideways to the bottom of the boat, still laughing quietly.

With an infuriated huff, Ythnel turned to Muctos and pulled his arms back inside the boat. She fought to conjure an idea, anything that might help them, but nothing came to mind. So she sat there staring blankly at the water dripping from Muctos's hands to form pools on the floor of the boat.

That was it! She could use the boat to hold the water. Energized by the plan, Ythnel began scooping handfuls of water into the boat with abandon.

"Wouldn't it be quicker to punch a hole in the boat," Kestus chuckled. "Or better yet, just tip us over."

"I'm not trying to kill us, idiot," Ythnel hissed as she continued to shovel in the water. "I'm going to save us." Kestus gave her a puzzled look, but kept quiet as she spent the next several minutes filling the boat with handfuls of water. When there was a sizable pool a couple of inches deep, Ythnel stopped. Positioning herself on the bow seat, she began chanting and moving her hands over the water. When she was done, Ythnel cupped her hand, dipped it into the puddle and raised it slowly to her mouth. Parting her dry lips, she took a sip.

It was fresh.

Crying with delight, she took another quick drink then moved to Muctos, raising a handful to his mouth and pouring it in. The mage sputtered, some of the water running down the sides of his face, but he drank most of it, and Ythnel gave him some more.

"I'm sorry."

Ythnel glanced over to see Kestus sitting back up, looking at her with an expression on his face she could not read. She nodded, and he leaned over to get his own drink. Then he helped Kohtakah.

Twice more that day, they filled the bottom of the skiff with water and Ythnel purified it. There was plenty to drink, but Kestus had been right. With nothing to eat, none of them had the strength to paddle the boat against the current. So they drifted.

On the fourth day, as the sun was nearing its apex, Ythnel spotted something on the northern horizon. It was little more than a dark speck, but it was moving.

"A ship!" Ythnel cried, startling the men from their doze.

"You could be right," Kestus said after staring at the speck for a few moments. "But how do we signal it?"

"I think I know a way." Muctos began to wave his hands, silently mouthing words. Ythnel thought she saw "help" among those passing his lips. When he was finished, he pointed to the north and a gust of wind suddenly swept past the four of them, heading the same direction.

"Now we wait."

They sat staring at the speck on the horizon for what seemed like hours, but when Ythnel looked up at the sky, the sun had barely moved. Looking back, she swore the speck looked larger. She said nothing, though, as it was likely a trick of her eyes either from gazing at the sun for too long or simply from her mind letting her see what her heart wanted. To take their minds off waiting, Ythnel suggested they purify more water. They were all scooping when Muctos shouted suddenly.

"I see sails."

They all paused to look. Ythnel was sure the speck was larger now. And there was a ripple along one side, like wind fluttering a bedsheet hung out to dry. It was gone as soon as she noticed, but she was sure she saw it. Caught in a moment of hope, Ythnel stood up in the boat and began waving her arms.

"We're over here! Over here!"

"Sit down, or you'll capsize us before they get here," Kestus scolded her lightly. She looked down to see the corner of his mouth twist up before he pulled her down. Then all four of them began to grin then laugh uncontrollably, tears streaming down their cheeks.

❖ ❖ ❖ ❖ ❖

The square-sailed, double-masted merchant ship *Lady Splendor* made port in Mordulkin two days after picking up Ythnel, Kestus, Kohtakah, and Muctos from their skiff in the middle of the Bay of Chessenta. The *Lady Splendor*'s captain, a foppish halfling who favored bright silk shirts regardless of the occasion, was most generous in loaning the use of his cabin to the four during the trip. They were well fed and clothed, and Ythnel felt fully recovered from their ordeal as they walked onto the docks of Luthcheq's smaller rival. The city looked similar to Luthcheq: its buildings of white stone crowded together, and its citizens moved about their daily business in an orderly manner, but the bounce in people's step and the ready smiles on the their faces told Ythnel that below the surface, Mordulkin was a much different place.

Kestus led them away from the docks and into the city. As they had discussed on the ship, the plan was to rent some rooms at an inn Kestus had stayed at previously, where they would wait while he tried to get word to his contact. The quartet walked down wide streets full of shops, taverns, and inns. Kohtakah had been given some crude crutches as a parting gift from the *Lady Splendor*'s captain, and he used those to amble along. Ythnel noted how none of the storefront signs were faded, the paint depicting bolts of cloth, steaming plates of food or liquid-filled vials was not chipped. Likewise, the building facades were clean and showed little signs of age. It was quite a contrast to her home of Bezantur, where only the large temples and the nobility could afford to, or cared to, keep up their property. Either the merchants of Mordulkin did well for themselves or the wealth was spread around by some larger governing body that sought to create an atmosphere of prosperity.

Their first stop was a squat building on a street corner with a sign hanging out front. Painted on it was a pile of coins sitting atop of an open book. The four walked in and found themselves in a cozy antechamber. A small fire smoldered in the hearth to the right, providing a comfortable level of heat for the room. In the center of the area was a writing stand. Through a doorway in the far wall, Ythnel could see the edge of a desk and hear the scratching of a quill on parchment.

"Just a moment. I'll be right with you," a dry voice called from around the corner in the office. The scratching stopped, and a thin, older man with wispy curls of white hair appeared. He wore a black jacket with sleeves that fell just short of his wrists over a plain linen shirt tucked into black pantaloons. When his eyes fell on the group, one thick, bushy eyebrow arched in a look that clearly questioned whether they belonged in his establishment. Ythnel realized their secondhand clothing probably made them look like beggars. The clerk opened his mouth, but Kestus spoke up before he could say anything.

"My name is Kestus Aentius. I have an account with you. I am here to make a withdrawal. As you can probably see, I and my companions need to refresh ourselves." The old man seemed to consider this for a moment before shuffling back into his office. He returned shortly, his arms wrapped lovingly around a thick, leather-bound book. He laid the book upon the writing stand and began to thumb through the first pages.

"Aentius ... Aentius ... Aentius. Ah, yes, here we are. Oh." Both eyebrows rose slightly. "Will you be making a large withdrawal today, Master Aentius? I may need some time to collect the necessary—"

"No, I just need one hundred authokhs."

The clerk breathed a sigh of relief. "Very well. If you will sign here?" The old man held a quill out for Kestus then indicated a place on the page where the mage was to sign. When he had done so, the clerk went once more to his office. He stopped before a section of the far wall and mumbled something Ythnel couldn't quite hear. The wall disappeared to reveal an iron door. The old man spoke again, and the door swung inward, a secret vault now visible beyond. He returned with two bulging coin purses and handed them to Kestus.

"Will there be anything else?" The clerk closed his ledger when Kestus shook his head. "Until your next visit, then, Master Aentius." He bowed slightly and shuffled back to his office. Kestus turned and headed out the door.

Their next errand took them to a tailor's shop a street over from the coinlender. Kestus had them all measured and ordered outfits made, despite Ythnel's protests. He then purchased clothing from the merchant's current stock to replace the ill-fitting hand-me-downs given to them aboard the *Lady Splendor*.

They finally came to stop before a sign that depicted a beast with the head of an eagle, the body of a lion, and wings of flame. The building was two stories high, with glass-paned windows on both levels and a black iron-hinged door that swung open silently at Kestus's touch.

"Olaré, gentlefolk." Behind a waist-high counter to the right of the entrance stood a man in a green tunic and brown linen vest, his thick mustache hiding the upper half of the broad smile he offered. "Welcome to the Flaming Griffon. Interested in a room or two for the night?"

"Two adjoining rooms," Kestus replied. "We'll need a cot in one of them."

"Of course. How long will you be staying?"

"We're not sure, but this should cover us for a few days." Kestus set the remaining coins in a stack on the counter. "Have dinner sent to our rooms when it's ready please."

"Certainly," the innkeeper fawned, scooping up the coins and dropping two keys in their place. "Your rooms will be up the stairs to the left there. Will there be anything else?"

"Uh, a bath would be nice," Ythnel suggested.

"I'll have water drawn right away, milady." With a knowing smile, the innkeeper rang a bell, summoning a flurry of servants. The trio made their way past the front desk and up the short flight of stairs while orders were being given.

The rooms were comfortable; each had two single beds, a writing table, an armoire, and a window that looked out onto the street. No sooner had Ythnel flopped on her bed than there was a knock on her door. She opened it to find a maid ready to lead her to the bathing room. Her new linen dress draped over her arm, Ythnel followed the older woman down the hall. Once inside the steamy room with the door closed, Ythnel shed her old clothing and slipped into the tub.

"To the trash with these, milady?" the maid asked, holding up the dingy garment between her index finger and thumb. Ythnel nodded before sliding under the water.

After braiding her hair, Ythnel joined the men in their room for dinner. Kohtakah and Muctos sat on their beds, plates of roasted mutton and stewed vegetables resting in their laps, while Ythnel sat at the writing table, shoveling the food in as fast as she could chew and swallow. At least she hadn't drooled as the first tendrils of aroma drifted to her nose. Not that either of the mages would notice, buried as they were in their own meals. Kestus had either already eaten or was not hungry because he paced the floor with an air of impatience. Ythnel was dabbing up the last pools of juice with a thick slice of bread when there was a knock at the door. Kestus practically ran to open it.

"Master Rueldarr said you had a dispatch to send?" A young boy stood in the doorway fidgeting.

"Ah, yes. Ythnel, if you wouldn't mind handing over that envelope on the desk."

Ythnel noticed for the first time a small envelope with the name "Crarl Ormane" scrawled on the front. When she grabbed it, her fingers pressed against a hard blob of sealing wax on the back.

"See that this gets to the Jedea Academy before sunset, boy. There'll be some extra coin if I hear it was so."

The youth nodded vigorously, grabbed the envelope from Kestus, and darted down the hall.

"So, I take it the recipient of that envelope is your contact?" Muctos asked from his seat on the bed.

"Crarl Ormane is the name I was given by my contact. That's who the letter is addressed to. I don't know if it's an actual person or just some sort of password." Kestus strolled back to his cot and sat down. While he had visibly relaxed after closing the door, there was still something pensive about his mood.

"What is the Jedea Academy?" Ythnel asked.

"It is the oldest school in Mordulkin for students of the Art," said Muctos. "It was founded by Soldim

Jedea, the first ruler of the city. The Jedea family has ruled Mordulkin since the rebellion that ousted Unther from Chessenta." Muctos paused, and his eyes suddenly lit up. "What if your mysterious benefactor is a member of the Jedea family?"

"Let's not get our hopes up," Kestus cautioned.

They retired to their rooms for the night. Ythnel inquired with a maid about a switch, which earned her a strange look, but one was retrieved from the inn's stables. She performed her nightly prayer ritual and slept soundly.

When Ythnel finished her prayers the next morning, Kestus was already out running some errands. He returned shortly after she finished a late morning-feast. He had with him a couple of new purses of coin and their tailor-made outfits. Ythnel asked if there had been any response to his letter, but the mage shook his head.

Lunch went by, and there was still no word. Ythnel wanted to get out and stretch her legs by walking through the city, but Kestus counseled patience. Everyone needed to be here and be ready to go should a reply come requesting an immediate meeting. Finally, as they were finishing dinner in the common room of the Flaming Griffon, a message was delivered. Kestus read through it silently while everyone else finished their meals. He set the note down on the table, pushed his chair back, and stood up.

"Let's go."

The brisk walk to the residential district, where the academy was located, took a little more than half a candle. The sun was just dipping below the skyline of the city, casting everything in shades of deep purple and golden orange. The houses that lined the streets ranged from simple, single-family dwellings to large mansions with landscaped terraces covering an entire block. As with the merchant district, all the buildings here showed similar signs of regular upkeep, and Ythnel wondered at the amount of coin it would take to maintain so much property.

The Jedea Academy grounds were even more immaculate than its neighbors'. Spring-green grass of uniform height surrounded the two-story complex and was split in the front by a white granite walkway that led from the curb to an ornate, oak door. Brilliant white stone, shining in the fading sunlight, was austere in its lack of decoration. Four square towers formed the corners of the academy, and its sloped roof was covered in tiles of twilight-gray slate.

Ythnel brought up the rear as the quartet walked single file to the door. Kestus looked at them over his shoulder then rapped his knuckles against the solid wood, producing a muffled sound that was barely audible to Ythnel.

"You're going to have to put a little more muscle into it, Kestus, if you expect anyone to hear you," she kidded. Muctos chuckled, which turned into a throat clearing when Kestus glared at him. The mage went to knock again, but the door opened and a young woman with long, straight black hair stuck her head out.

"I'm sorry, but the library is closed for the night. Please come back tomorrow."

"We're not here to look at books," Kestus interjected, pulling the note from a pouch on his robe. "We have an appointment with Crarl Ormane."

The woman's face scrunched up in a mix of puzzlement and frustration as she took the paper from Kestus. "Wait here," she said after glancing at it. The door closed, leaving the four to stand waiting out in the gathering night.

"Certainly a hospitable bunch," Ythnel said. Kestus opened his mouth, but the dark-haired woman reappeared at the door before he could say anything.

"Follow me, please."

Just inside the door was, indeed, a library. Ythnel gazed in awe at the shelves upon shelves of books that stretched across the carpeted floor. She felt insignificant, surrounded by the collected volume of knowledge, and cringed inwardly as the muffled tread of the group passing through the room disturbed the silence that hung in the air like a mantle of respect.

They came to a door and the dark-haired woman knocked once before ushering them into the small office beyond. Piles of books covered most of the floor, with paths cleared between the door, a reading chair, an overflowing bookshelf, and a desk. The desk was occupied by an older man who thumbed through a dusty tome by the light of a brightly glowing quill that rested in an inkpot set on the corner of the desk.

"Master Thilymm, these are the people here to see Crarl Ormane."

The old man looked up, seemingly aware of his visitors for the first time. He placed a marker in the book, closed it, and set it on the desk before standing and dismissing their escort with a nod. He wore a conical hat that covered any hair that might still be on his head, which made his thick, white mustache stand out even more. A jeweled medallion hung around his neck, the multifaceted sapphire reflecting the light of the enchanted quill on the desk as it rested against the silky fabric of his light blue tunic.

"Welcome, welcome. I am Ovros Thilymm, Head Librarian of the Academy."

"Where is Crarl Ormane?" Kestus asked.

"He is not here."

"What? But the note said we were to meet him."

"No, the note said to come to the academy."

Ythnel tensed. This conversation was taking an uncomfortable turn. They had no weapons, but she was sure she could take the old man out before he could call to any hidden allies.

"Don't play word games with me," Kestus fumed. "The note was signed by Crarl Ormane."

"I assure you I am not playing a game. Crarl Ormane is not here because it would be impossible for him to. He is nothing but a name."

"You were right," Muctos muttered. Kestus nodded, but frustration still showed on his face.

"Fine, so we're not going to meet Crarl. Who are we going to meet? Or was there some other reason we were invited here?"

"You can relax," Ovros said, looking right at Ythnel as though he had read her mind. He was more observant than she gave him credit for. "You are going to meet the person you came here to see. Let's go upstairs." He scooted past them and led them back out through the library to a door in the middle of the back wall. The librarian put his medallion against the wood of the door and uttered something unintelligible. A chime sounded, and the door swung open as the single, clear note faded away.

Ovros followed the hallway behind the library to the right until it came to a flight of metal stairs that led both up and down. He began to climb, the clanging of his steps echoing off the stones of hall. The four looked at each other before Kestus started up the stairs. Muctos shrugged and began his ascent, followed by Kohtakah, who navigated his crutches awkwardly. With a quick look back down the hall, Ythnel brought up the rear.

The stairs ended at a landing with another door. Again, Ovros put his medallion to the wood and spoke the command to open it. Another hallway stretched beyond, lined with doors on either side every ten feet or so. Ovros stopped before the third on their left and knocked.

"Come in," came the response in a deep, commanding voice. The door swung open at the librarian's touch, and he stood aside to let the four enter.

"I'll be here when you are finished," he said and turned to leave.

The room they were in appeared to be some sort of lounge. There were four overstuffed chairs set about the room, each with their own end table and candelabra. Thin bookshelves stood against the walls at odd intervals. Another door stood closed in the far wall.

The dominant feature of the room, however, was the imposing figure who stood in the center of it. Thick, shoulder-length gray hair framed a square face and was held back by a gem-encrusted gold band at the temples and forehead. Bushy eyebrows drooped over sparkling eyes, and a neatly trimmed beard ran along the jawline before surrounding a broad mouth. A thick cape dyed red hung over a loose silk robe of deep purple.

"I apologize for all the secrecy," the man said in the same strong voice Ythnel had heard from outside. She started in surprise just the same then blushed when she realized she had been staring, captivated by the physical specimen before her. "If my presence here, my connection to you, were to be known, much planning would be ruined and lives possibly lost."

"Who are you?" There was something in Kestus's voice, as if he already knew the answer, but couldn't believe it. "We know Crarl Ormane is a phantom."

"I am Hercubes Jedea, king of Mordulkin."

Kestus nodded slowly, his face betraying his inability to come to terms with the revelation.

"So you were going to help us," Muctos breathed.

"Yes, I answered Kestus's inquiries through a third party, so as to remain anonymous. Don't look so shocked," Hercubes said to Kestus, in response to the furrowing of the mage's brow. "I've known about the society for a while, but I didn't dare to make contact until everything was in place. In fact, I know more than you may realize, Kestus Aentius, Muctos Dapritus, and Ythnel Duumin, though I am surprised to see the werecreature is still with you."

Ythnel could not keep her jaw from dropping open. It was one thing for him to know the mages' names, but how would he know about her. She had never set foot outside of Thay until a few tendays ago.

"Well, you waited too long, your majesty." Anger bolstered Kestus's voice, and there was a fire in his eyes. "The society is dead."

"But you are here," Hercubes replied, "and that will do." He met Kestus's gaze, but his voice softened as he continued. "I am truly sorry for the loss of your friends. Do not turn your anger upon me, though. The Karanoks are the ones responsible. We can still exact vengeance upon them."

"I'm listening," Kestus said.

"Mordulkin and Luthcheq have long been enemies, as I am sure you are aware. While we have been able to turn away invasions, we were too small to mount an offensive of our own. So we waited, biding our time until the fanaticism of the Karanoks created enough instability in the city that we could strike.

"That time has come. What we lack in armies, we make up for in arcane resources. This academy, which my ancestor built, has produced many skilled wizards loyal to Mordulkin and her cause. Luthcheq's edict against magic will end, and the Karanoks will be destroyed.

"There is one obstacle still in our path, however."

"Witchweed," Kestus answered.

"Yes, witchweed. The Karanoks have enough of the cursed plant to stop a legion of wizards. We cannot succeed as long as it remains in the Karanoks' possession. My agents have learned the location of three stockpiles kept within the city limits. If those were eliminated, the forces of Mordulkin could sweep in and take Luthcheq long before new crops grew come next harvest.

"That was what I was hoping your society would accomplish. It is what I'm still hoping you will accomplish."

"What about your agents?" Muctos asked.

"Unfortunately, I have not heard from them in tendays. I fear they may have been discovered and disposed of."

"And you expect us to go back into that city of madness? Forget it. Unlike Kestus, I lost everything when I left. I'm not about to throw away my life trying to return."

"I understand," Hercubes said. "You will be welcome here in Mordulkin, if you wish to stay. What about you?" he asked Kestus.

"I'll do it," Kestus said. "I owe it to the others to see this through. I'm not sure if I can do it alone, though."

"I would go, but I think I would be more of a hindrance in my present condition," Kohtakah said, disappointment thick in his voice.

"I'll go," Ythnel said. They all turned to look at her.

"There is retribution to be meted out and a debt to be paid." Ythnel braced herself for the inevitable protest, but all she got were knowing nods from both Kestus and Hercubes.

"Then it is decided. There are a few details to see to, but they can be taken care of in the morning. Tonight you will return to your rooms at the Flaming Griffon and sleep well. What aid I can give will be waiting for you when you leave.

"Farewell, my friends. May Mystra watch over you."

THE PRIESTS

The carriage rolled past the East Gate and into the city at a leisurely pace. The streets of Luthcheq were filled with revelry, its citizens out in force to celebrate Midwinter. Ythnel pulled her fur jacket tightly around her; the carriage did little to keep the chill of the air out, or the dull roar of the festivities.

"It will probably snow before the night is over," Kestus commented from his seat opposite Ythnel. "There's enough moisture in the air."

Ythnel nodded, wondering what snow would look like. It was a distracting thought, and she shook her head to be rid of it. They were here on dangerous business. A misstep would mean the end. Nervous, she played with the ring given to her by Hercubes Jedea. The three rounded, red stones embedded in the silver band were smooth under her fingertips. The ring stored spells that the wizard had told her would aid in her mission. She had already cast one as they waited in line to enter the city. Her hand moved subconsciously to touch the soft, unmarred skin of her right cheek.

"You look . . . beautiful."

The pause caught Ythnel's attention, but Kestus looked away when their eyes met.

"If I had never met you before, I'd . . . I'd never recognize you."

He was right, of course. She looked nothing like the woman who had come to Luthcheq as a governess. Her golden hair was full and shiny, falling in waves just past her shoulders. Deep blue eyes looked out from long eyelashes, separated by a button nose and complemented by lush, pouting lips. A blouse and trousers of flimsy, pale blue silk clung to curves she was not born with. It was all a ruse, bait for a trap.

The carriage came to a halt with a lurch. Kestus opened the door and stepped out then turned to lend a hand to Ythnel. Their breaths were puffs of white in the air between them.

"Are you ready?" Kestus asked, continuing after she nodded. "Naeros favors three taverns in his carousing: the Black Mercy, the Vampire's Tooth, and Bale's Bones. Two of them are a few blocks north of here; the other is on the southern end of town. Be careful. I'm not going to be there to back you up."

"I know."

"No, I mean I won't be helping with the rest. Taking care of the witchweed is going to be up to you. I have my own score to settle first, and I don't know how long it will take me. Hells, I don't even know if I'll succeed." Kestus gave a quick laugh.

"I understand," Ythnel said calmly. "You do what

you have to. May Loviatar bless your endeavor." She gave him a small kiss on the cheek and stood back. There was a question in his eyes, and his mouth twisted as though he wanted to say something, but he merely nodded and got back into the carriage. Ythnel watched it pull off down the street and disappear into the frolicking masses. Then she turned and headed north.

The Vampire's Tooth was a sailor's tavern. It sat right across from the piers, a long, squat building that blended well with the dockside warehouses surrounding it. Thin slashes of light escaped through the warped wood of shuttered windows and the battered door. Ythnel's nose wrinkled at the unique combination of salty sea air and fermented alcohol that exuded from the Tooth like the poisonous breath of some great green dragon. It was hard for her to imagine that a self-important noble such as Naeros would patronize such an establishment. Of course, the most unlikely people always wound up where you least expected them. Some of the visitors to the manor back in Bezantur would have certainly raised eyebrows were their appetites ever to be made known publicly.

Steeling herself, Ythnel pushed through the door and hit a wall of sound. What had been only a muffled hodgepodge of noise outside transformed into a roar of distinct activities: the knocking of wooden tankards, the booming of raucous laughter, the skidding of heavy furniture dragged across the floor, and the angry shouting of patrons demanding the fulfillment of their desires. Ythnel stood in the doorway, stunned. Waves of silence rippled out from her as those closest took notice and all eyes were turned upon her.

"If you're lost, darlin', I'll be more'n happy ta take ya home." The anonymous catcall brought a chorus of chuckles and snapped Ythnel out of her momentary daze. Disguised as she was, she could not afford to be caught off guard in a place like this. Confidence would be her greatest weapon. Holding her chin up, Ythnel strode toward the bar, ignoring the lecherous leers from patrons and the hateful glares of the wenches who normally serviced the Tooth's clientele. She scanned the booths and tables as she crossed the sawdust-covered floor but saw no sign of Naeros.

When she reached the bar, there was nowhere to stand or sit. A tall, husky man with a clean-shaved pate and a gold hoop in his right ear shoved another patron who had passed out on a stool. A puddle of drool had formed around his head as it lay on the bar. The push sent the unconscious drunk to the floor, where he continued to snore. Ythnel nodded and took the seat, ordering a tankard of ale from the scruffy bartender.

"So what brings a pretty lady like yourself to this fine establishment?" the husky man asked.

"I'm meeting someone here," Ythnel said, avoiding the man's gaze by searching the crowd.

"Ya shore ya in da right place?" the tavern master asked when he returned with her drink.

"Actually, no," she replied, turning to look at the round face covered in splotches of short, bristly hair. "Is Lord Naeros here?"

"I ain't seen 'im," the bartender said, a knowing grin growing on his mouth, "an' I don' reckon 'e gonna be 'ere tonight." Ythnel nodded, set down her untouched tankard along with a few coins, and got up to leave.

"Where you goin', pretty?" The husky man was suddenly in front of her, his stained vest and the barely contained flesh underneath filling her view. "Just 'cause your 'lord' ain't here don't mean you gotta leave."

"You're quite right," Ythnel said, smiling. "I could certainly enjoy myself with such a fine specimen as yourself." She leaned in, her eyes smoldering, and wet her lips with a lick of her tongue.

"Now, that's what I'm talking abou—uhn." The man grunted as Ythnel delivered a blow to his solar plexus, followed with a heel to his left knee. She gave him another fist just under his sternum, and the man crumpled to the floor on his side. Ythnel stepped over him, ignoring the gaping jaws of the remaining patrons, and left the Vampire's Tooth.

The Black Mercy was only a few blocks west of where Kestus had dropped her off. It was a flat-roofed, single-story building of white stone from which rolled the sounds of merrymaking to mix with the noise of the crowds in the streets outside. Ythnel stood across the street for a few moments, watching well-dressed men and women coming and going from the tavern. With its strategic position near the palace and the apparently higher class of clientele, Ythnel was certain she would find her prey here. She made her way through the celebrants and entered the tavern.

A minstrel played upon a stage to the left. There were tables spread across the center of the taproom, booths on the right wall, and the bar in the back. She spotted Naeros almost immediately. Dressed in a fur-trimmed cloak over a black tunic with the Karanok crest embroidered on his left breast, he sat at a table on the far side of the stage near the bar. A wench snuggled in his lap while he drank and joked with three of his thugs. Ythnel let her gaze stay on Naeros long enough to make eye contact when he finally looked her way. Then she casually looked away and headed for the other end of the bar, feeling his eyes on her the whole way. Ordering a tallglass of wine, she turned to watch the minstrel's performance, keeping track of Naeros from the periphery of her vision. In predictable fashion, he unceremoniously dumped the wench as he stood and sauntered toward her, waving off his henchman when they rose hesitantly to follow. Ythnel continued to ignore him until he spoke.

"I don't believe I've seen you around before. My name is Naeros Karanok." He offered her a smile she was sure he thought was his most charming.

"I know who you are," she said, sparing him a quick glance before taking a sip of her wine and returning her attention to the stage, a coy smile on her lips.

"Well, then, you have me at a disadvantage, and I hate being at a disadvantage. Might I know your name?"

"I am Reary."

"It is a pleasure to meet you, Reary." He took her free hand and brought it to his lips. "Would you care to join me?" He motioned to the wall of booths.

"They are all full, my lord."

"Something I will remedy immediately." Naeros moved to the nearest both and cleared his throat. The occupants looked at who was standing before them and quickly vacated. Naeros smiled at Ythnel and offered her a seat first; then he sat opposite her. A serving girl appeared, and Naeros ordered a bottle of wine for them. When the serving girl returned with the bottle and an empty tallglass, Naeros refilled Ythnel's glass then poured his own. He sniffed the bouquet then clinked his glass off hers and took a sip.

"So I haven't seen you before, and your name is not common to this region. I'm guessing you're a visitor to our fair city. Is this your first time to Luthcheq?"

Ythnel took a sip of her wine and smiled. The man

was quite astute. She would have to be careful and not give herself away. "No, my lord. I've been here once before."

"And what brought you back, business or pleasure?"

"A little of both. Truth be told, you're the reason I came back." Ythnel knew she was taking a gamble. Being this forward might put him off or make him suspicious.

Fortunately, it appeared his ego was quite large enough to accept that a beautiful woman would come back to Luthcheq just to meet him. He arched his eyebrow at Ythnel and leaned toward her, placing his hand over hers.

"Really? Why would that be?"

"You have quite a ... reputation. I wanted to see such a man for myself." Ythnel smiled through her eyelashes, her foot rubbing against Naeros's calf under the table.

"Well, you've seen me now. What do you think?"

"That there is more to you than I could possibly learn about sitting here in this tavern."

"That, my dear, is certainly true, but I think I have a solution. Why don't we spend the rest of the evening at my tower?" Without waiting for an answer, Naeros slid from the booth and held his hand out for Ythnel. She smiled and accepted it.

They walked out of the Black Mercy alone, Naeros having dismissed his men. His arm and cloak were draped over Ythnel's shoulder as they maneuvered through the crowd. She half-listened as he went on about himself, going over in her head what she wanted to happen next. So far, everything was moving in the direction she had planned. For a moment, she wondered what Kestus was doing and if she would see him again.

That train of thought was interrupted by a sudden crawling of the skin between Ythnel's shoulder blades. Someone was watching them. She glanced behind them but couldn't see anyone suspicious amongst the revelers.

"What is it?" Naeros asked, stopping.

"Oh, nothing really," Ythnel lied. "I'm just amazed at the enthusiasm of the people. It must be freezing out here, yet no one seems to care."

"Chessentans do love their celebrations, and the citizens of Luthcheq even more so." Naeros smiled and led her on again. They crossed the manicured grounds of Naeros's tower, the sounds of the Midwinter festival suddenly distant as they passed under the great trees that formed a semicircular barrier between the Karanok home and city. They stopped before a single wooden door at the base of the tower. While Naeros fumbled for his key, movement back in the trees caught Ythnel's eye. She studied the shadows but couldn't make out anything except thick trunks and leafless branches. A click signaled Naeros's success at unlocking the door, which he held open for Ythnel. Shaking her head at whatever phantoms her nerves were conjuring, Ythnel turned and walked inside.

Therescales weaved his way through the celebrants, his cloak wrapped tightly around him, his focus straight ahead. It was time to leave Luthcheq. Jaerios had been dropping some not-so-subtle hints that Therescales' usefulness to him was quickly waning. With the Mage Society gone, that left Therescales as the only remaining wizard within the city, and Jaerios was ready to concentrate his efforts on purging the arcane elsewhere. He did not want to have to worry anymore about its presence at home.

So, always trying to stay one step ahead of the madman, Therescales decided to make his exit. Tonight, under the cover of the citywide festival, was the perfect opportunity. There were just a few things to pick up from his home first.

He climbed the steps to the front door of the house once owned by his former mentor. The irony of the choice to live here after Haraxius was executed by the Karanoks had always amused Therescales, though in hindsight, he was surprised it had never aroused suspicion among the society. With a shrug of his shoulders, Therescales unlocked his door and walked inside. It was nothing he had to worry about anymore.

Lighting a candle at the entryway, Therescales headed down the hall to his bedroom. He grabbed a couple of changes of clothing and shoved them in a pack. He went to the kitchen next and stuffed some bread and dried meat into an empty sack. All that was left were a few items to gather from the study. He crossed the living room and spoke the command that opened a secret panel in the wall.

"Hello, Brother Asp."

Therescales whirled back to the living room, searching for the source of the voice, but no one was there. Then he heard chanting, and a figure appeared before him. He reached for his dagger, but his limbs felt like lead. In seconds, he was unable to move except to breathe, paralyzed by the intruder's spell. Forced to look straight ahead, he studied the man who now stood before him. The face, with brown hair, a square jaw, and intense, dark eyes, was unfamiliar. He wore a gray, undecorated tabard over a robe of purple. Most striking, however, was the gray tint to the man's skin. Whoever he was, he had to be a mage. That was the only way he could have known Therescales' secret identity.

"I doubt you recognize me," the man said, "but you know what I am, don't you." He walked toward Therescales as he spoke. Therescales could see the hatred, the vengeance, burning in his eyes. Realizing this man meant to kill him, Therescales struggled in his mind to overcome the enchantment that held him.

"How could you betray us to the Karanoks?" The man circled Therescales, his arms folded into the sleeves of his robe. "Were the rumors true? Did you turn in Haraxius as well? No, it does not matter. There is still the blood of the society on your hands. I am here to see that the cries of those who died because of you are answered."

The mage stopped and brought up his hands. He began to weave a pattern in the air with them, his voice intoning Draconic syllables. Therescales recognized the incantation, and his adrenaline surged. By sheer force of will, he broke the spell that held him and in one motion, grabbed his dagger and flung it at the spellcaster. The mage didn't even flinch as the blade struck him in the chest with the chink of metal against stone and bounced harmlessly away. A ball of fire began to grow in the air between the man's hands. Therescales crouched, searching for some way to avoid the coming attack. The mage finished his spell and sent the growing fireball hurtling toward Therescales. At the last moment, Therescales leaped backward, and the fireball rushed over his diving form, singeing the front of his clothes as it passed. Seconds later, it impacted on the far wall of the living room, exploding in a shower of flames and creating a hole big enough for a man to walk through to the outside.

Dazed and his ears ringing, Therescales scrambled to his feet, bracing for another arcane blow, but the shockwave of the explosion had knocked the mage prone as well, and the man was just now struggling to get up. Taking his chance, Therescales dashed through the still-burning hole in the wall and out into the street, running for all he was worth and not looking back.

Kestus stood and cursed. The man was as slippery as his Mage Society namesake. Through the flames licking the far wall, he could see Therescales fleeing down the street and knew the man had too great of a head start.

That wasn't about to stop him.

From a pouch on his belt, Kestus produced a licorice root. He had hoped to save this spell as a means of escape should things have gone bad, but now it was his only hope of catching Therescales. Reciting the incantation, he waved his other hand over the root before tossing it into his mouth. It dissolved on his tongue instantly. Then Kestus took off running.

The feeling was exhilarating. Crisp winter air rushed passed him as he sped after Therescales. Once again, the magic made him feel alive. He laughed with the pure joy of it.

Therescales must have heard him, for the man looked over his shoulder and gave a startled cry when he saw the mage closing the gap between them. He darted down a lane to their left, but Kestus followed right behind. Kestus rounded the corner and found himself at the edge of a sea of revelers. Therescales had already waded in and was about halfway through.

Not about to give up now, Kestus shoved his way through, earning sour looks from those he jostled. He didn't bother to apologize. By the time he broke through, Therescales had reached the end of the street. Kestus growled in frustration. He could feel the magic that granted him the extra speed starting to dissipate. If he didn't catch up quickly, he would lose Therescales for good.

That's when a patrol of city guards appeared from the cross-street Therescales was nearing. Upon spotting them, the rogue shouted at them and began pointing back down the street at Kestus. The guards looked his way and began marching toward him. Therescales once more ran off into the night without looking back.

"Azuth's beard," Kestus swore. Several nearby citizens gave him odd looks at the mention of the patron of mages. When they noted his stony skin, they gasped and backed away. "If they think that's bad," he muttered, "wait until they see this." Pulling some dried bat guano and a pinch of sulfur from his pouch, Kestus began casting the same spell he had used in Therescales' home. The ball of fire formed in the air before him, and he sent it hurtling toward the approaching guards. The crowd behind Kestus gasped when it exploded as it reached the patrol. When the smoke cleared, four charred bodies lay in the middle of the street.

"It's a wizard," someone cried, which brought several screams from individuals in the crowd. The reaction was not unexpected, but it still caused Kestus's heart to ache. Why couldn't they realize what he already knew? On an impulse, he decided to show them. He turned to the crowd.

"Don't be afraid," he called out to them. "Magic is not evil. That is a lie propagated by the Karanoks. It is a tool, like a smith's hammer or a carpenter's saw. It can create beautiful things." Kestus evoked a cantrip he had learned long ago and sent a dazzling flare of light high up into the night sky where it burst like a falling star. Murmurs of appreciation rose from the crowd.

"I was born and raised in this city," Kestus continued, drawing the crowd's attention back to him. "I have been persecuted by the Karanoks because of my ability, my craft." He was working them now. A glance at the buildings around him had reminded Kestus that he was practically in the center of the merchant district of Luthcheq. Sister Rat's report on the tension between the city's business class and the Karanoks sprang to mind. Perhaps he could get the anger seething just under the surface to finally erupt.

"I am tired of that persecution, and I'm making a stand. The Karanoks can no longer impose their tyrannical will on me. And you should stand up to them as well."

"Why?" someone shouted. "We're not wizards." That brought a few nervous chuckles from the crowd.

"No, but you are oppressed just the same. The Karanoks have increased the taxes they levy against you in order to fund this crusade of theirs. They fear magic, and they are desperate to be rid of it. If we got rid of them, however, not only would those taxes be lifted, but it would no longer be illegal to use magic or trade with those who do."

Kestus could hear the gathered citizens start to talk amongst themselves. His heart raced. Had he gotten through to them? Were they going to follow him against the Karanoks? He held his breath.

The tromping of metal-shod feet echoed from down the street. Kestus turned to see a large contingent of city guards appear, bristling with crossbows and spears. Swept up by the idea of leading a rebellion, he called to the crowd once more.

"Now is our chance to rise up and throw off the chains the Karanoks have wrapped around our necks. Are you with me?"

A couple of errant crossbow bolts whizzed over the heads of the crowd and bounced off nearby buildings. As one, the crowd screamed and ran the other way. Kestus swore. He looked back to the approaching guards. There were too many to take out before they reached him. Kestus sprinted after the crowd, his speed back to normal now that the spell had worn off. He made it back to the street where Therescales' house was and paused, trying to decide what to do. He wondered how Ythnel was faring. Even though his personal quest for vengeance had failed, perhaps he could find her and help her still.

First he would need to lose the guards. Word of a wizard loose on foot in the city would spread quickly. He needed a better way to get around.

He spotted an unattended carriage parked by the curb another block up.

The sounds of celebration spilled from the building as Kestus approached. No one was standing around outside, so he climbed into the driver's seat and took the reins in hand. As he slapped the horses into motion, a man stepped from the alley next to the building, frantically lacing up the front of his britches.

"Hey, stop! Where are you going with that carriage?"

"Consider it your Midwinter present to me!" Kestus hollered over his shoulder as he sped down the street.

"And these are my chambers." Naeros swung the ornate, wooden door inward, revealing a large, four-poster bed draped in silk sheets of dark red. He let Reary enter in front of him, pausing in the doorway to watch her as her eyes swept across the room. He smiled at the thought of how undoubtedly impressed she had to be with his collection of handcrafted furniture; a matching armoire and desk completed the set he had had imported from the forests of the Great Dale. He closed the door behind himself with a soft click and came up behind Reary, putting his hands on her now-bare shoulders. Her creamy white skin was smooth and warm to his touch. He leaned in to inhale the fragrance of her hair, but she pulled away, striding over to one of the stone walls.

"What's this?" She asked, examining a loop of braided leather attached to a six-inch handle hanging on the wall. Every few inches along the braid, a metal bead was embedded.

"That is whip. I collect them," he said proudly, sweeping his arm out to encompass the room. He studied Reary for a reaction as she noticed for the first time the various whips hanging at intervals on the walls of the chamber. "It's a hobby of mine."

"I never realized there were so many different kinds." There was genuine surprise in her voice. And something else was there as well—interest. Her face registered no shock, however.

"Well, that concludes the tour." Naeros put on a sly smile and once more approached Reary. "What do you think?"

"You are a very interesting man, Lord Naeros," Reary breathed. She turned to face him, draping her arms around his neck. The puffy, diaphanous material of her sleeves tickled his neck when her hands slid up to lock behind his head. Naeros ran his fingers along the tops of her arms, following the sleeves to where they ended at a pair of straps connecting them to the bodice of her blouse. Then he stroked her hair with his right hand while his left moved down to her waist. "Do you bring all the girls up here?"

"Yes." Naeros grinned and pulled her to him, kissing her savagely. She returned the embrace with equal force. He swept her up and carried her to the bed, falling on top of her. She ripped off his shirt, laughing, and he could feel desire burst into flame within him. They rolled on top of the sheets, kissing and grappling with abandon. Reary maneuvered herself to a straddling position atop Naeros then pulled away, breathing heavily.

"Don't tell me you're tired already," Naeros chided.

"Hardly." Reary smiled wickedly and lunged for him. As they kissed, she grabbed his lip between her teeth and bit hard. Naeros tasted something coppery in his mouth and shoved her back. He touched his finger to his mouth and came away with blood.

"What the . . ." he snarled, sitting up. Reary laughed, and Naeros felt his face flush. He backhanded her across the cheek, and her head snapped to the side with the impact, the long tresses of her blonde hair whipping around to cover her face. She sat there silently for a moment, her head hanging within the shrouds of her hair.

"You shouldn't have done that." Naeros's brow furrowed, frustrated by this strange woman.

"So you're the only one who gets to play rough, then?" Reary still hadn't moved, and there was something different about her voice. "That's rather selfish, don't you think." Naeros's eyes widened as Reary's blonde hair shimmered and darkened, the locks on the left side of her head disappearing to reveal a serpent tattoo stretched across her bare scalp.

"In fact, I'm willing to bet you're as much a child in bed as you are in your little torture chamber." Reary's head swung around, and Naeros's jaw dropped when he saw two familiar scars running down the right side of her face.

"You!"

The Loviatan he had once held prisoner in his dungeon laughed again and raised her right hand. Naeros glanced at it and saw it was surrounded by a dark halo of energy. He cried out as she slammed it into his chest. He could feel the energy disperse throughout his body, causing his muscles to convulse. With his last ounce of control, he shoved the cleric off of him, sending her to the floor at the foot of the bed. Then he collapsed back onto the bed, his muscles quivering like jelly.

The Loviatan rose like a specter from the floor to gaze down on him with eyes that promised retribution. She turned and moved quickly to stand before a wooden-handled instrument with a single, thick braid of rope almost two feet long that tapered before flaring out in an oval knot at the tip. She removed it from its hook and held it in her right hand, letting the leather fringe where the rope fastened to the handle play across her fingers as she rolled her wrist back and forth, testing the weapon's balance.

"You don't see nagaikas much anymore," the cleric said, walking casually back to the bed. "Some genius thought they might make a good riding whip, but they're a little heavy. You could really hurt an animal if you didn't know how to use it just right." Her smile was cruel and mocking. "No, they're much better suited for doling out punishment."

Naeros pushed himself up. He felt exhausted, as if every muscle had been taxed to its limit and there was nothing left. The Loviatan lashed out with the nagaika, striking him solidly in the cheek. He reeled with the blow but was unable to catch himself and rolled off the far side of the bed. His face throbbed where the knot struck; any harder and his jaw might have broken.

"Where are you going, Lord Naeros? Surely you're not tired already."

"I'm going to kill you, whore." Naeros struggled to raise himself up on all fours, his limbs trembling.

"Oh, I doubt that." The cleric rounded the corner of the bed, her slippered feet coming into Naeros's view. "It looks like you can barely hold yourself up." He raised his head in time to see the nagaika descend, and he flinched defensively, but instead of the knot slamming into him, he felt a sudden sting on his shoulder. It came again and again across his exposed back, until his flesh burned and Naeros could feel trickles of warm wetness running down his sides. He moaned and collapsed to the cool stone of the floor.

"I should have known you could dish it out but not take it," the Loviatan sneered. "If I had the time, I'd see just how far I could take you. There are other things I have to attend to, however. Fortunately, they'll likely bring you as much suffering as any beating I could administer." She bent down, raised his chin with her fingers, and kissed him hard, breaking his lip once more between her teeth as she pulled away. Then she stood, walked to the wall, exchanged the nagaika for a bullwhip, and left the room without looking back.

Naeros lay there panting until the sound of the

cleric's footfalls had long faded. When strength began to flow back into his muscles, he pulled himself along the floor to the side of the bed and propped himself up against the post. He closed his eyes again, concentrating on the rise and fall of his chest with each breath he took. Whatever the witch had done to him was starting to wear off. A few more seconds and he'd go after her. Then he'd show her a beating she'd never forget.

"My, my, what have we here?"

Naeros's eyes sprang open at the sultry voice, his heart beating wildly with fear that the Loviatan had returned. When he turned to look, he let his breath out and sagged back against the bed. It was only his sister, Saestra, dressed in a black, lacy gown that flared at the wrists and ankles.

"Go away, Saestra. I'm not in the mood for your games right now."

"Oh, I'm sorry. Did your conquest not go well tonight?"

"That's none of your damn business. Besides, what are you doing here anyway?" Naeros let his frustration edge his voice. His sister leaned against the door frame, staring at him with a wild look in her eyes. "Are you going to just stand there, or are you going to help me?" He frowned and shifted, uncomfortable under Saestra's gaze.

"Help you?" She laughed. "How delightful. Dear brother, where were you when *I* needed help?"

"What are you talking about?"

"Have you forgotten so quickly? It wasn't that long ago. A sister follows the advice of her older brother and meets her young lover in The Crypts for a late-night tryst. The pair investigates an open mausoleum, only to be locked inside by the older brother. When they cry for help, they are answered with cruel laughter. Surely you remember all that?

"What you don't know is that while seeking a way out, the two lovers found a secret passage that led to a hidden chamber below the tomb. Within that chamber, they came face-to-face with its undead resident. The creature savagely killed the sister's lover and made her its servant." Saestra shivered, and her eyes, which had been looking somewhere far off, came riveting back to lock on Naeros. He shrank back at the feral death he saw within them.

"I'm sorry, Saestra. It was just a practical joke. I never meant for anything to happen."

"Shut up!" She snarled, and Naeros saw the fangs hiding behind her lips. "You left me to die that night. And I did. I became a monster because of you! I can still feel his cold embrace. Do you know what that's like?"

Naeros shook his head frantically.

"Then why don't I show you." She lunged for him.

THE **P**RIESTS

Ythnel crept down the stairs, her back to the wall and the coiled whip in her right hand. That fool Naeros had made the task of locating the witchweed stockpile much easier with his little tour. The one place he had not taken her was down to the cellar of the tower. As there was nowhere for the witchweed to be stored in the places he had shown her, that left the cellar as the only place it could be.

Most of the servants had been dismissed for the night, allowed to attend the city's Midwinter celebrations. Still, when she reached each landing, she paused and peeked her head around corners or through doorways. Quick glances confirmed that the tower was relatively empty, and reassured, Ythnel moved on. She came to the main floor and glided across the foyer between the tower entrance and the parlor, her slippers thankfully muffling the sounds of her steps. Before she could start down the next flight of stairs, however, there was a noise at the door. Ythnel ducked into the parlor and flattened herself against the near wall just as the thick, wooden entry door swung open and Naeros's three henchmen strolled in, chuckling about something. Ythnel tensed and let the whip uncoil from her hand.

A shout echoed down the stairs leading back to Naeros's chambers. From her vantage point, Ythnel watched as the three men raced upward, calling out to their lord. Ythnel let go of a breath she hadn't realized she was holding and slid back around the wall. Darting a glance over her shoulder, she descended once more.

Torches set in black iron sconces at the base of the stairs cast their flickering orange and yellow light across the stone walls, vainly attempting to soften the cold, hard reality. The cellar was a single hallway dug out of the earth, the stonework ending with the last step. Three steel doors stood closed along the hall, one at the far end and the other two opposite each other about halfway down from where Ythnel stood.

Not knowing which one led to the witchweed, she was forced to open each door. Behind the first one was a room full of casks of ale and racks of wine bottles. Some burlap sacks marked as dry goods of various sorts were stacked in one corner.

Ythnel opened the second door and sucked in her breath. Down a short flight of steps was the torture chamber where Naeros had beaten her. The chains which had once held her hung limp and empty from the ceiling. The flesh of her wrists itched from the memory.

For a moment, Ythnel was frozen with emotional turmoil. Anger and fear swelled together, fighting each other for control. The conflict did not have the strength to sustain itself, however. Ythnel had already fought this fight, had accepted the pain and suffering, had endured it to come out tempered and honed on the other side. What had happened in this room seemed so long ago now. It had no power over her. Anger and fear fled, replaced by a resolve as hard as cold steel.

Ythnel closed the door and moved to the end of the hall. This was the last room; the witchweed had to be in there. She flung the door open, suddenly impatient to be out of the tower. Inside were stacks of crates, barrels, and sacks. Ythnel ripped open a sack and found dried leaves stuffed inside. It was the witchweed. She jogged back down the hall and grabbed one of the torches from its sconce. When she returned to the room, she held the torch's flame to the open bag until the leaves shriveled and the burlap began to burn. Then she set the torch down and quickly moved the ignited bag next to a stack of crates. She ripped open several more bags, scattering their contents around the room and laying the sacks at the base of a group of barrels or crates. Satisfied with her effort, she picked the torch back up and lit more of the sacks until small blazes were crackling all over the room. Ythnel stepped out of the room, tossed the torch back over her shoulder, and slammed the door shut.

Ythnel bounded back up the stairs to the main level and skidded to a halt in the foyer. On the stairs across from her appeared one of Naeros's men. Caught by surprise, she could only stare as he stumbled into the foyer. He held his blood-soaked hands in front of him, shock registering on a face smeared in blood as well. Ythnel could not tell if it was his or someone else's.

There was so much. He finally noticed her at the top of the steps, but before she could react, he dropped to the floor and lay motionless.

Something inside Ythnel yearned to go up those stairs to see what had happened. She hesitated, pulled between curiosity and duty. With an imperceptible shake of her head, Ythnel turned to the door and left the tower.

She sprinted across the grounds; there was no time to waste. Who knew how long the Midwinter celebrations would last? She needed the distraction just a little longer. Where there had been milling citizens before she entered the tower, however, there was only an empty street. Fear gripped Ythnel. Had she taken too long? A group of people ran by, and Ythnel yanked aside a straggler.

"Where is everybody?" When the young man gave her a strange look, she added, "I was hoping to still do some celebrating."

"Oh, there are still plenty of festivities. There's a gathering over by the palace where some minstrels are playing. We were going to check out this building that's on fire. You want to join us?"

Without thinking, Ythnel looked back over her shoulder to the tower, expecting to see smoke billowing out the top. There was nothing.

"It's over there." He pointed to the southwest, and Ythnel saw a pillar of smoke rising from somewhere in the middle of the quarter.

"As interesting as that looks, I think I'll head over to the palace." Ythnel let the youth go, and he hurried off to catch up with his friends. As she turned down the street toward the palace, she wondered what else might be going on in Luthcheq and whether it would help or hinder her mission.

There was indeed a large crowd gathered before the palace, and several minstrel groups were playing various instruments. Those who had long since shed their inhibitions through alcohol were dancing with abandon to the music of their choice. To Ythnel, some looked as if it were to music only they could hear. Others, paired off on the fringes, embraced their partners for warmth or more intimate purposes. Ythnel waded into the middle. She was often jostled by flailing revelers, but she shouldered her way through undaunted. She had to stop and stand on her toes to orient herself on the palace every so often; the shifting and bumping of the dancers kept throwing her off course. Finally she broke through and found herself in a small space of calm surrounding the palace gate. A single guard stood watch there wearing his ceremonial helmet and breastplate and carrying a spear. Thinking quickly, Ythnel held the whip still in her hand behind her back and lurched toward the guard.

"Halt, you are not allowed—"

Before he could finish, Ythnel stumbled into him. She reached up as if to kiss him and whispered the command to trigger one of the spells stored in the ring Hercubes had given her. There was no flash of light or ringing chime to signal it had worked, but Ythnel felt the guard relax slightly against her.

"What did you say?" he asked.

"You're going to make me say that again? Out here where everybody could hear?" She blushed and batted her eyelashes. The guard looked at her in confusion, which changed to understanding when she pushed up against him.

"Well, I can't say as you're exactly the prettiest girl I ever seen, and if the captain finds out I left my post, I'll be in a heap of trouble."

"He doesn't have to know," Ythnel purred. "And we just have to go somewhere no one will see us. Like behind those bushes on the other side of the gate. C'mon. Don't make me wait."

"All right, all right. If you want it so bad, I'm not about to be the one to say no."

He fumbled with his keys, unlocked the gate, pulled Ythnel through, and closed it behind them. While his back was to her, Ythnel darted behind a nearby hedge. He turned around, a look of surprise on his face, as he scanned the grounds for her. She extended her arm so he would see where she hid, her finger crooked in a come-hither motion. He chuckled and followed her.

When he came around the hedge, Ythnel was waiting for him. She snapped the bullwhip out, lassoing his ankle and yanking his feet out from under him. His head hit a paving stone with a crack and bounced once. Ythnel walked up to his motionless body and unwrapped the whip. Then she stripped off his armor and put it on over her own clothes. The helmet was a little loose, even with her hair stuffed up inside. Thankfully, her chest was no longer enhanced by the transmutation spell to the point where the breastplate would have been painfully uncomfortable. When the straps were securely fastened, Ythnel hung the whip off her belt, grabbed the spear, and headed to the palace.

As she climbed the steps to the palace doors, Ythnel scrambled for a plan. The palace was easily twice the size of Naeros's tower, and she had no idea where the stockpile of witchweed might be stored within. She was going to have to risk asking someone and pray that the armor was enough for her to pass as a guard.

The great bronze doors at the top of the grand

staircase swung inward ponderously but quietly, their hinges obviously well cared for. Ythnel found herself in a large entryway decorated with marble statues of nude athletes in each of the four corners. Another set of doors stood closed in the far wall, though these were of polished wood with the Karanok crest carved in bas-relief at eye level. Two single doors were located on the right and left walls.

Beyond the inner doors was a high-ceilinged room that appeared to serve as some sort of lounge. Two low tables were surrounded by several comfortable-looking chairs. Ythnel weaved her way through the furniture to a single door in the far wall. She paused for a moment, a kernel of inner doubt questioning whether proceeding was the smartest plan. The only way you'll convince anyone you're a guard is if you walk with confidence, she reminded herself.

Nodding to herself, she pulled the door open and stepped into a vast hall with arch-vaulted ceilings. She had caught only a glimpse of it the last time she was here, before she had been ushered through the double doors across from her, twins of the set that led into the palace from the entryway. She craned her neck, taking in the sweeping arches of white stone from which hung multicolored banners and exquisite tapestries decorated in floral patterns that framed various scenes of athletic competition.

Footfalls echoed from down the hall to Ythnel's left, jerking her from her inspection of the ceiling. A guard wouldn't be gazing at the architecture. She turned to face whoever approached and saw someone in the black-and-gold-trimmed white livery of House Karanok. The corner of her mouth quirked up in a half-smile; bluffing a servant would be much easier than if she were to face another guard.

She met the man halfway, putting her hand up to stop him. His look of annoyance changed to one of confusion, mixed with a hint of fear when he realized who had stopped him. His bowl-cut hair and large nose made it was almost comical.

"What can I do for you, sir? Is everything all right?"

"Nothing for you to worry about. I just need to know where the witchweed is kept."

"I-I don't know. I just clean the family chambers upstairs."

"Then who would know? I don't have time to be stopping everyone wandering in the halls and ask."

"Whoever's on duty downstairs in the guard post would know. You should check with them." The servant was looking up at her strangely, but he glanced back at his feet when she narrowed her eyes.

"You've wasted enough of my time, then. I hope you aren't this disrespectful with the other guards. I've half a mind to report you."

"Oh, no, sir. I didn't mean anything. I'm terribly sorry." He bowed hastily and scuttled away.

Ythnel sighed. She should have known better than to think it was going to be easy. It looked as if she would have to try to bluff her way past the guards after all. Recalling the stairs she had climbed from the palace dungeons on her previous visit, Ythnel moved down the hall to her right until she came to the first door past the entrance to the audience chamber. It opened to a torch-lit corridor that angled to her right and ended in a flight of steps leading under the palace.

At the base of the stairs, she found herself in a large space separated from the rest of the dungeon by walls of bars on two sides. To her left were the cells, one of which she had been kept in. The room itself held a table with a couple of chairs, a desk, and a cot. A guard sat hunched over the desk.

"What do you want?" he asked disinterestedly. Apparently he had heard her coming down the stairs. Uncertain how to answer, Ythnel cleared her throat. The guard stopped whatever he was doing and turned to face her. It was Corporal Urler from before!

"Do I know you?" he asked, squinting at her from his seat.

"Uh, no, I'm normally stationed out on the west wall."

"What are you doin' here?"

"There have been some fires in the city." Ythnel's mind scrambled for words, ideas coming each time only as she started to open her mouth. "One of the fires is at Lord Naeros's tower. His stockpile of witchweed was torched. I was sent over here to guard the palace's storeroom in case it was also a target."

"There's no way anybody could git past the palace gate, let alone make it down here," Corporal Urler bragged.

"I'm just following orders," Ythnel shrugged. "If you want to vouch for—"

"All right. No need fer that." He got up and moved to the gate that led farther into the dungeon. "You waitin' fer an invitation? Come on."

The hallway was lit by a single torch about halfway down its length. They passed a closed door on the right, followed by an open archway that led into a large chamber hidden in shadows. As they neared the end of the hall, a door stood in the left wall. Corporal Urler stopped before it, removed a ring of keys from his belt, and unlocked the door.

"Here you go."

Ythnel spoke two harsh words born in the depths

of the Abyss and struck out with her hand, grabbing a hold of the guard's face. The dark aura of the Power exploded around wherever her flesh touched his, and small gashes began to appear on his exposed skin. With a strangled cry, he stumbled away from Ythnel, but the damage was already done. Blood poured from open wounds as he backpedaled into the wall and slid to the floor. By the time he hit the ground, he had stopped breathing and his eyes were rolled back into his head.

Ythnel dragged Corporal Urler's body into the room. It wouldn't do to have someone come down the hall and notice him there. Grabbing the torch from its place on the wall, Ythnel set to work. When she had several fires going, she closed and locked the door behind herself. On her way out, she tossed the keys into the corner of one of the far cells then headed back up the stairs.

Once more in the great hallway, Ythnel turned to leave the palace but paused. Something nagged at her in the back of her mind. A memory stirred of her standing bound in the audience chamber before Jaerios Karanok. From his robe he withdrew a medallion in the shape of a scourge. It was her medallion, and here was her opportunity to retrieve it.

It was a crazy idea. The likelihood that he even still had it was remote. The chance that she could find it if he did was even smaller. Yet she had to try. It was one more thing the Karanoks had taken from her, and she meant to have it all back. The servant had said the family lived on the second floor. She would start looking there.

From where she stood, Ythnel could see a stairway that led up just past the protruding corner of the audience chamber. She darted across the hall and ascended.

The stairs ended in another great hall much like the one below. The numerous tapestries hanging along the full length of the hall, however, depicted members of the Karanok family, often in locations Ythnel guessed were somewhere in the city. While she recognized a few faces, there were many she did not. She hoped the unfamiliar ones were from generations past. It was an unsettling thought that this fanatical family might be so prolific that the woven portraits represented numbers in their current ranks.

Even if it were so, there was nothing Ythnel could do about it. It was best to concentrate on the problems at hand, and her largest one was determining which of the many doors lining the hall led to the chambers of Jaerios Karanok. Checking each one would not only take an incredible amount of time she did not have, but it would also greatly increase her risk of discovery. Yet she had no way of knowing otherwise.

Caught by indecision, Ythnel remained rooted at the top of the stairs. There were three doors within twenty feet of her, two to her left at the end of the hall and one straight ahead. While she debated which one to open, a noise at the bottom of the stairwell caught her attention. Someone was coming upstairs, and whoever it was, was moving quickly. Forced to choose before she was discovered, Ythnel moved briskly to the end of the hall and tried the door on her right. It opened, and she stepped inside without looking, just as she heard whoever was behind her reach the top of the stairs. She left the door cracked enough to peer back out into the hall. An older man in a white night robe, his head crowned in a wreath of gray hair, swept around the corner from the stairs and headed down the hall away from Ythnel. At about fifty feet, he turned to his left and disappeared down a passage

Ythnel hadn't realized was there. Moments later, she heard the distant echo of someone knocking, and a muffled voice calling for Lord Jaerios. Then there was silence.

While Ythnel waited, crouched behind the door, it occurred to her she didn't know where she was hiding. She turned, half expecting to see the room's occupant glaring at her balefully. Fortunately, there was no one. Moonlight spilled in from a window in the wall to her left, just five feet from the door. It appeared she was in some sort of study. Bookcases lined the right and back walls. A large desk sat in the middle of the room, with a high-backed chair on the far side and a single, nondescript chair on the near wall. A marble bust stood next to an unlit candelabrum, both bathed in the pale luminescence of the moon. The bust looked familiar, but she couldn't quite place who it was supposed to be.

Voices in the hall returned Ythnel's attention to the door.

"The fire in the palace is contained to the dungeon, my lord. However, with at least two other fires burning in the city, I thought it prudent you were notified."

The older man in the robe she had seen earlier came into view first, talking over his shoulder to someone behind. Before he finished speaking, Ythnel saw who followed. Lord Jaerios's gray-streaked dark curls were tousled, and he wore a silk robe of deep crimson over his night clothes. His current state was a far cry from the regal commander she remembered seeing, but there was no mistaking the man who had condemned Ythnel to death. The pair was trailed by a single guard as they made their way to the stairs. It was all Ythnel could do not to rush out and attack them. Her retribution on Jaerios would have to take another form, however. She could not risk an alarm being raised now.

Once the three passed beyond range of her hearing, Ythnel slipped out of the study and down the hall to Jaerios's chambers. The short passage off the main hall led about twenty feet before turning sharply to the right to end at a closed door. It was the room beyond the open door at the corner of the passage that Ythnel entered. The long, rectangular room had two windows in the far corner, one on each wall. While less ostentatious than his son's room, Jaerios's bedchamber was still richly furnished. The four-poster bed against the wall to the right of the door was a dark-stained wood with beautiful grain and lightly gilded trim along the head- and footboards. A matching bureau stood just to the left of the door. In the far corner was a writing desk and chair, positioned so that whoever sat at it would have excellent views of the palace grounds out both windows.

Closing the door to prevent anyone from hearing her search, Ythnel rummaged through the bureau drawers first. She pulled handfuls of neatly folded clothing from their resting places and tossed them to the floor, but her efforts yielded nothing. Her scourge medallion was not tucked beneath a stack of underclothes, nor did any of the drawers have a false bottom in which something could be hidden.

Frustrated, Ythnel stormed over to the writing table. She gave a cursory glance to a freshly inked letter that seemed to be informing an ally or family member that the purging of Luthcheq had finally been accomplished. With a dismissive snort, she set it back down and inspected the other objects that sat on the desktop. A small ceramic jar held a dark fluid that Ythnel guessed was ink, but was too narrow at the neck to have stored her medallion. The slender, wood box next to it kept Jaerios's writing quill. Ythnel sighed, ready to give up. The desk had a center drawer, but at this point, she felt certain the medallion wouldn't be found. Shrugging to herself, she decided to check anyway, opening the drawer only partway with a half-hearted tug. A ream of blank parchment was stacked inside, slightly skewed from the force of the drawer opening. Ythnel started to push the drawer shut when she noticed a slight bulge in the center of the stack of paper.

Opening the drawer the rest of the way, she lifted the corner of the pile and looked underneath. There lay the small scourge, nine straps of five-inch long leather secured to a four-inch handle of iron. Ythnel smiled triumphantly as she scooped up the medallion and fastened it around her neck by two of the leather straps. She felt whole again with it tucked under her breastplate and nestled against the flesh of her chest; an emptiness in her heart she had tried to ignore was now filled. Regardless of what she had been taught during her time at the manor, this symbol of her faith had become a link to her goddess she could not do without, and she intended to never lose it again.

Her purpose accomplished, all that was left for Ythnel was to figure out how to leave. Walking back out the front door was not going to be an option. The fire in the witchweed storeroom had likely alerted the palace to the presence of a malicious agent, and anyone who could not be readily identified would be stopped and questioned. She would have to find an alternate means of escape. It was not an easy task considering she was unfamiliar with the layout of the palace. Standing around in Jaerios's bedchambers was not going to change that, though it might certainly increase her chances of getting caught. Still pondering what to do, Ythnel left the room and headed back down the hall toward the steps. She paused at the head of the staircase, listening for the sound of anyone approaching. She could hear the echoes of footsteps and the murmurs of distant voices, but the sounds came and went, with no one appearing at the bottom of the stairs.

Perhaps they were still fighting to contain the fire in the dungeon, Ythnel thought. Even so, that did not change her options. The activity below told her that she would be discovered before she could cross the great hall.

Feeling exposed, Ythnel decided to hide in the empty study to think things through further. She left the door cracked again so she could hear in case someone climbed the stairs to this level. For several moments, she paced in silence before the single window, which was divided into many square panes by thin strips of wood and stretched from floor to ceiling. The grounds outside extended off into the darkness. A single outbuilding sat a few yards away at the edge of visibility. Ythnel paused and looked up into the night sky. Clouds were converging, the stars no longer visible and the moon a pale haze behind the billowy, dark gray forms. No torches or lanterns where lit on this side of the palace. It was as though this small section of Luthcheq was cut off from the rest of the world.

Inspiration struck Ythnel, but she would have to move fast. The fire would occupy the attention of people inside the palace, but what she planned would probably make enough noise that anyone outside might come to investigate. She moved to the chair on the near side of the desk but changed her mind and went to the pedestal that supported the marble bust. She had finally recognized who it was and thought it fitting that Lord Jaerios would aid her escape. Ythnel tried to rock the pedestal, but it wouldn't budge. For a moment, she panicked, unsure if she could get her idea to work. But she swung around so she was between the window and the pedestal and began to slide the bust to the edge. It was incredibly heavy, and she wondered if she would drop it once its full weight was brought to bear. She paused for a moment to gather her strength, and with one last effort, Ythnel pulled the bust from its pedestal, letting the statue's weight and the momentum pivot her around. She released the bust as she turned toward the window, and the marble piece crashed through the glass and wood to fall head-first, so to speak, almost twenty feet to the paving below and shatter.

There was no time to catch her breath. Ythnel shoved and tugged the heavy desk toward the broken window until it was just a few inches from the ledge. Taking her whip from her belt, she tightly wound the tapered end around one of the desk's legs. She gave it a few hard tugs to make sure it wouldn't come undone and the desk didn't move. Then she tossed the handle out the window. Peering down, Ythnel saw it come up short, leaving her a good drop of at least six feet. For a moment, she considered running back to Jaerios's bedchamber and grabbing his sheets, but she decided it would take too long. Knocking several large pieces of glass out of the way, Ythnel let her spear fall to the ground outside, swung over the edge and lowered herself down the whip. She dangled for a breath when she reached the handle, looking at the ground below, before letting go to land on the balls of her feet. Forced to leave the whip behind, Ythnel retrieved her spear, darted to the corner of the palace, and glanced at the gate. A group of guards huddled there, but they broke apart as she watched, some heading back out into the streets and others to the palace. Ythnel ducked back behind the corner, and when she checked again, only one guard remained.

Ythnel skirted along the front of the building, keeping her back to the stone, until she reached the side of the grand staircase. Then she drew herself up and moved boldly out into the courtyard toward the gate.

"It's starting to get crowded in there," she said gruffly as she neared the gate guard. "Captain ordered me back to my regular station."

Without waiting for a reply, Ythnel jerked the gate open and walked into the street. Citizens still clogged the area, but any celebrations had ceased, and most were craning their necks to catch a brief glimpse of what was happening beyond the gate. Some were whispering to one another in anxious voices about what was going on. They parted easily for Ythnel in her guard disguise as she headed south toward the Temple of Entropy.

THE PRIESTS

Walled off on its own but not gated, the Temple of Entropy stood just south of the Karanok palace. The main building was nearly three stories tall, its center rising well above the outer section. Thick, fluted columns formed a portico around the exterior, winding around the squared-off, U-shaped entrance and disappearing around the sides of the structure. An annex was connected to the north end of the temple, and a single outbuilding squatted to the south. The grounds were dark and quiet; no celebrations were going on here. Ythnel strode through the silence like a nocturnal predator stalking its final prey whose scent was so intense and all-consuming, its presence so close that no other thought entered her mind except to take it down. She sprang past the short flight of steps and slipped into the shadows of the giant columns. The great bronze doors were closed and locked, so Ythnel rapped the butt of her spear against one of them and waited. Soon she heard the click of a key turning in a lock on the other side, and one of the doors came open enough for a robed figure to emerge. Light from inside the temple flooded out onto the portico, forcing Ythnel to squint in the brightness as her eyes struggled to adjust.

"Yes, what is it?" The figure's features where hidden in the shadow of a cowl, but Ythnel knew it was a man from his voice. She could also tell he was not pleased with having to answer the door.

"Someone is setting fires in the city." Ythnel had been rehearsing what she was going to say as she walked to the temple. Her voice was confident but disinterested, as though she were just following orders. "Both Lord Naeros's tower and the palace were targets, and the witchweed stored there was burned. I've been sent to check on the stockpile kept here." She waited expectantly for the invitation to come in.

"Tell your commander that everything's fine. I'm sure we'll be able to handle anyone who tries to break in. Good night." It was obvious from his tone of voice that the temple clergy did not have a high opinion of the city guard. Before Ythnel could protest, the door was closed and locked once more.

She stood there for a moment, stunned. Anger and indignation welled up, and she proceeded to hammer the door with her spear shaft until it swung open again.

"What is going on out—you!" The man who had first answered the door shouted over Ythnel's pounding, his head sticking out past the door. "Why are you still—"

Ythnel swung the butt of the spear and slammed

it against the side of his face. The force of the blow knocked the other side of his head against the closed door, and the man dropped to the ground unconscious. Ythnel grabbed him by the shoulders and dragged him out into the shadows, where she stripped the robe off of him and put it on over her armor. She wrested the ring of keys from his hand, entered the temple, and closed the door behind herself.

Once the doors had been locked, Ythnel turned her attention to where she was. She stood in a bare narthex with walls of flat, white stone. There was a plain, wooden door set opposite the main entrance and three simple, open archways in the left wall that led into the nave of the temple.

What rested in the apse at the far end of the nave explained the lack of decoration, for it commanded Ythnel's attention as soon as her eyes crossed it. Floating just above the floor of the dais was a huge globe of absolute blackness more than twenty feet in diameter. It rested there, unmoving, and Ythnel was reminded of a hole. Absently she wondered, if it were a hole, where did it lead? The stray thought lingered and grew. Perhaps she could spare a goodly breath or three just to satisfy her curiosity. This was, after all, a divine entity, and she had never been in the presence of one, not even Loviatar.

Ythnel took a step into the nave and cast her glance around. There was no one else there, but she wasn't so absorbed by the sphere as to throw caution entirely to the wind. She crept along the gallery on the right side of the nave, using the shadows to mask her movement, though the white priest's robe with its gold trim limited her ability to melt into the background. Her eyes were fixed on the sphere, but it had not changed since she first saw it. She paused at a door about halfway down the gallery, a voice in the back of her head insisting she had spent too long gazing at this object of someone else's worship. There was another reason she was here, a more important task to complete.

A door at the front of the nave creaked open, and out filed a line of robed clerics, Kaestra Karanok in the lead. Ythnel froze in a half-crouch; there really wasn't any good cover between her and the dais. Fortunately, it appeared the Entropists were giving their undivided attention to the sphere. The clerics knelt on the floor at the base of the dais, while Kaestra climbed the first few stairs. Her back to those below, the high priestess raised her arms with her palms toward the sphere and began to chant. The other clerics started to genuflect, adding their own chants as a counterpoint to Kaestra's. The acoustics of the nave sent the echoes bouncing off one another, rendering the meaning of the chants indecipherable to Ythnel. There was nothing further she could gain by standing there, so she tip-toed backward until she felt the rough wood of the door behind her. She opened it in minute increments and slipped through as soon as there was enough space, gently closing the door behind herself.

The side passage she was in ran the length of the nave and rounded the corners at both ends. It was probably a utility corridor, much like those at the manor back in Bezantur, which allowed the clergy and servants to move about the temple without disturbing any worship services that might be going on. Ythnel guessed that the door she had seen in the narthex opened to the hall somewhere behind her, while the door that the Entropists had used to enter the nave lay ahead around the corner. What she really wanted to know was where the witchweed was kept. At the manor, all the storerooms were below the main floor. The layout of this temple was not at all like the manor, so she was reluctant to rely upon any comparisons. She needed to find someone who knew where things were located but wouldn't question inquiries from someone in a robe. She needed a temple servant.

At the manor, the servants' quarters were a floor below those of the members of the church; there were no other buildings on the grounds. A hunch told Ythnel that the Entropists liked to keep themselves separated. Having to share space with servants would be an irritant, something to avoid as much as possible. Giving them their own building where they could spend their off-duty time would be the preferred solution.

Ythnel headed back down the hallway but passed the door that led to the nave. She did not want to go back out the front. The southern end of the temple had jutted out beyond the entrance, and Ythnel was sure there was a side door somewhere farther down the hall that the servants used to enter and exit the building. Sure enough, as she rounded the corner, she found another door on the outside wall. It was locked, but she fumbled through the keys she had taken and found one that worked.

She crossed the distance between the temple and the outbuilding at a trot. Using the same key as before, Ythnel let herself in and tried to get oriented quickly. Stairs to her right led up to a second floor, while a hall lined with doors ran away from her. It had the definite feel of a dormitory to her.

There were several servants milling about in the hall next to some of the doors, speaking amongst themselves. They all seemed to be women. Some noticed her and gave quick curtsies before ducking into their rooms and closing the doors. Not wanting to be left with having to drag somebody out of their room, Ythnel advanced down hall, analyzing the remaining women, trying to decide who to enlist.

When she was about halfway down the hall, a door to her right opened, and a young girl charged out, her eyes on the floor. Oblivious to the presence of anyone around her, she barreled into Ythnel's side. Ythnel turned and grabbed the girl to keep both of them from falling. The girl's eyes widened when she saw the robe. She began to cry, dropping to her knees and stammering an apology between gasps. Ythnel's eyes widened as well. The hair was straight and bobbed at the chin, and the face was a little dirty, but the girl weeping for mercy at her feet was Iuna Saelis.

Once more, the dream from the swamp and Iuna's voice asking Ythnel to show her crystallized in her mind. Ythnel was to be Iuna's instructor, her guide in the teachings of Loviatar. That she should stumble into the girl here only affirmed the revelation. It was a clear sign that Loviatar's hand was behind the recent events in Ythnel's life. But first she had to finish her business with the Karanoks.

"Enough of that," Ythnel said gruffly, falling into the character of a stern priestess. "Stand up." She helped Iuna to her feet, careful not to lean too close and reveal herself just yet. "I need some help, and you've just volunteered yourself, girl."

"Yes, Mistress. I'm so sorry. Whatever you need, I will do my best."

"Hmm, we'll see about that. Follow me." Ythnel led Iuna back across the grounds to the temple and entered through the service door. The past few tendays had been hard on Iuna, it seemed, for this change in demeanor was nothing like the spoiled little girl

Ythnel had first met. She wondered if Kaestra had broken Iuna's spirit, or if that fire had just been banked, the embers waiting for something to breathe life back into them.

"So, Mistress, what is it you need of me, if I might ask?"

Ythnel started, not realizing she had paused while her mind wandered. The question was one she had been avoiding. She knew what she needed, but wasn't sure that the clerical robe alone would be enough to come straight out and ask without raising suspicion. However, she hadn't come up with another way.

"Preparations need to be made to move the witch-weed. The stockpiles at the palace and Lord Naeros's tower have been sabotaged, so extra measures are being taken to protect what remains."

Iuna let a frown wrinkle her brow for a moment, but it vanished when she saw Ythnel looking at her. "Wouldn't that be a task better suited for one of the men, or at least someone bigger than—?"

"Are you questioning me?" Ythnel snapped, though she smiled inside at Iuna's moment of resistance. The girl had not been broken after all. "Consider this penance for your earlier rudeness. Do not make me add to it."

"Yes, Mistress," Iuna said meekly. She stood there, and Ythnel realized she was waiting to follow her.

"Well, get moving. We don't have all night."

Iuna jumped and nearly sprinted down the hall away from the entrance to the nave. Surprised at the girl's fleet-footedness, Ythnel took a moment to follow. When she caught up, Iuna stood before another door. Ythnel unlocked it with the same key from her key ring and pulled it open to reveal a spiral staircase leading down. She motioned for Iuna to go first. The girl grabbed one of the small, lit lanterns that hung in the hall and descended, Ythnel following a few steps behind. At the bottom, a cavernous room spread out before them, easily one hundred feet long and half that length across. Crates, barrels, and sacks were stacked neatly, almost to the ceiling in some cases, divided into areas by the category of goods they contained. There were various dried goods, foodstuffs, drinks, and temple sundries. Iuna wound through the maze without hesitation, and Ythnel did her best to keep up. She was struck with déjà vu as she recalled the day in the marketplace when Iuna had plowed through the crowd on the way to the dressmaker, Ythnel fighting to stay within sight.

Rounding a corner, Ythnel nearly knocked over Iuna, who had stopped before several pallets of burlap sacks stacked against the wall. She didn't need to ask what was inside.

"Go fetch some lantern oil," she commanded. Iuna ran off, the light she carried bobbing in and out of view, marking her progress. In minutes, she was back with a couple of flasks in her hand.

"What do you need these for? There's plenty of—"

"Quiet! It is not your place to ask what I need. Now stand back." Ythnel took the two flasks, removed the stopper and dumped their contents over the front of the pallets; the dry burlap quickly absorbed the liquid. "Now give me the lantern." She held her hand out expectantly. Iuna hesitated, but Ythnel put her fist on her hip, and the young girl reluctantly produced the lantern. Ythnel smashed the glass encasing the flame on the corner of a nearby crate then held the naked fire to the soaked burlap. It caught quickly, the blaze leaping across the stacks, hungrily devouring the oil and dry materials. Ythnel stepped back and smiled.

Iuna screamed.

Ythnel grabbed the girl before she could dart away and clamped a hand over her mouth. Iuna struggled, but Ythnel had her tightly. Tears were forming in her eyes, which were wide and panicked, the pupils fully dilated.

"It's all right," Ythnel tried to soothe, but the girl shook her head frantically. "I can explain everything. If I remove my hand, do you promise not to scream?"

Iuna looked at her for a moment then slowly nodded. Ythnel withdrew her hand, but held it ready to slap back in place if necessary.

"Mistress Kaestra will kill me if she finds out about this," Iuna whimpered.

"No, she won't. She won't be doing anything to you anymore because you're leaving this place. You're coming with me."

Iuna looked straight at Ythnel, her brow furrowed in obvious puzzlement as she tried to make out the face in the shadow of the cowl. With a deep breath, Ythnel removed the hood, bathing her face in the light of the growing fire. She searched Iuna's eyes for some sign of recognition. Would the girl remember her? Would she fear her? Or would the hate return? Would she blame Ythnel for all that had happened and betray her once more to the Karanoks?

"Ythnel?" The question was one of many contained within Iuna's hopeful face. Ythnel nodded. Iuna jumped toward Ythnel, wrapping her arms around the Loviatan's neck in a hug any mother would envy. Then the girl broke down sobbing, clinging to Ythnel's neck. Ythnel embraced her back and lifted her up. It was time for them to leave.

Ythnel hurried back the way they had come. The fire now covered the entire stock of witchweed and threatened to leap onto the surrounding piles of stored goods. It provided more than enough light for Ythnel to maneuver through the room, and she soon reached the edge of the stacks.

Before she could cross to the stairway, however, a pair of clerics appeared at the foot of the steps. They stopped whatever conversation they had been involved in to take in Ythnel, Iuna, and the roaring blaze.

"What is going on here?" One of them demanded. Ythnel didn't bother to answer. She pulled her medallion out from under her breastplate and channeled divine energy, directing it at the clerics with a shouted command. The two threw up their arms in a startled effort to protect themselves, but Ythnel's target had not really been them. The base of the stairs was suddenly engulfed in impenetrable shadow, extending out far enough to catch Ythnel at its edge. She retreated a few steps and was once again able to see. The clerics inside cried out to each other, lost and sightless within the darkness.

Ythnel backtracked to the middle of the storeroom. Even as far away from the blaze as they were, she could still feel the heat from the fire. She set Iuna down, and looked around frantically.

"Is there another way out of here, Iuna?" She barely got the question out before a fit of coughing took her. Smoke was starting to fill the room, making breathing difficult. She tore a large chunk of fabric from the hem of her robe, ripped that in half, and gave part to Iuna. "Hold this over your mouth and nose," she said, showing the girl what she meant by doing so with her own piece.

Iuna covered her face with the cloth then tugged at Ythnel's sleeve, pulling her farther into the storeroom. Ythnel walked in a crouch, trying to keep her head below the rising smoke. They reached the far side of the room, and Iuna pointed to another stairwell. Ythnel gave Iuna a shove forward, and they both charged up the steps. The door at the top was locked, but Ythnel was able to open it with her keys. Once they were out, Ythnel slammed the door shut. They lowered themselves to the floor, gasping for breath. Ythnel let them sit there for a few moments before picking herself up. She shed the smoke-stained, torn robe in favor of the guard's armor underneath and picked up the spear she had leaned against the wall.

"Come on. We're not out of here yet."

They raced back down the service hall, Ythnel in the lead this time. A door in the wall that was shared with the nave opened as they rounded the corner, and Kaestra Karanok stepped out. Ythnel saw her, but had no time to stop. They both went down in a tangle of limbs.

Kaestra was the first to recover, disengaging herself from the jumble and getting unsteadily to her feet. Ythnel looked up from where she sat on the floor to see the high priestess staring down at her, her mouth agape.

"You! I don't know how you survived Adder Swamp, but it was foolish to come back here. What did you hope to accomplish?" Kaestra finally noticed Iuna, and her eyes narrowed. "Did you come for the child? How pathetic. She's certainly not worth throwing your life away. And be assured, I will see you dead this time." Kaestra started an incantation, her fingers weaving patterns in the air. Ythnel struggled to get up, to throw herself at Kaestra in an attempt to disrupt the casting, but her limbs suddenly began to stiffen. She instantly recognized the enchantment and fought against its compulsion with all her will. Slowly, she lifted herself off her knees and straightened. Kaestra's eyes widened in horror as Ythnel threw off the effects of the spell with a sinister grin. She took one step toward Kaestra, and the Entropist turned and fled back into the nave.

Ythnel gave chase, shouting for Iuna to follow. She could not afford to let Kaestra get away. It appeared, however, that escape had not really been the priestess's intention. Kaestra stood on the far side of the dais, next to the sphere of Entropy.

"Did you think me so easily defeated? That was but one of the minor powers Entropy has bestowed upon me. Now you shall see the real power at my command." Kaestra began to chant once more. She was too far away to reach in time by running, and Ythnel did not want to throw away the only weapon she had, so she readied herself for whatever was coming. Then she remembered Iuna.

"Run, child," she ordered. "I will meet you outside when this is over. Now run." From the corner of her eye, Ythnel saw Iuna sprint down the nave and disappear through the arches.

Kaestra completed the incantation and waited expectantly. Ythnel glanced around, wondering if she was about to be struck by a blast of divine fire or suddenly transported to some nether plane, but nothing happened. Had Kaestra somehow failed to properly execute the necessary ritual? The triumphant look on her face said no. Ythnel took a hesitant step forward then another and another until she was at the base of the dais directly below the sphere.

A dull white, scaled claw emerged from the sphere, followed by a similarly colored, clawed foot. A bony, devilish face appeared next. The top of the skull was divided into three ridges, with a pair of pointy ears on the sides that lay flat and angled toward the back of the head. Its large, slanted eyes were without pupils and glowed red. A flat nose extended forward to merge with a slight muzzle that snapped open and shut to reveal rows of razor-sharp teeth.

"Behold your death, Loviatan," Kaestra cackled. The summoned devil stepped fully from the sphere, revealing a pair of batlike wings protruding from its back and a thin, barbed tail that whipped about its body constantly, as though it were a living, sentient being all its own. "Kill her," Kaestra commanded, pointing at Ythnel. The infernal creature stared at its mistress for a moment, hissing, then locked its gaze upon Ythnel. It took a step down the dais toward her, and she moved backward to match it.

"Loviatar, protect me," she breathed, clutching her medallion. The words were more than a simple plea. Ythnel drew upon the Power, shaping it into a ward against the extra-planar being approaching her. Sensing the barrier, the devil hissed but continued its advance.

Your puny shield will not stop me, fleshling. The serpentine voice echoed in Ythnel's head. *I will take your soul back with me to Baator and torture it in ways your goddess could not imagine.* It halted within three feet of Ythnel, its forked tongue flicking around the teeth exposed by its malicious grin. She found herself drawn to the deep, red pools that were its eyes. Unable to break the gaze, she was suddenly in yet another contest of wills as fear grasped for her heart. She fought again, as she had against Kaestra, and the fear receded, though Ythnel was shaken up by the contact.

Another hiss was all the warning she got before the devil's tail streaked out at her. She knew it was too late to dodge and prayed the ward would hold. The tail's barb connected, slicing Ythnel's left arm open from bicep to shoulder. An intense chill seeped in through the wound, and Ythnel looked down to see frost forming around the gash. She staggered back a step, her arm hanging limp at her side.

You are mine.

In desperation, Ythnel stabbed at the abishai. That was what it was called, she remembered, chuckling to herself. Of all the information stored somewhere in the recesses of her mind from lessons on outsiders, all she could come up with was what the damned devil was called.

The spearhead connected with the abishai's scaly hide but failed to penetrate. At that same instant, Ythnel sensed her ward fail. She cursed herself for the tactical error. She backed away, hoping to put more distance between her and the devil and buy some time in the bargain. Feeling was coming back to her arm, but it would be several minutes before she could make any use of it.

Your weapon is useless.

"Drop!" The command came from the abishai's mouth, rather than inside her head. It sounded like a knife scraping against a whetstone, and so surprised Ythnel that her mental defenses were caught unprepared. She felt her hand release the spear and heard the weapon clatter to the ground.

If Ythnel had been a warrior who relied only upon steel and strength, she likely would have fled at that point. As it was, those things were only minor tools in her armory. Her greatest weapons were the link to her goddess and the Power she could call up through it. Matching the abishai step for step in an effort to keep it from closing the distance between them, Ythnel summoned the Power to her. It responded in a rush of exhilarating pain, the familiar sting of a thousand tiny lashes. Ythnel rose above the pain, shaping the Power into a manifestation of pure force. The air before her shimmered, and the Power coalesced in the form of a nine-tailed scourge tipped with wicked-looking, inch-long barbs. The weapon hovered there between the abishai and Ythnel, awaiting her command.

Your spirit weapon cannot harm me. The taunt lacked the confidence that had been behind the previous ones. It was as though uncertainty had crept into the devil's mind. And perhaps a little fear had edged in as well.

Ythnel sent the scourge whirling toward the abishai. The strike caught the infernal creature across the chest, and the weapon's barbs dug deep, tearing off scales as they raked the demon's hide to leave ichorous paths in their wake. The abishai hopped backward beyond the scourge's reach and crouched there. It seemed to be waiting for something, but nothing happened. It gingerly touched the open wounds on its torso with a claw, bringing the bloody tips up to stare at them in apparent surprise.

With a hiss of rage, it leaped in the air. Ythnel sent the scourge up to meet it, the tails whipping across the devil's face to leave oozing stripes of ichor. The abishai landed off balance, and Ythnel pressed her advantage. The scourge hurtled toward the abishai. It brought its wings around to shield its body, and the weapon dissipated upon contact.

Ythnel gasped in horror. The abishai slowly unfurled its wings, letting out a low, hissing laugh as it realized what had happened.

"Enough of this!" Kaestra screamed from the dais. "I command you to kill her now!"

The abishai glared at its mistress but obeyed, leaping into the air once more. Ythnel dived forward as it came down on top of her. Its claws scored on her back nonetheless, and she grunted as the nerves of her rent flesh burned with pain and froze at the same time from the chill of the strike. The maneuver worked though, as she now lay within reach of her pitchfork. Behind her, the sound of the abishai's wings flapping told her it had risen again for another attack. Grasping the weapon in the crook of her good arm, she swung around and propped herself up into a sitting position, the butt of the shaft braced against the floor at a forty-five degree angle.

Once more, Ythnel called upon the link to her goddess, called upon all the Power she could channel. Crying out for vengeance, she focused all the pain that had been visited upon her, the suffering that demanded retribution, into the spear she held. It began to glow an angry red that pulsed faster and harder as Ythnel pushed every last thought of punishment she could conjure into the wood and metal weapon.

The abishai, thinking its victim finished, was already hurtling toward Ythnel when she brought the spear to bear. Unable to stop its descent, it slammed into the glowing weapon. The monster's momentum carried it down the shaft, the spearhead piercing internal organs and breaking through the scales of the abishai's back. In a final pulse of red energy, the spear and the devil exploded, showering Ythnel in gore and splinters.

"Run, child," Ythnel ordered. "I will meet you outside when this is over. Now run." Iuna sprinted down the nave but paused at the doors that led out of the temple and turned back to look one more time. Mistress Kaestra had completed her spell and stood at the top of the dais grinning in triumph while Ythnel approached warily.

Then the monster appeared out of the midst of Entropy and Iuna decided it was time to leave. She slipped out the door and closed it behind her. Her heart was racing with fear as she leaned up against the door.

What should she do now? Ythnel had told her to wait, but Iuna wasn't sure the woman would survive. If she was killed, Iuna would be left to fend for herself. Not a very promising prospect, Iuna admitted to herself. More than likely, she would be recaptured and be severely beaten, if not worse.

"She has to win," Iuna whispered to herself. "She promised she would take me away from here." Tears started to well up, and she scrubbed at her eyes defiantly. She was not going to cry. She was going to be strong—like Ythnel. If she could suffer all that she had and still come back to challenge Mistress Kaestra, then Iuna could, too.

Iuna decided to move a little ways down the portico and tripped over the body of the priest who had answered the door for Ythnel. When she realized what it was, Iuna screamed, but quickly clamped her own hand over her mouth to cut herself off. Ythnel was in there fighting for their lives, and she didn't need Iuna alerting anyone else that something was wrong at the Temple of Entropy.

❖ ❖ ❖ ❖ ❖

"No!" Kaestra screamed. Her face was a mask of fury. "I will not be denied this victory." She strode down the steps of the dais, her right hand raised in a clenched fist, a black haze forming around it. Ythnel scrambled away, pushing herself to her feet and turning to face Kaestra. The Entropist struck out with her hand, and Ythnel staggered backward, barely avoiding the blow. Enraged, Kaestra lunged, her hand outstretched. The move was sloppy, and Ythnel dodged aside easily. The momentum carried Kaestra past Ythnel, and Ythnel stuck her leg out, hooking the Entropist's ankle with her own foot. Kaestra tumbled to the floor face-first. As she struggled to get up, Ythnel kicked her in the ribs, putting plenty of force behind the greaves of her armor, and heard bone crunch. Kaestra groaned and tried to get up again, but Ythnel stomped on her arm just below the triceps, snapping the bone. Kaestra cried out, clutched her broken arm, and rolled onto her back to face Ythnel.

"Consider yourself denied," Ythnel panted.

Kaestra's lip curled in a snarl. "I am not through yet."

"No, I think you're quite finished."

"Think again." Kaestra raised her good arm. Ythnel leaped back, mistaking the gesture as some sort of attack. Then she heard a rumbling behind her and turned to see the dark sphere of Entropy moving through the air toward her.

"Let's see how you fare against a god," Kaestra cackled. The sphere advanced inexorably through the nave. It came into contact with the front row of pews, and the wooden benches disappeared, their forms twisting and distorting as they were sucked into the sphere.

Ythnel gasped, eliciting another laugh from Kaestra. The high priestess sat up and motioned again. Entropy picked up speed, coming straight for Ythnel.

She dived to the floor, and the sphere passed over her by inches, leaving a path of destruction in its wake. Ythnel tried to crawl away, but Kaestra sent the sphere after her. She rolled to the side, and Entropy flew past her into the near wall, leaving a gaping hole. The wall trembled then collapsed in a shower of stone and mortar. Ythnel managed to hide among the ruins of the wall before the dust cleared enough for the high priestess to see her.

There was no way she could defeat Entropy, Ythnel knew. Neither could she keep dodging its charges. She was tiring and would eventually make a mistake or react too slowly. If she couldn't beat the sphere, though, she could finish off Kaestra. It appeared that Entropy was responding to the high priestess's directions. Without her guidance, perhaps it would return to its former stasis.

"You cannot hide, Loviatan!" Kaestra called out. "I will destroy this whole temple if I have to."

Ythnel believed her. She cast about for something to use as a weapon. A glint caught her eye, and she saw the steel tip of her spear resting not far from her on the floor. However, reaching it meant moving from the small cover she was hiding behind. Deciding to risk it, she darted for the spearhead.

Kaestra spotted Ythnel and immediately sent Entropy after her. Ythnel grabbed the short length of shaft still attached to the spearhead and stood, swiveling to face Kaestra.

"I've had just about enough of you and your god," Ythnel said and hurled the spearhead at Kaestra. The high priestess opened her mouth in surprise, and her eyes widened as the makeshift weapon flew true, burying itself in her breast. Blood blossomed across Kaestra's white tabard, and her eyes fluttered. Her mouth worked in an effort to say something, but all that came out was a trickle of blood. She sagged back against the end of a pew and died.

Ythnel let out a sigh of relief then remembered Entropy. She looked to her left and saw the sphere hovering motionless less than a foot beside her. "That was closer than I would have liked."

With one last look around the nave, Ythnel staggered out of the temple and into the night. She leaned heavily against one of the columns outside to catch her breath and let her eyes adjust to the darkness. The air was chill, and she felt gooseflesh rise along her arms and legs.

"Ythnel!"

The shout brought Ythnel's head up, and she saw Iuna coming toward her from the shadows of the portico. Ythnel pushed herself up off the column and embraced the girl with her good arm.

"It's snowing, Ythnel. I've never seen snow before."

Ythnel looked out into the night to see flakes of white coming down in a steady flurry. The ground was already covered in a light dusting.

"I've never seen snow before, either." She smiled down at Iuna. "Come on. Let's get out of here." They walked out under the snow toward the waiting street. Ythnel wasn't sure how they would get out of the city, but she was too tired and sore to think about that now.

A black carriage pulled up to the gap between the walls surrounding the temple, blocking access to the street. Ythnel halted as soon as she saw it, shoving Iuna protectively behind her. Between the snow and the shadows, she couldn't identify who was driving.

"Get inside. We don't have all night. Or would you rather walk?" Kestus hopped down from the driver's seat of the carriage, a welcoming grin splitting his face. Ythnel breathed a sigh of relief and jogged to the carriage, pulling Iuna along behind her. Kestus helped them both inside, closed the door behind them, and climbed back up to take the reins. Then the carriage took off once more into the night, heading toward the South Gate and out of Luthcheq.

THE **P**RIESTS

EPILOGUE

Aznar Thrul sat at his dining table, sipping the bowl of soup before him with disinterest. He really wasn't hungry. Well, at least he was not hungry for food. There was time to kill, however, so he went through the motions of taking his evening meal. When Aznar had nearly finished half the bowl, his chamberlain appeared to announce that his guest had arrived and was waiting in the bedchamber. Aznar nodded his acknowledgment and continued with the meal. When the last of the soup had been drained, he dropped the spoon into the bowl with a clink, pushed back from the table, and rose.

He forced himself to maintain a leisurely pace as he strode down the hall to his chambers. Tonight's meeting had occupied his thoughts all day. It was a long time coming, and the possibilities excited him. This would not be just another conquest. It would be the start of something bigger.

At the door to his room, Aznar paused to compose himself. It was important that he remained in control, and letting too much emotion show could jeopardize that. Satisfied that his face revealed nothing more than he wanted it to, he opened the door and step inside.

Headmistress Yenael sat on the bed, her body half-turned toward the door. As was customary for all visitors to the zulkir's chambers, whatever clothes she had worn to the Citadel had been left in the care of his chamberlain. In their place, Yenael was given a sheer white gown. The practice was for security reasons, of course, but Aznar certainly didn't mind the additional benefits it occasionally presented him. Even after twenty years, Yenael's body was still firm and quite attractive. He didn't bother to hide a smile of pleasure as he walked to the center of the room.

"So, do you have something to report, or was this visit simply a social call." He watched her from the corner of his eye. She had made no pretenses at modesty when he entered, and he had expected none. That was the other purpose of the gown. Being naked in the presence of others who were dressed was often unsettling enough for people that they let their guard down and gave away things they hadn't intended to. Yenael's face was placid, and her body language said she was perfectly comfortable. Aznar wondered why that didn't anger him.

"My agent was successful, O Mighty Tharchion, Mightier Zulkir." She used the proper address, but her tone of voice did not hold any acknowledgment of the weight behind those titles. "I'm sure your own intelligence sources have already informed you that Mordulkin's forces are on the move."

Aznar nodded and moved over to an end table that held a tray with a decanter of Thayan brandy and two glasses. He offered one to Yenael, but she shook her head, so he poured for himself and set the decanter down. Picking up the glass, he turned to Yenael and took a sip.

"So, the question now is whether Mordulkin will remember its promise once Luthcheq falls."

"I would not worry about it, O Mighty Tharchion, Mightier Zulkir. Hercubes is a man of his word. He will honor the agreement. The city will stand, as much as it chafes him. And you will be allowed to establish an enclave by whomever is installed as governor."

"A governor I will have chosen," Aznar laughed, "though Hercubes will think it was his own decision."

"Of course," Yenael agreed.

Aznar downed the remainder of his brandy and returned the glass to its place on the end table. He was almost giddy over the success of his plan. The enclave would be the first of many he'd sponsor. No longer would he have to worry about his rival zulkirs gaining some advantage over him through this enterprise. As a bonus, he would be ridding Faerûn of the fanatical Karanok family and their insane dream of purging the world of wizards. It was certainly a cause for celebration if ever there was one, and he said as much out loud.

"Did you have something particular in mind, O Mighty Tharchion, Mightier Zulkir?" Yenael asked, her eyebrow arched.

"It has been a while since I was last subject to your ministrations," Aznar mused. "I'd be interested in seeing how much your skills have progressed."

Yenael smiled and patted the top of the bed next to her.

Saestra Karanok leaned against the back of the chaise lounge with her right arm folded under her breasts while she played absently with the dagger in her left hand. She wore a backless lace blouse with frilly sleeves that matched her violet eyes, tucked into a black, mid-thigh-length leather skirt. The skirt was practically indecent, but she enjoyed it. A pair of French doors leading to a balcony in the wall behind her had been swung open, allowing the light of the full moon and the occasional wintry gust of wind to enter the room. She watched as a wisp of cloud crossed the face of Selûne and sighed.

Things were starting to unravel in Luthcheq. Kaestra, her twin sister, had been found dead in the Temple of Entropy, the black sphere itself hovering just a few feet from her. There were rumors and whispers that the god had killed its high priestess in displeasure for the church's crusade against the Art. These were reinforced by the alleged "wizard attacks" this past Midwinter and the reports that the forces of Mordulkin were now on the move against the city.

To make things worse, with the removal of the Mage Society, Saestra's father, Jaerios, no longer ordered witch hunts within the walls of Luthcheq, effectively eliminating the story she used to cover up her nightly forages. She desperately needed to find a new means of discarding the bodies and misdirecting any inquiries made about their disappearances.

The creaking of old wood brought Saestra's attention back to her room. Against the left wall stood two matching sarcophagi of darkly stained wood. Stylized images of a Mulhorandi pharaoh and queen were carved into the covers of each. Saestra had imported them a while ago to decorate her apartments, though the pharaoh's sarcophagus had been in storage until recently.

Its cover now swung open, revealing the body of Naeros Karanok in a stately repose. Saestra smiled, her tongue playing over her fangs.

"I wondered when you were going to wake up."

Naeros's eyes fluttered open, and he glided forward, the cover of the sarcophagus closing behind him. Slowly his feet settled to the stone floor, and his arms unfolded. "Good evening, Mistress," he said, turning to look at Saestra. "What is your will?"

"Yes, yes." She stood up and wandered over to the balcony. The nights were still quite chilly, but Saestra was unaffected by such things. She glanced wistfully out across the stair-step skyline of the city.

"Do you think we should leave, dear brother?"

"Why would we have to leave?"

"Because things are becoming too risky to remain here for much longer. With each feeding, we move closer to discovery."

"Who cares?" Naeros snarled. "They cannot hurt us. We should just kill them all."

Saestra frowned. She thought turning Naeros into a spawn would be a wickedly cruel revenge at first, but he was just as much a bore undead as he had been while alive. Violence was always his answer, without any consideration of the consequences. She wished now that she had just killed him along with his thugs.

"And what about Father? Should we welcome him into our new family, or just kill him with the rest."

Saestra didn't bother to keep the irritation and sarcasm from her voice, though it was wasted on Naeros anyway. She did not wait for his answer. "Never mind. I'll think of something." She walked back into the room and came over to Naeros.

"I bet you're hungry after sleeping for so long." She petted his head as she would a lost puppy. He nodded eagerly, a wide grin revealing his own set of fangs.

"Why don't we go find something to eat then, hmm?"

Iuna, Kestus, Kohtakah, Muctos, and Ythnel all sat around the table in the dining room of the Flaming Griffon. War was the topic of most hushed conversations amongst the inn's patrons; the city buzzed with preparations. Even without an official declaration, the signs were impossible to miss. Mordulkin was moving against Luthcheq.

The companions were making an effort not to talk about it. Everyone buried themselves in their meals, avoiding eye contact as they ate, struggling for something to say that had no connection to war during the awkward moments when everyone looked up at once.

"The leg looks nice," Ythnel said to Kohtakah after finishing her bowl of five-bean soup.

Kohtakah looked up, realizing she was speaking to him. "Yes. Thank you. Lord Jedea put up the coin for one of the local temples to regenerate it. In return, I agreed to join ... the army...." His voice faded as he realized he had spoken about the taboo subject. They all sat in relative silence for a while, their attention back on what was left of their meals.

"How are things over at the academy?" Kestus

asked Muctos a few minutes later. Muctos had been appointed as an adjunct to the Jedea Academy while Kestus and Ythnel had been away.

"Oh, I'm really enjoying the work. I find teaching to be very fulfilling. My only complaint is the increase in class sizes due to how many professors ... have enlisted...." Muctos smiled apologetically.

"Why are you all so afraid to talk about the war?" Iuna blurted out. The four companions looked at each other and at Iuna, shocked by the question. Then they burst out laughing.

"Because some people think that if they don't talk about something, it's not really happening," Ythnel said, smiling fondly at the girl.

"That's stupid," Iuna replied.

"Yes, it is." Ythnel drew in a deep breath and met Kestus's gaze. "So when are you leaving?"

"Not for a few more days. The vanguard is already on the move, but there is still some planning to do before the main force marches. In fact, I have another intelligence meeting to attend in a couple of hours." Kestus had been asked by King Hercubes to help lead part of the assault against Luthcheq because of his intimate knowledge of the city. "What about you?"

Ythnel drained her ale tankard and sat back in her seat, a warm feeling of satisfaction washing over her. It was good to be among people who accepted her again, people who she could call friends. That she would be leaving them behind was painful, but Loviatar taught that life was full of pain and only the weak tried to avoid it.

"There is a ship leaving for Bezantur on the morrow. I've purchased passage for Iuna and myself aboard it. This will be our last night in Mordulkin." The others nodded, and a comfortable silence settled over the group. A serving girl came by, and they ordered another round of drinks.

They spent the rest of their time together reminiscing over their tankards. Finally Kestus stood up from the table and shook hands with Kohtakah and Muctos, saying he would see them in a day or so. When he turned to Ythnel, he paused. She could see the question in his eyes. It was the same question that had been growing in her heart since their return from Luthcheq, but she had no answer. Their paths were diverging, and the charge Ythnel had been given over Iuna was not something she would lay down for anyone.

"May Loviatar bless your endeavors," she whispered in Kestus's ear as they embraced warmly. Muctos cleared his throat and the two pulled apart.

"Good night, everyone." Kestus nodded and smiled then left.

"We should be going, too," Muctos said, standing. "Take care of this one," he said to Iuna while motioning to Ythnel. "She needs a lot of looking after."

He winked at her, and she smiled back. Kohtakah said his good-byes, and the two men left. Ythnel stared at the entrance of the Flaming Griffon for a few moments after they disappeared. She sat back down in her chair and gazed at the empty seats around the table. It was hard to believe this was it. Tomorrow they would be leaving. Tomorrow they would be returning home. Ythnel couldn't wait to see the faces of her sisters, to be back in the halls of the manor once more. She hoped Iuna felt as excited as she did.

"Well, I guess that leaves just us," Ythnel said, looking over at her young ward. "Why don't we head upstairs and get ready for bed. We have an early rise in the morning."

"Yes, Mistress Ythnel."

An excerpt

The Fighters

MASTER OF CHAINS

JESS LEBOW

Ryder ran his hand over Samira's soft black hair. He felt her arms tighten around his middle.

"Don't go," she said.

He returned her squeeze. "I must."

Samira looked up at him, her beautiful brown eyes filling with tears. "Then promise me you'll return. Promise me that you're not going to get yourself killed doing something foolish."

Ryder smiled. She loved him. She loved him dearly, but knowing that only strengthened his resolve.

"I promise you, Samira, I will return to you." Though it pained him to do so, he pushed her gently away. "I will be back before nightfall." Then, grabbing his belt and sheath from the table, Ryder kissed his wife good-bye and stepped out the door into the afternoon sunshine.

"Close the bar behind me, and don't let anyone in until I get back," he said over his shoulder.

He could hear the extra-heavy crossbeam slide into place behind him as he crossed the dirt road. On the other side, Liam was leaning against a heavy tree, his arms across his chest.

Ryder slapped him on the arm as he approached. "You ready, little brother?"

Liam tapped the hilt of the sword dangling from his belt. "Ready."

Ryder nodded, satisfied. "Then let's go meet the others."

Liam knelt in the bushes alongside the well-traveled, packed dirt road that ran west from Zerith Hold, Lord Purdun's fortress in Duhlnarim, through Furrowsrich village and out of Ahlarkham. Six other men knelt beside him, including his brother. They were waiting on a carriage that was reportedly leaving Zerith Hold with a diplomatic letter bound for High Watcher Laxaella Bronshield, the still-mourning baroness of Tanistan. Liam and the others intended to make sure that letter never reached it's destination.

Liam, Ryder, and the rest of the Crimson Awl had made significant headway in the past few months against Lord Purdun's elite guard. The last thing they needed was for Lady Bronshield to add her might to that of Purdun's. The Awl would worry about one barony at a time, starting right here at home. But to do that, they had to make sure the neighboring lords didn't broaden the scope of the fight too soon. That was why they were all here, to stop that letter, which reportedly was a request for aid, from getting through to Tanistan.

In the near distance, Liam heard the telltale sound of horse hooves and rough wooden wheels rolling over the packed earth.

His brother must have heard it too. "This is it," said Ryder. "You all know your jobs. There should only be two guards. If we're swift about this, nobody needs to get hurt."

Liam looked over the other men, locals all of them. They nodded at Ryder's last minute instructions. All of them that is except Kharl.

The young man, the son of a local merchant, had never been on a raid before. He hadn't heard a word Ryder said, his eyes focused on the road, his right hand gripping the hilt of his long sword so tightly his knuckles were turning white. A line of sweat had started to form along the edge of his golden blond hair, and he looked a little pale. Liam could have sworn the kid was shaking.

Ryder must have noticed it too. "Don't worry," he said, smiling at Kharl. "You won't even have to use your sword."

Kharl nodded. "But what if they give us trouble?"

Ryder shrugged. "Then I suppose you'll get the opportunity to use your sword after all."

"No," Kharl replied, shaking his head. "I mean, what if they don't give us the letter? What do we do then?"

Jarl, a great big bear of a man with a tattoo of a mermaid on each forearm spoke up. "We take it from them lad."

The other men nodded their agreement.

"But..." Kharl stuttered. "But...do we...?"

Ryder put his hand on the young man's shoulder. "Kharl, I won't ask you to kill anyone in cold blood, if that's what you're asking."

Kharl nodded, his shoulders relaxing a bit.

"But if things do get out of hand, you may have to defend yourself." Ryder got suddenly serious. "If that happens, if you find yourself in the position where it's your life or his—" Ryder looked up at each of the other men, his eyes lingering on Liam a moment longer than the rest, then back at Kharl—"then I expect you to kill that man dead. I won't be losing anyone on this raid. Is that understood?"

Kharl nodded, and the other men grunted their assent.

"Good." Ryder chuckled, the moment of seriousness passed. "You know, Kharl, you can do me a favor."

"Really? What?"

"You're mother makes the best beef stew in all of Erlkazar. When you get back, see if you can't get her to make a pot and invite Samira and I over for dinner."

The worry on Kharl's face faded. "Sure, Ryder. I'll do that."

Liam shook his head. His brother always had a way with people. "Hey, Kharl."

The blond man leaned back to look at Liam. "Yeah?"

"I want some of that stew too."

Kharl threw his arms out wide. "You're all invited."

The sound of horses and wheels grew louder as it came around the bend, transforming into a well-appointed carriage. Pulled by a pair of majestic-looking horses draped in the livery of Lord Purdun, the coach wasn't in any hurry. The doors were painted with the familiar shield-and-double-crossed-sword crest that turned Liam's stomach every time he saw it. It was the official seal of Lord Purdun, the owner and master of the land on which all of his family and friends lived and had to pay taxes for. Just as Ryder had said, there were only two guards and the driver. Whoever rode inside was concealed by a series of velvet drapes covering the windows. Liam imagined the occupant was some corpulent, bloated diplomat with a double chin and greasy fingers. Who better to deliver a letter of alliance from the bastard Lord Purdun to one of the other regional dukes?

The carriage drew nearer, and Ryder rose onto the balls of his feet, still concealed by the tall bush. He held his hands to his face and whispered, "Before you can truly move forward, you have to be willing to live with the consequences." Liam doubted the other men heard him.

Then Ryder smiled and took one last look at the other men. "It's time to give it to old Firefist." He dropped into a crouch, then sprang out of the bush. "Now!" he shouted, pulling his long sword from its sheath as he came down only ten yards in front of the carriage.

Liam didn't hesitate. He was the second of the eight men to reach the road and draw his weapon, taking his position beside his brother.

As Liam had expected, the horses were startled by the sudden appearance of armed men on the road. They bucked, and the driver had to struggle to keep control of them.

"Halt!" shouted Ryder, holding his palm out to the coach.

The other men leaped out of their hiding spots—two more up front, the final four behind, boxing the coach in on the packed dirt road.

The guards on the carriage had to hold onto the seat to avoid being tossed from their perch because of the startled horses. But as the horses came to a stop, they stood up and drew their weapons.

"Don't be foolish," shouted Ryder. "We're eight. You're only two. Just drop your weapons and give us the letter you carry, and there will be no need for you to be harmed."

Liam wished he was as eloquent as his older brother. Ryder had a simplicity with words. No wasted effort, no beating around the bush, just the facts, plain and simple.

The guards stood motionless, still gripping their swords. They looked far more relaxed than Liam thought they should. Hells, they looked more relaxed than he felt right then.

"I said drop your weapons!" shouted Ryder. He stepped to the side of the coach, the afternoon sun glinting from his polished blade.

The guards looked at each other, then lowered their weapons, placing them on the wooden bench beside them.

"The letter is inside," said one of the guards, lifting his hands in the air. "The countess carries it. Please don't harm her, we're responsible for her safety."

Ryder glanced back at Liam, a smirk on his face. Then he nodded. Without a word, Liam followed his brother to the door.

Ryder knocked on the wooden door with the hilt of his sword. The heavy pounding scratched the paint from the door, marring Lord Purdun's crest.

The door remained closed.

Liam spared a glance back at Kharl. The young man was shifting his weight side to side, but he kept his eyes squarely on the two guards, his sword drawn, just as he'd been instructed to do. That night, in the pub, the young man would be telling stories of his bravery to the other revolutionaries, and the nervousness would be nothing but a distant memory.

Ryder knocked on the door again. "We seek only the letter you carry," he said. "Surrender it, and you will not be harmed."

Still the door remained shut.

Ryder's simple smile had faded, replaced with a look of serious contemplation. It was a dangerous look. Liam had seen it many times—whenever his older brother didn't get his way. Liam had feared that look since they were both little boys. It meant Ryder had reached his limit. It meant he no longer intended to play nice.

"Countess, this will be your last warning," said Ryder. "You have to the count of three to come out here and deliver that letter, or we *will* come in."

Liam gripped his sword. This was not the way they had hoped this would go.

"One . . ."

Time seemed to slow down. Liam could hear his heart pound in his chest. They knew this was a possibility, but nobody wanted things to get rough.

"Two . . ."

The door burst open and slapped against the wall of the carriage. Right behind it poured out half a dozen of Lord Purdun's elite guards. Six more jumped out the door on the opposite side.

Ryder's sword came up and parried the first guard's blow as he backstepped away from the carriage and called, "It's a trap!"

The other men jumped into action.

Liam stepped up beside his brother, stopping Ryder's retreat. The two of them lunged forward. Unable to stop his onrush, the guardsmen's eyes went wide. He managed to bash aside Liam's blade, but he was too slow to catch Ryder's. The tip of his long sword found a crease in the man's half-plate, and it sank into the flesh below. Twisting sideways, he pulled himself off the blade like a piece of skewered beef, dropping his sword and giving way to the other five armored men behind him.

The baron's elite guards spread out in a circle, surrounding the brothers, three training their swords on Ryder, two on Liam. Liam spun around, placing his back up against Ryder's. It wasn't the first time they had fought in that way. Liam hoped it wouldn't be their last. Both men began turning a slow circle, holding their attackers at bay with the points of their swords.

Standing in the middle of a ring of armed soldiers, the eye in the center of a raging storm, Liam caught sight of Kharl. The young man was battling the two carriage guards. They had regained their dropped swords, and they had the young man locked into combat. One was circling around to the side, attempting to pin Kharl between them. For a relatively inexperienced fighter, Kharl was holding his own. He parried a blow from each side, then took a large step back, keeping the guards from flanking him. Despite the young man's terrific effort, he was still losing ground. He was in a fight he couldn't win, but he hadn't realized it yet.

Liam scanned the area, hoping someone else could get to Kharl before it was too late, but the other men were busy with guards of their own. Not counting the carriage driver, there were fourteen armed elite guardsmen to eight freedom fighters. Kharl was on his own.

If they were just typical thugs, it wouldn't have been an issue. Liam would put any one of those men up against two local thugs. It would be no contest. But the baron's elite guards were trained soldiers. They had good weapons and the best armor—and they knew how to win a fight.

The sound of Ryder's sword bashing aside a guardsman's blade brought Liam back to the fight at hand.

A pair of soldiers rushed the brothers, one from each side. Ryder stepped left, Liam right. They moved together like a multi-headed creature sharing a single spine. Their blades moved in synchronicity, striking out at different foes. Liam didn't need to see what his brother was doing. They had been practicing that style of fighting since they were boys.

Liam held a tree branch tightly in both hands. It was his eighth birthday. As a present, his uncle had made him a toy wooden sword. But that sword was in the hands of Tyler, the local bully.

Liam could feel his brother's back against his as they turned a slow circle, looking out at Tyler and his three pals.

"Don't worry Liam," reassured Ryder, also with a branch in his hands. "I'm a good fighter, so you will be too."

Liam nodded. If his big brother said it, it must be true.

"Hey, kid," taunted Tyler. "You want this?" He shook the toy sword in Liam's face.

Liam's chest burned with hate.

"Don't fall for it, Liam," directed Ryder. "Let them make the first move."

"What? Are you chicken?" Tyler laughed. "Too afraid to come get your little toy from me?"

Liam gripped the branch tighter in his hands. He wanted so badly to swing it, to bring it down on Tyler's head and make him give back his birthday present. But more than anything, Liam trusted his older brother.

"What's the matter, Tyler?" taunted Ryder. "You've

got us outnumbered. Looks like *you're* the chicken."

Tyler lifted Liam's wooden sword over his head. "I'll show you who's chicken." Then he came running right at Ryder.

The three other young thugs followed the bully's lead, and came rushing in.

Liam felt something in the pit of his stomach clench, then he just lost control. His arms reacted without him willing them to. He watched as the branch swung wildly from side to side. The whole thing didn't seem real. He wasn't in control, and he didn't know the outcome, all he knew for sure was that his brother's back against his was the most reassuring feeling in the whole world.

From behind him Liam heard a loud crack, and just like that the whole thing was over. The young punks retreated, not wanting to get hit by the flailing branch. Liam stopped swinging when they took a step back. Then he followed their gazes over his shoulder.

Tyler lay on the ground, blood pouring from his nose, Liam's sword on the ground beside him.

"I'll take that," said Ryder. He leaned down and picked up the birthday gift. The branch he held in his other hand was broken in two.

Ryder turned and grabbed Liam by the shoulder. "Come on," he said. "I think these guys have had enough."

Liam's blade danced, parrying blows. He could feel his brother's back against his own. It was a familiar thing. Despite their teamwork, the guards they fought were not going to fall for any cheap tricks. They knew how to deal with other, well-trained swordsmen. They came in at the same time, thrusting in short bursts, trying to overpower the brothers. They kept Liam off balance, never giving him an opening. He had time to only defend himself.

The guard to his left feigned high, then went low. Liam brought his sword down, smashing the attack to the dirt. The other guard came in high. Liam dodged to the side, bringing his sword up in a long arc and bashing away his opponent's blade with a flourish. The two elite guardsmen took a step back, regained their composure, then lunged together. Liam employed Bonfellow's defense, bringing the forte of his blade around in a short circle, catching the tip of both blades with his and flinging them toward the sky. Had there been only one attacker, Liam would have lunged for a riposte. As it was, he'd be opening himself up to one of the two guards if he did, so he held tight. He wouldn't fall for the ploy.

He could hear Ryder's voice inside his head: Let them make the first mistake.

That back and forth went on for what seemed a long time. The guards would rush, and Liam would fight them back, threaten a bit, make them retreat, then they would return with a different strategy.

Liam could feel Ryder step, lunge, retreat, parry, then lunge again. From the pattern, he could tell that his brother was fairing similarly with his three. Defense was one thing, but there was no way they were going to win the fight if they didn't make some headway soon.

The guardsmen came in once again. Liam dodged both blows in swift order. Then he made his first mistake. Stepping away from his brother, he lunged, sticking the tip of his long sword into the hip of the soldier on his right. The man wailed and stepped back, but the other guardsman took advantage of the opening, swinging his sword at Liam's exposed middle.

Liam retreated, bashing aside the first attack, but the soldier pressed his advantage, swinging his sword again. The second blow slipped past Liam's guard, catching him in the shoulder. His chain mail tunic took the brunt of the attack, but the tip ran up under the short sleeves, cutting a shallow wound into his arm. Liam hissed at the pain, pulling sideways and away from his brother.

Ryder spun around, knowing his little brother had been hit. "Liam!"

Liam pulled his arm in toward his side, trying to minimize the pain. But in doing so he opened up his back. Two of the guardsmen lunged at the same time, taking advantage of his exposed body. Liam swung down with his right hand, in an attempt to parry the attacks, but his wounded arm slowed him down.

Both blades came in, slipping past his defense.

Liam tightened his gut, preparing for the pain. Out of the corner of his eye, he caught sight of Ryder's sword. It came out of nowhere, a silvery flash that caught one guardsman across the forearm and slapped aside the other's blade. With his other hand Ryder shoved Liam hard.

Liam stumbled forward, crashing into the guardsman he'd already injured. The two of them tumbled to the ground. Liam tucked his sword up tight against his body as they careened across the ground. When they came to a stop, he rolled forward with all of his might, pushing away from the soldier. He made two quick turns then leaped to his feet, twenty paces from where he had begun. The guard's heavier armor had weighted him down, and he struggled to get up from his back like an upside-down turtle.

"Run, Liam!"

Liam looked up at his brother. He was surrounded by four guards with no one to watch his back. Ryder turned a quick circle, flinging his blade out to keep the guardsmen at bay.

Liam took two steps toward his brother.

"Look out," shouted Ryder.

Liam looked down just in time to see the injured guardsman on the ground swing at his ankles. He leaped in the air, jumping over the blade. In midair he turned his long sword over. Coming down on the prone soldier, he drove the tip through the man's helm, pinning his head to the ground.

Putting his boot on the fallen soldier's shoulder, Liam pulled his weapon from the man's ruined skull then turned to help his brother. His eyes came up just in time to see Ryder lunge at one guard just as another lunged at him. Ryder's blade hit its mark, driving deep into his target's neck. The guardsman's blade also struck home, slicing Ryder across the belly.

"Ryder!" Liam broke into a run.

Ryder dropped to one knee, his left arm holding his stomach, his hand covered in blood. He looked down at the wound in his belly then looked up at Liam. He looked so sad, so scared, like a lost child. Liam had never seen his brother like that, and it sent a shiver down his spine.

Liam skidded to a stop.

"Run, Liam." Ryder pointed away from the carriage with his chin. "Go." Then he turned his attention back to Lord Purdun's elite guardsmen.

Liam couldn't move. He just stood there, watching his brother's blood spill to the ground.

Ryder couldn't stand, but he held the remaining three guardsmen at bay from his knees. He swung his long sword in a wide arc, then jabbed at them with the sharp tip. Each strike was accompanied by another splash of blood. The guards took a step back, and Ryder turned to look at Liam.

"Look after Samira. Tell her I love her."

With Ryder's attention turned away, the biggest of the three guardsmen charged forward.

The blood in Liam's veins suddenly ran cold.

"Ryder, look out!"

"Run, Liam." Ryder turned and brought his blade up, right into the guardsman's gut.

The big man let out a screech as he impaled himself. Ryder held the hilt of his sword as best as he could, but the guardsman in all of his armor was just too heavy, and the big man fell forward, smothering Ryder.

For a moment, every inch of Liam's body tingled. It was as if he was trying to fight against the forward movement of time, and it tore at his skin. It was the moment in which he would lose his brother. It was the moment of his greatest failure, and he desperately wanted to go back, to stop everything before that instant, to replay the moments of his life over and over again, always stopping before he reached that last part.

Four more soldiers came around the back of the carriage.

Liam stood there stunned, the fibers of his body struggling to keep him rooted in time—but it was no use. It was a fight he could not win.

The other guards wasted no time, charging in, stabbing at Ryder's prone body. Liam winced, the wounds of his brother stung doubly for Liam. He wished desperately that it could be him lying their on the ground. He wished he could trade places with his brother, take his place under the killing blows of the guardsmen.

The whole thing had gone terribly, terribly wrong. His face grew hot, and he began to see red. The trap was yet further proof of the treachery of Lord Purdun.

Liam's lip curled up into a sneer. His body was steeled by the hatred and pain coursing through his body. The baron would pay, but first his guardsmen would all be sent to the Nine Hells. Liam lifted his sword.

"Liam . . ." came a strangled voice.

Liam looked to the ground to see Kharl. The young man was still alive, but he was bleeding from a large wound in his side.

"Liam . . . please help me."

Liam looked back at Ryder. His brother had stopped moving. He lay on the ground, his torso bent back over his heels, still gripping the hilt of his sword. The big guardsman lay on top of him, impaled on the tip of his blade. The fury that had momentarily taken hold of him suddenly fled. His hatred turned to sadness, and his arms felt tired and weak.

"I'll tell her," he said. "I'll make sure she knows."

With what little strength remained in his body, Liam turned away from his brother and helped Kharl up from the ground.

Coming September 2005
from Wizards of the Coast

NEW TALES FROM FORGOTTEN REALMS CREATOR
ED GREENWOOD

THE BEST OF THE REALMS
Book II

This new anthology of short stories by Ed Greenwood, creator of the
FORGOTTEN REALMS Campaign Setting, features many old and well-loved
classics as well as three brand new stories of high-spirited adventure.

CITY OF SPLENDORS
A Waterdeep Novel

ED GREENWOOD AND ELAINE CUNNINGHAM

In the streets of Waterdeep, conspiracies run like water through the
gutters, bubbling beneath the seeming calm of the city's life. As a band of
young, foppish lords discovers there is a dark side to the city they all love,
a sinister mage and his son seek to create perverted creatures to further
their twisted ends. And across it all sprawls the great city itself: brawling,
drinking, laughing, living life to the fullest. Even in the face of death.

SILVERFALL
Stories of the Seven Sisters

This paperback edition of *Silverfall: Stories of the Seven Sisters*, by the creator
of the FORGOTTEN REALMS Campaign Setting, features seven stories of
seven sisters illustrated by seven beautiful pages of interior art by John Foster.

ELMINSTER'S DAUGHTER
The Elminster Series

All her life, Narnra of Waterdeep has wondered who her father is. Now
she has discovered that it is no less a person than Elminster of Shadowdale,
mightiest mage in all Faerûn. And her anger is as boundless as his power.

www.wizards.com

ED GREENWOOD

THE CREATOR OF THE FORGOTTEN REALMS WORLD

BRINGS YOU THE STORY OF

SHANDRIL OF HIGHMOON

SHANDRIL'S SAGA

SPELLFIRE
Book I

Powerful enough to lay low a dragon or heal a wounded warrior, spellfire is the most sought after power in all of Faerûn. And it is in the reluctant hand of Shandril of Highmoon, a young, orphaned kitchen-lass.

CROWN OF FIRE
Book II

Shandril has grown to become one of the most powerful magic-users in the land. The powerful Cult of the Dragon and the evil Zhentarim want her spellfire, and they will kill whoever they must to possess it.

HAND OF FIRE
Book III

Shandril has spellfire, a weapon capable of destroying the world, and now she's fleeing for her life across Faerûn, searching for somewhere to hide. Her last desperate hope is to take refuge in the sheltered city of Silverymoon. If she can make it.

www.wizards.com

ADVENTURES IN THE REALMS!

THE YELLOW SILK
The Rogues
Don Bassingthwaite

More than just the weather is cold and bitter in the wind-swept realm of Altumbel. When a stranger travels from the distant east to reclaim his family's greatest treasure, he finds just how cold and bitter a people can be.

DAWN OF NIGHT
The Erevis Cale Trilogy, Book II
Paul S. Kemp

He's left Sembia far behind. He's made new friends. He's made new enemies. And now Erevis Cale himself is changing into something, and he's not sure exactly what it is.

REALMS OF DRAGONS
The Year of Rogue Dragons
Edited by Philip Athans

All new stories by R.A. Salvatore, Richard Lee Byers, Ed Greenwood, Elaine Cunningham, and a host of **Forgotten Realms®** stars breathe new life into the great wyrms of Faerûn.

Go Behind enemy lines with Drizzt Do'Urden in this all new trilogy from best-selling Author R.A. Salvatore.

THE HUNTER'S BLADES TRILOGY

The New York Times *best-seller now in paperback!*

THE LONE DROW
Book II

Alone and tired, cold and hungry, Drizzt Do'Urden has never been more dangerous. But neither have the rampaging orcs that have finally done the impossible—what for the dwarves of the North is the most horrifying nightmare ever—they've banded together.

New in hardcover!

THE TWO SWORDS
Book III

Drizzt has become the Hunter, but King Obould won't let himself become the Hunted and that means one of them will have to die. The Hunter's Blades trilogy draws to an explosive conclusion.

THE THOUSAND ORCS
Book I
Available Now!

FROM *NEW YORK TIMES*

BEST-SELLING AUTHOR

R.A. SALVATORE

In taverns, around campfires, and in the loftiest council chambers of Faerûn, people whisper the tales of a lone dark elf who stumbled out of the merciless Underdark to the no less unforgiving wilderness of the World Above and carved a life for himself, then lived a legend...

THE LEGEND OF DRIZZT

For the first time in deluxe hardcover editions, all three volumes of the Dark Elf Trilogy take their rightful place at the beginning of one of the greatest fantasy epics of all time. Each title contains striking new cover art and portions of an all-new author interview, with the questions posed by none other than the readers themselves.

HOMELAND

Being born in Menzoberranzan means a hard life surrounded by evil.

EXILE

But the only thing worse is being driven from the city with hunters on your trail.

SOJOURN

Unless you can find your way out, never to return.